The Lochmore Legacy

One Scottish castle.
Four breathtaking romances through the ages.

The bitter feud between the Lochmore
and the McCrieff clans is the stuff of legend.
And Lochmore Castle has been witness to it all.

The battles, the betrayals, the weddings,
the wild passions.

But with the arrival of a new owner to Lochmore,
the secrets buried deep in the castle
are about to be revealed through four romances,
as we fall back in time through the
Victorian, Regency, Tudor and Medieval eras...

Discover more in

His Convenient Highland Wedding
by Janice Preston

Unlaced by the Highland Duke
by Lara Temple

A Runaway Bride for the Highlander
by Elisabeth Hobbes

Secrets of a Highland Warrior
by Nicole Locke

Author Note

I was delighted to be asked to write this first book of the four that make up The Lochmore Legacy. The idea fascinated me—a mystery that is unraveled as we go back in time through history and, as a huge bonus, the other three titles were to be written by Lara Temple (Regency), Elisabeth Hobbes (Tudor) and Nicole Locke (Medieval). The four of us are already good friends who, with five others, run the Unlaced Historical Romance Group on Facebook, so this was perfect.

But then the doubts set in. All my books to date have been set in Regency England, but this book is set in 1848, well into the Victorian era and the Industrial Revolution, and the series is centered around a fictional castle on the west coast of Scotland. I am so happy I ignored my doubts, though, because the research has been fascinating and I have learned so much—but I won't list the topics I researched here or I might spoil some elements of Lachlan and Flora's story!

I hope you fall in love with The Lochmore Legacy— I certainly have and I simply cannot wait to read the other three books to find out exactly how the mystery unfolds.

JANICE
PRESTON

His Convenient
Highland Wedding

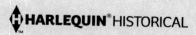

Special thanks and acknowledgment are given to Janice Preston for her contribution to The Lochmore Legacy series.

Recycling programs
for this product may
not exist in your area.

ISBN-13: 978-1-335-63505-1

His Convenient Highland Wedding

HARLEQUIN®
www.Harlequin.com

Printed in U.S.A.

Janice Preston grew up in Wembley, North London, with a love of reading, writing stories and animals. In the past she has worked as a farmer, a police call handler and a university administrator. She now lives in the West Midlands with her husband and two cats and has a part-time job with a weight-management counselor—vainly trying to control her own weight despite her love of chocolate!

Books by Janice Preston

Harlequin Historical

Mary and the Marquis
From Wallflower to Countess
Regency Christmas Wishes
"Awakening His Sleeping Beauty"

The Lochmore Legacy

His Convenient Highland Wedding

The Beauchamp Heirs

Lady Olivia and the Infamous Rake

The Beauchamp Betrothals

Cinderella and the Duke
Scandal and Miss Markham
Lady Cecily and the Mysterious Mr. Gray

The Governess Tales

The Governess's Secret Baby

Men About Town

Return of Scandal's Son
Saved by Scandal's Heir

Visit the Author Profile page at Harlequin.com.

Prologue

December 1841—Castle McCrieff,
the Highlands of Scotland

'But... Father... I can help... I can help you to think of ideas—'

'Out!'

Flora McCrieff flinched at her father's roar, but he did not raise his hand to her. This time. Her younger brother, Donald, pulled a mocking face from behind their father's back. Father would listen to Donald's ideas, no matter how stupid they were, simply because he was a boy and would be clan chief one day. But that didn't make him wise...his ideas were always foolish, like the time he persuaded their two younger sisters, Aileen and Mairi, to sneak away with him to explore a wreck that had washed up in a nearby cove. He'd not even thought about the tide turning and cutting them off and if Flora hadn't followed her instinct that something was wrong, and gone in search of them, they would all have been drowned.

Not that her father had ever acknowledged it.

She left her father's business room without another word, shutting the heavy iron-studded door behind her.

It was no use trying to change his mind once it was made up. The air in the room had swirled thick with her father's anger and she'd sensed he was battling to rein in his temper. Better to leave before he lost control. Financial worries, made worse by the slow but steady loss of tenants—leaving the Highlands to try their luck in America and Canada— had made his temper touchier than ever.

A sense of injustice pounded in Flora's chest. Her head was full of ideas and she *knew*, if only he would listen, that she could help Father find new ways to raise money for the clan and to repair Castle McCrieff, their home and the ancestral home of the McCrieffs. But no one ever paid her any attention, unless it was to order her about. It had always been that way. Lasses should be seen and not heard—one of Father's favourite phrases and Mother never contradicted him. Not about that. Not about anything. Well, Flora knew she had more sense in her little finger than Donald had in his entire brain. At eleven, he was only a year younger than her, but when it came to common sense he was more like five years her junior.

Flora stood irresolute in the hall, which covered much of the ground floor of the keep and where a fire was kept blazing day and night, summer and winter, in the huge fireplace with its carved-stone mantel. The castle remained much the same as when it had been built, centuries ago, with a few additions. She shivered. It might be fanciful, but sometimes she imagined she could *feel* those people of long ago—their joys and their heartaches; their passions; their rage and their laughter—their emotions absorbed by the massive stone walls that were still hung in places with faded tapestries in the old style.

'There y'are, Flora, lass.' Maggie bustled from the direction of the kitchen, a tray in her hands. 'Will ye no' take this to your mother and your sisters for me? We've a mountain of food to prepare for the evening meal yet.'

Without waiting for a reply, Maggie thrust the tray, with its three bowls of broth and plate of bannocks, into Flora's hands and hurried away. Flora sighed. She didn't mind helping Maggie, their cook, but she was so tired of being overlooked by everyone.

When I am married I will be a fine lady. I will rule my household and everyone will pay attention to me and marvel at my ideas and have respect for me.

It was a favourite daydream of hers. Father was an earl and, as the eldest daughter, she would marry a man of her own station, which would mean she would be a countess or even higher. Maybe even a duchess.

She trod carefully up the stairs, heading for her mother's sitting room, where her little sisters were keeping warm as they recovered from influenza. They were much better now, but lacked the energy to do much other than sit by the fire while Mother read to them.

The bowls of broth safely delivered, Flora left the room and then hesitated. It was bone-chillingly cold outside, with a brisk wind blowing ragged clouds in off the sea. If she went downstairs, for certain Maggie would find something to keep her busy, but that resentment at her father's dismissal of her still lingered, making her restless. She turned away from the staircase and wandered along the passageway, pausing at a window to gaze out over the hills to the east. It was a majestic view, but a lonely one. She pulled her woollen shawl closer around her shoulders as a shiver coursed across her skin.

A movement from below attracted her attention—Father, clad in his black greatcoat, striding for the stables, followed by Donald, his shorter legs scurrying in an attempt to keep up with Father's longer stride. Bitterness scoured Flora's throat. Donald always got to do the interesting things. He was always toadying up to Father and he was always putting Flora down. He was jealous of her, that's what he was. She flung away from the window and the unfairness of life before running blindly down the passageway.

She rounded a corner and then, slightly breathless, halted in front of the door that led into the Great Tower. It was forbidden. It was always kept locked and, in her memory, only Father—and his father before him—had ever gone inside. It was unsafe, he said, and not even the servants were allowed to enter. But Flora knew where the key was kept, because she had seen her father take it from a wooden chest set in a window embrasure further along the passage. And she had watched as Father had gone inside. That was last year and she had thought nothing of it at the time but, recently, when she had been out riding her pony, she had glimpsed a man at the window right at the top of the tower. Her heart had nigh on stopped in terror, but then he had swept a hand over his head and she had recognised the gesture.

It cannot be so very dangerous if Father went up there.

Before she could talk herself out of it, she hurried along the passageway to the chest and opened the lid. Inside, wrapped in a tartan cloth of the McCrieff colours of brown, lilac and moss green—the colours of the Highlands, Father always said—was a large iron key. She grabbed it, closed the lid and looked all around. There was nobody there. In fact, the castle seemed almost eerily quiet today. At that thought, a shadow swept over her and she started, her heart leaping into her throat as she clutched the key to her chest. A glance out the window showed a huge, black cloud had covered the sun and she laughed at her silly fancy that, somehow, Father knew of her disobedience and was signalling his displeasure. He'd left the castle. He couldn't possibly know.

Nevertheless, a war waged within her breast. Defiance of her father could result in punishment and yet...that lingering feeling of being constantly overlooked prodded her into doing something that would prove, if only to herself, that she could not so easily be dismissed.

And humming beneath those two opposing emotions of fear and bravado was something else. Something... *other*. And it was growing stronger. And it was urging her to follow her instinct that *this*—her fingers tightened around the key—was right. This was what she needed to do...must do. It urged her on. No. That wasn't quite right. Flora shook her head in frustration...she couldn't quite grasp the meaning of that compulsion... She concentrated, hard, and then she gasped. And straightened her spine. That gut feeling—her instinct—was not *urging* her to go into the tower. No. It was drawing her there... beckoning her...

She hesitated no longer. Her instincts had never let her down. She ran to the door, inserted the key into the lock and turned it.

Inside, the windowless room was utterly dark, other than the light admitted by the open door. The room smelled musty and, as her eyes adjusted, she could see it was completely empty apart from a door set at right angles to the outer curved wall. Flora closed the door to the tower behind her and, in the dark, felt her way around the wall—the stone cold and rough against her fingertips—until her questing touch found the roughly hewn frame of the door within the room. It was not locked. She sucked in a deep breath and lifted the latch, the loud grating sound stirring her fears all over again. But the urge to go further...to seek...to, somehow, put things right...was near overwhelming, and she pulled the door open, revealing stone steps spiralling up into the tower.

Light from above lit the way and Flora crept up the stairs, keeping as quiet as she could even though there could be nobody there to hear her. Her breaths sounded harsh in the silence and she fancied she could hear her heart drumming in her chest. At the top of the stairs she halted, disappointed at the empty room that met her gaze. There was no mystery here. She crossed to the window—which at some time had been enlarged from the original arrow slit—and gazed out over the bleak hills and the glens with their pewter-grey lochs to the snow-capped mountains to the north. Then she remembered having seen Father at this very same window and she ducked away in case she, too, might be seen.

She swept the room again and her breath caught in her lungs as she realised it wasn't quite circular, although the tower itself was definitely so. She frowned, trying to persuade herself she was imagining it, but there was no mistake: the curve of the wall opposite the window was different. And why did a tapestry cover one end of that shallowly curved wall in this deserted tower?

Her feet moved, seemingly of their own volition, to that tapestry. Its faded colours depicted scenes of men doing battle with swords and claymores—a familiar enough sight to one brought up with tales of past ferocious battles between the clans—against the backdrop of a magnificent castle. Without further thought, she pulled the tapestry away from the wall. Dust billowed into the air and she held her nose between finger and thumb and squeezed her eyes shut until the urge to sneeze passed.

She opened her eyes, but they were blurred with tears and, without warning, a wave of sorrow crashed over her. Still holding the tapestry, she rubbed away the tears with her other hand. Behind the tapestry was a simple wooden door. She opened it and slipped behind the tapestry and through the door into a narrow space lit by two tall, narrow windows—arrow slits from which her ancestors had fired upon their enemies, long ago.

Then her eyes dropped and a high scream whistled from her lungs before she clamped her hand over her mouth. She wanted to run, but her legs locked tight. The skeleton gleamed white among the frayed and rotting cloth that had once shrouded it, but had now fallen away to expose the bones. It lay on a stone shelf built out from the wall and Flora could not tear her gaze away as grief, anger and aloneness battered her.

Her gulping breaths sobbed into the silence as she strove to move.

To get away.

To leave that dreadful sense of desolation behind.

The light outside abruptly brightened and a stray sunbeam penetrated one of the arrow slits to touch the skeleton, and a gleam from among the shredded linen caught Flora's eye.

As if in a dream, she saw her trembling hand reach out. As her fingers closed around a metallic object, she was all at once released from that awful paralysis. She whirled around and ran, never pausing until she reached the sanctuary of her bedchamber. She leapt on to her bed, scrambling back until she was up against the headboard. She bent her legs and clasped her arms around them, resting her forehead on her knees as the tears leaked hot from her eyes and her chest heaved.

A sharp prick in the palm of her right palm finally shook Flora from her terror. Slowly, she released her legs, becoming aware that she clutched something in her right hand. She opened her fingers, hardly daring to look.

There, on her palm, rested a brooch fashioned from silver. Her breathing slowed and steadied, and calm gradually overcame her fear. She swung her legs from the bed and crossed to the window to examine the disc-shaped brooch more closely. The surface was decorated with a plant she recognised—a thrift, with its tuft of leaves and its distinctive flowers aloft on slender stems. Two swords crossed at the centre in an X, with the letters R and A at either side.

A drop of blood sat in the centre of Flora's palm, where the pin of the brooch had pierced her skin. She bent her head to lick it away and, as she did so, her head swam and utter anguish rushed through her. She clutched her hands to her chest until that feeling subsided, then studied the brooch once more, willing it to give her some clue as to what she might do to set everything right. She rubbed the surface with her thumb and felt calm descend as she made a silent vow to take care of it.

She wrapped it in one of her embroidered handkerchiefs and laid it in the bottom of her drawer. Even had she not sworn that vow, she would never dare replace the brooch—the thought of seeing that skeleton again made her quake with terror.

Father must know it is there. Who is it? Why is it in our tower?

On that thought, Flora realised she must go back and lock the tower door before anyone found it open but, after that, she would never, ever venture near the Great Tower again.

But neither would she ever forget what she had seen.

Chapter One

October 1848

The tall, broad-shouldered figure standing before the altar sent shivers crawling up and down her spine. In desperation, Lady Flora McCrieff turned to her father, the Earl of Aberwyld, whose grip around her arm had not relaxed once on the five-minute walk from the castle to the kirk.

'Father...'

She quailed under that implacable green glare. Then her father bundled Flora none too gently to one side of the porch. Out of sight. Out of hearing.

'Ye'll not disgrace me again, Flora,' he hissed. 'D'ye hear me?' He shook her arm. 'Ye'll do as I bid ye—for the love of your family and your clan. Think of your brother and your sisters. You owe them this.'

Her stomach roiled so violently she had to swallow several times to prevent herself being physically sick. She mentally scrabbled about for more of the persuasive arguments she had rehearsed in her bedchamber as her maid had prepared her for this wedding. *Her* wedding. To a man she had never met. To a man whose name she had never heard until Sunday—two days ago—when her father had announced her forthcoming nuptials.

All her protestations had fallen on deaf ears. The banns had already been read and finally she understood why she had been forbidden to attend church services on the past three Sundays.

'Father...please...'

Why didn't I run when I had the chance?

But where would she have gone? She had nowhere and no one. And the shock of discovering the future had been mapped out for her was only just beginning to wear off. Misery squeezed her heart as her father's grip tightened painfully.

'No. You will do as you are told, lass, and wed McNeill. Ye will not care to experience my displeasure if you refuse to obey me in this.'

Tears scalded Flora's eyes and her father sighed, loosening his grip. He lifted Flora's veil and brushed a tear from her cheek.

'I need you to do this, Flora. McNeill seeks a well-born wife and he is wealthy enough to take you without a dowry.' He cleared his throat and glanced apprehensively at the door. 'He has promised to fund the repairs to the keep roof—you've seen how much damage has already been done by the leaks. *And* he'll provide dowries for Aileen and Mairi. Surely ye want to see your little sisters make good matches? Ye *owe* it to us after that business with Galkirk.'

A seed of hope germinated. Might this finally persuade her family to forgive her for letting them down so badly last year? Would obeying her father mean they would finally stop blaming her? But it still hurt that her own family appeared to view her as a brood mare, expecting her to sacrifice the rest of her life to a man she had never met.

Lachlan McNeill.

Her bridegroom. A rich man. A businessman.

And a plain mister—a poor match for the eldest daughter of an earl…even an impoverished one like her father. Her inner voice taunted her, telling her it was no more than she deserved. She had spoken out against the Duke of Galkirk last year and the consequences had been disastrous. Since then, she had become more accustomed than ever to keeping her opinions locked inside. It was less painful that away.

She longed to defy her father but, in truth, she had no fight left. She sucked in a deep breath, swallowed past the lump in her throat and nodded. Her father smiled, lowered her veil and—this time—he crooked his arm for her to take rather than grasping her arm. They entered the kirk and began the short walk up the aisle towards Lachlan McNeill.

Dread churned Flora's insides. What manner of man would take a bride unseen and even pay money for her? All too quickly, they reached her bridegroom and a swift sideways peek at his profile reassured her in his appearance, at least. His black frock coat was fashionably nipped in at the waist and well-tailored—the attire of a gentleman. His black hair was thick and wavy on the crown, but neatly trimmed to collar length, and his sideburns—not bushy in the fashion favoured by some men—reached to the hinge of his jaw. His profile was stern and slightly forbidding with its straight nose, strong jawline and firm lips, but Flora's keenly developed sixth sense told her he was not a man to fear even though his dark eyebrows were slashed low.

Flora wiped her mind of all thought as the marriage ceremony commenced.

* * *

Lachlan McNeill couldn't quite believe his good fortune when he first saw his bride, Lady Flora McCrieff, walking up the aisle towards him on her father's arm. Her posture was upright and correct and her figure was... delectable. The tight bodice and sleeves of her wedding gown—her figure tightly laced in accordance with fashion—accentuated her full breasts, slender arms and tiny waist above the wide bell of her skirt. She was tiny, dwarfed by her father's solid, powerful frame, and she barely reached Lachlan's shoulder when they stood side by side in front of the minister. True, he had not yet seen his new bride's face—her figure might be all he could wish for, but was there a nasty surprise lurking yet? Maybe her features were somehow disfigured? Or maybe she was a shrew? Why else had her father refused to let them meet before their wedding day? He'd instead insisted on riding over to Lochmore Castle, Lachlan's new home, to agree to the marriage settlements.

Their vows exchanged, Lachlan raised Flora's veil, bracing himself for some kind of abomination. His chest loosened with relief as she stared up at him, her green eyes huge and wary under auburn brows, the freckles that speckled her nose and cheeks stark against the pallor of her skin. His finger caught a loose, silken tendril of coppery-red hair and her face flooded pink, her lower lip trembling, drawing his gaze as the scent of orange blossom wreathed his senses.

She is gorgeous.

Heat sizzled through him, sending blood surging to his loins as he found himself drawn into the green depths of her eyes, his senses in disarray. Then he took her hand to place it on his arm and its delicacy, its softness, its fragility sent waves of doubt crashing through him, sluicing him clean of lustful thoughts as he sucked air into his lungs.

For the first time he doubted this plan of his to wed an aristocratic lady with useful connections in Scottish society—connections he needed to help his fledgling whisky distillery succeed. He had never imagined he'd be faced with one so young…so dainty…so captivating… and her beauty and her purity brought into sharp focus his own dirty, sordid past. Next to her he felt a clumsy, uncultured oaf.

What could he and this pampered young lady ever have in common? She might accept his fortune, but could she ever truly accept the man behind the façade? He'd faced rejection over his past before and he'd already decided that the less his wife ever learned about that past, the better.

He barely noticed the walk back down the aisle. Outside, his new in-laws—Lord and Lady Aberwyld and their three other children—gathered around them and his lordship thrust out his hand, grasping Lachlan's in a strong grip.

'Ye'll join us for a bite to eat to celebrate your nuptials before ye set off?'

'Thank you. Yes.'

'It's only a short step from the kirk. It wasna worth harnessing the carriage.'

They set off walking—Aberwyld and Lachlan, followed by Flora and the rest of the family. Lachlan would by far prefer to walk next to his bride but, with a shake of her head, she had made it clear he should fall in with her father's wishes. It didn't take Lachlan long to realise Aberwyld expected his entire family to bend to his demands.

Castle McCrieff was a massive tower house with a

flight of stone steps leading up to a heavy wooden door. Inside, although there had been some efforts at modernising, with plastered walls and carpet squares, much of the old stonework was still exposed and the passages and rooms had stone flag floors. The others disappeared into a side room, but Aberwyld stayed Lachlan with a hand to his arm.

'It looks old-fashioned to your eyes, nae doubt, after Lochmore.'

Lachlan shrugged. 'You'll have funds to modernise it now.'

Aberwyld grunted. 'Aye. I dare say.'

'And you'll help me find patrons for Carnmore Whisky?'

It was his only reason for marrying Flora McCrieff—the influence such aristocratic connections would bring him.

'Aye. I'll put in a word for ye when I can.' Aberwyld's gaze slid shiftily from Lachlan's, leaving him to doubt his new father-in-law's words. 'And ye'll have Flora to help ye.' A heavy hand landed on Lachlan's shoulder. 'Well, lad…go on in with the others. I'll join ye in a wee while.'

He left Lachlan to go and find the rest of the family. As he neared the door they had gone through, he heard Lady Aberwyld say, 'Och, Flora. If only ye hadn't refused the Duke. You were always too stubborn for your own good and now see what it's brought ye…a plain mister as your husband.'

Lachlan stalked in, putting an end to the conversation. His bride looked on the verge of tears and her mother—a wishy-washy female—looked flustered. Well, good. How dare she upset her daughter with her spiteful remarks? On her wedding day, too.

The wedding breakfast lacked any sense of celebration or joy. Nobody even raised a glass to toast their marriage or to wish them happiness. Probably they saw nothing to celebrate—an earl's daughter marrying a man such as Lachlan McNeill.

No. Nothing to celebrate at all.

Aberwyld had joined them soon after Lachlan did and it quickly became apparent that Lachlan's initial appraisal of him as the sort of dour patriarch who expected unquestioning obedience from his family was correct. He held forth on a variety of subjects, the rest of the family barely speaking unless it was to agree with him. Lachlan had come across his type many times—bullies who threw their weight around until someone had the courage to stand up to them. It was clear none of his family possessed that courage. Except…

Lachlan eyed his bride, sitting quietly at his side, her eyes downcast. She had refused a duke. Maybe she had more courage than her manner suggested?

He was relieved when Aberwyld finally stood, saying, 'Ye'll no doubt be in a hurry to get away home before night falls, McNeill.'

They trooped outside to where Lachlan's carriage waited at the bottom of the steps, Flora's hand on Lachlan's arm. Aberwyld beckoned and a woman carrying a wicker basket stepped forward.

'Maggie's packed provisions for your journey.'

Lachlan glanced at his coachman. 'Barclay. Load the basket, please.'

A choked off sob from Flora reached Lachlan and her fingers tightened on his sleeve. Her expression did not change, but a sidelong glance showed him her clenched jaw and the rapid rise and fall of her breasts as she held her emotions at bay. He covered her hand with his and squeezed. She was his now, to protect and to cherish, and he would do so.

He was mystified as he studied Flora's family. There were tensions here he did not understand. Were they not upset to see her leave? They kissed her goodbye with little show of emotion. Perhaps that was normal for aristocratic families? His own family had been boisterous and loving…until hunger and poverty had ground their spirit.

Lachlan handed Flora into the carriage. She thanked him quietly. She waved to her family and then settled back, staring resolutely out of the window as they drove away from Castle McCrieff.

'Why did you not wed that Duke?'

The question had been clawing at Lachlan ever since he had overheard Lady Aberwyld's words.

His bride visibly started. He couldn't blame her—they'd not exchanged a single word since they'd set off on the journey home to Lochmore Castle. Their eyes had not even met—she staring from the window on her side of the carriage and he from his. She was a long time answering him…was she already regretting their marriage? Was she disappointed in him? His mouth twisted in a wry smile. Of course she must be. He was a poor lad from the slums of Glasgow—albeit a wealthy one now. Hardly the sort of husband a young girl would dream of, particularly when measured against a duke…

'Well?'

The demand sounded harsh, but he wouldn't soften it. Better to wait and see what she had to say for herself.

'The Duke of Galkirk made me an offer last year. I refused him.'

Her voice was quiet, with the slightest hint of a Scots burr—not the harsh Glaswegian accent from his youth, but softer…like the early morning breeze, redolent with the scent of heather, that whispered down from the hills and out across Loch Arris whenever there was a lull in the onshore winds that so often battered Lochmore Castle. Her green eyes searched his face before dropping to her gloved hands, folded in her lap.

'Why did you refuse?'

She tucked her bottom lip under her teeth—small, even, white—and gave a tiny shake of her head. 'Does it matter? We are wed now.' Again she surveyed his face, her expression revealing nothing of her thoughts, before she resumed her perusal of the passing scenery.

Lachlan took the opportunity to study his new wife.

Wife! How peculiar that sounded. Him, a married man. He, who had always prided himself on needing no one, for hadn't he proved that over the past fourteen years? He'd had nothing but himself and his wits to rely on, and he'd made a success of his life. Pulled himself out of the swamp of despair that had drowned so many and broken their spirit. No doubt they would find a way to rub along together in this marriage of convenience and, with luck, Flora would soon get with child and her attention would be on family matters while he would have his business interests and his search for Anna to occupy him.

The thought of his one remaining sister twisted his heart with guilt and grief. Where could she be? He had searched and searched for her ever since his return to Scotland. If only he had come home sooner. If only he hadn't been so determined to prove himself and make a success of his life. If only—

With a silent curse, he wrenched his thoughts from the past. He rarely allowed himself to dwell on it and, if it wasn't for the constant fear of what had become of Anna, he would have banished all thought of the past fourteen years by now. He hauled in a deep breath, pushing that ball of gnawing worry aside, and returned his attention to his new bride.

She appeared demure enough—docile even—but...it must have taken some spirit to refuse a *duke*. He frowned. Maybe she had hidden depths? Her mother had called her stubborn—was it that trait keeping her silent? He thrust his conjectures aside. They were two strangers now bound together for life and it was only fair to get to know her better before judging her.

He continued his scrutiny, remembering his body's reaction to her wide-eyed gaze in the kirk and the doubts that had swamped him. The memory rendered him even more tongue-tied than ever. He had no experience of how to treat a real lady, especially not one who now belonged to him body and soul. The responsibility didn't set well on his shoulders. He wasn't a man who developed friendships with ease, let alone a relationship such as this. Husband and wife.

'Pardon?'

She had spoken. Or he thought she had. But he had been inside his own head and missed her quiet comment.

'Where are we going?'

Her simple question stole his breath. All this time he'd been wallowing in his own awkwardness and discomfort and yet she—nineteen years of age and married to a man she had never met—did not even know where he was taking her.

'We are going home.'

She frowned, her smooth forehead wrinkling.

'How far?'

He glanced out of the window. They had left the coast behind and were now heading south from Loch Machrie through Kilmachrie Glen, bordered to the west by the ocean—currently invisible—and to the east by rugged green hills, moors and glens. They were passing the standing stones he had noticed on the journey to Castle McCrieff, and he knew they would not see the sea again until they turned off this road and headed south-west, towards the rugged promontory on which Lochmore Castle was built.

'About two hours. Maybe a little more.'

She lowered her head and her hand crept up to touch a brooch pinned to her travelling cloak.

'Where did you get that brooch?'

Her head snapped round as her hand closed around it. 'It is mine.'

'I don't doubt it. But it was not on your cloak earlier.'

Her face flamed and he recalled the tremble of her hand as he handed her into the carriage. He gentled his voice.

'I shall not take it from you. It was a harmless enough question, I thought. One that surely deserves an answer?'

He smiled at her, keen to ease this tension that shimmered between them.

'It was in my pocket. My father said it was unsuitable for my wedding day.'

'May I see it?'

Lachlan reached for the edge of Flora's cloak. He withdrew his hand when he saw her flinch.

'Are you *afraid* of me?'

Those green eyes sought his. 'A…a little.'

'Your father…he is a strict man?'

'H-he has very strong ideas of correct behaviour.' Her eyes blazed before her lashes lowered to shield her emotion. 'I did not always behave as he wished.'

'You refused a duke. And your father was…what? Angry? He punished you?'

'They were all angry.' Her voice dropped to a whisper. 'I let them all down.'

'Well, I tell you this, Lady Flora McNeill. I do not believe in physical punishment—' he had seen enough of that to last him several lifetimes, on board the convict ship and afterwards at the penal colony in New South Wales '—and you need never fear I will raise my hand against you.' He put his hand on her leg. 'You have my word.'

She released a quiet sigh. 'I thank you.'

But her thigh was rigid beneath his hand and he wondered if some of her fear might be of the night to come. She was a maiden and she might not even know what to expect of the marriage bed. Had her mother instructed her? Allayed her fears? He returned his hand to his own lap. There were no reassurances he could offer that would not result in embarrassment for them both—he must hope that once the hurdle of their wedding night was out of the way she would relax in his company.

Flora's stomach tied in ever tighter knots the further they travelled from the only home she had ever known. Her throat tightened and the tears that had lurked beneath the surface for the past two days threatened to spill—her family might have been resentful and critical of her over the past year, but at least they were familiar. She gulped, holding back the tears by sheer force of will.

Lachlan's voice broke into her thoughts.

'Are you hungry? You ate very little at the wedding breakfast. I can instruct the coachman to halt for a few minutes.'

He was well spoken: his voice deep and melodious

with a barely discernible Scottish burr. About to refuse, for she was eager to reach their destination and escape the close confines of the carriage as soon as possible, Flora realised maybe it was he who was hungry.

'Thank you. Yes, that would be welcomed.'

She couldn't stomach a thing, but maybe a drink would help moisten her dry mouth and throat. Lachlan rapped on the carriage ceiling and, after a few minutes, the vehicle turned off the road. Lachlan jumped out, lowered the steps and handed Flora from the carriage. She noted once again the strength in his grip. His arm under her hand as they had walked back down the aisle had been rock hard—he had a powerful physique and, despite the anxiety stringing her nerves tight, she couldn't help but feel a quiver of anticipation at the thought of their wedding night.

The two men on the box climbed down—the coachman checking the horses and the groom hurrying to the rear of the carriage to unstrap the basket Maggie had provided.

'Would you…er…?' Lachlan gestured vaguely in the direction of a low clump of bushes some twenty yards from where they stood.

Flora's cheeks burned. 'No. Thank you. I… I just need to stretch my legs a little.'

He nodded and she walked back along the road. She cast her gaze around her at the magnificent brooding landscape, the broad glen bordered by rugged hills. There was no sign of human habitation. Nowhere to run to, nowhere to hide. And, even if there was, there was nowhere she could go. She belonged to him now.

Her husband.

A stranger.

And she was now Lady Flora McNeill, not the lady of rank she had once imagined in her future.

And whose fault is that?

She quashed that taunt. She had been right to reject the Duke of Galkirk—her instinct had warned her against him even before he proved himself a despicable lecher on the very evening their betrothal was to be announced. And she had publicly denounced him, not realising at the time how great was the financial need of her family and their tenants. Needs that had worsened in the past year after blight hit the local potato crop yet again. The blame, disapproval and disappointment of her parents and her siblings—not to mention other clan members—had worn her down until the burden of shame had grown almost too much to bear. She had retreated into herself—speaking only when spoken to and accepting the chores heaped upon her shoulders without complaint.

And now, that same instinct that had prompted her to refuse Galkirk was telling her that Lachlan McNeill was a good man and she trusted his word that he would never raise his hand to her. The past twelve months, however, had taught her there were worse punishments than the strike of a man's hand. At least that was over and done with, if painful and humiliating, unlike the consistent drag on her spirits of knowing how she had let her family down.

How much would she see of her family in the future? Her father expected obedience from his wife and children and he'd already demonstrated his ability to cut those who displeased him from his life after his sister, Tessa—having defied their father's plan to marry her to the Duke of Lochmore—had been sent to live with relations in Glasgow. Neither Grandfather nor Father had ever forgiven her and Flora had never even met her aunt.

That incident had added yet another grudge to the ancient feud between the McCrieffs and the Lochmores—a feud that the marriage of Lochmore and Tessa had been intended to heal.

Flora glanced back at Lachlan, who was consulting with the coachman. He was her future and it was up to her to make the best of it and not look back. She slowly retraced her steps. She did not want him to regret marrying her, so she would try hard to make him happy. But did that mean she must obey him blindly in all things, as her mother obeyed her father? She did not think she could bear such a marriage, but she realised her future was in her hands. She would tread softly to begin with, however, until she knew her husband better.

Lachlan met her gaze as she approached. He was so tall—he towered over her—and he was so formidable looking with his stern expression and his brooding dark eyes under straight black eyebrows. She had seen him smile just the once, when he'd asked her about her brooch, but it had been a forced smile that didn't reach those deeply intense eyes.

And have you smiled at him?

A gust of wind caught at her cloak and she shivered, gathering it around her again. Beneath, she still wore her wedding gown—an old white-silk evening gown of Mother's, trimmed with Honiton lace—neither as fine nor as romantic as she had once dreamed of for her wedding, but then this union was not romantic, was it? It was a marriage of convenience. A lock of hair fell loose, tumbling across her forehead, and she tucked it beneath her bonnet. She forced herself to smile at Lachlan. His eyes widened, then he strode to her to take her arm. She hid her wince as he touched the painful bruise left by her father.

'It is cold out here. We will sit in the carriage to eat.'

'As you wish, sir.'

'Lachlan.' The rejoinder came swift and fierce. 'I do not wish to be "sir" to you.'

'Very well. Lachlan. It is a good Scottish name. As is McNeill.'

He nodded in acknowledgement, but offered none of his background. As they neared the carriage, the groom was on the roof, handing another basket down to the coachman.

'What is it, Barclay?'

'There's something in it, sir. It moved.'

He unstrapped the lid. It lifted an inch and a black nose emerged, followed by—

'Bandit!'

Nothing could stem the tears now. Flora fell to her knees and hugged the squirming terrier to her. She had begged her father to allow her to bring Bandit, but he'd forbidden it. So who…?

She set Bandit down and he bounded away before settling to the serious business of nosing the ground to investigate the fascinating smells. Flora pulled the basket to her and rummaged inside. Under a cushion she found a folded piece of paper. Her breath caught as she opened it.

Thought you might need a friend. D. x

Flora scrambled to her feet, clutching the note, joy coursing through her. Donald had defied Father. Through blurred vision she saw Lachlan watching her, a frown creasing his forehead.

'Bandit?' One brow lifted.

'Please say I may keep him.' If he said no, there would be nothing she could do. 'He is well behaved, even though he's only young.' He would be two in the spring and was a bundle of energy, but how could anyone resist his lop-sided ears and the black eye patches that had inspired his name?

Her new husband frowned. 'There are cats at the castle. And poultry roam freely in the grounds.'

'Bandit is used to livestock.' Flora tilted her chin at her white lie. He *was* getting better at not chasing after other animals.

'Very well. Watch he doesn't stray while we eat, Barclay.'

Lachlan handed Flora into the carriage, then followed her inside with the picnic basket. He opened it to reveal bread and cheese and a quart stoneware bottle of ale, but no vessels from which to drink. He appeared momentarily at a loss.

'I am not so fine that I cannot drink from the bottle,' Flora said, with a smile. The world had taken on a brighter hue.

Dull red flagged his cheekbones. 'It is not how I imagined toasting our union.'

His voice was gruff and a muscle ticked in his jaw. Out of nowhere came the urge to comfort him and Flora reached out to touch his hand. They had each removed their gloves in order to eat and the feel of his strong, hair-dusted hand…the heat of his skin…the sight of his neat square fingernails…sent her heart leaping and a tingle up her arm. He started at her touch and raised his gaze from the bottle to capture hers, his dark eyes puzzled. She braced herself against the natural instinct to snatch her hand from his and, instead, she stroked, tracing the solid bones of his hand with her fingertips, learning the feel of him. The air appeared to shimmer between them.

'We can toast our union when we are home,' she said

softly. 'Will you tell me a little about it? You called it a castle...have you lived there all your life?'

He tugged his hand from beneath hers. 'No.'

He offered her bread and cheese and, although still not hungry, she accepted a portion of each, wondering what she had said to cause his abrupt withdrawal. He opened the bottle and offered it first to Flora. She took it and drank gratefully, then nibbled alternately at the bread and the cheese, waiting for him to elaborate.

He tipped his head back, drinking a deep draught, before he continued. 'I bought it a year ago.' He looked at her again, his expression a mix of defiance and pride. 'It is a castle, yes. Lochmore Castle.'

'Lochmore?'

Chapter Two

Lachlan frowned at Flora's gasp. 'Did your father not tell you? He had a good look round when he rode over to discuss the settlements.'

'No, he did not.'

Father had always claimed nothing would induce him to set foot in the castle of his old enemy, ever since the proposed match between Flora's Aunt Tessa and the current duke had failed. It was a matter of pride, he had said, and if there was one thing Highlanders possessed in abundance, it was pride.

'I never imagined…but, how did…? You are a McNeill. Why do you own the ancestral seat of Clan Lochmore?'

Did Father view this as some kind of victory over the Lochmore—a McCrieff to be mistress of Lochmore Castle after all?

'Clan Lochmore?' Lachlan raised one dark brow. 'I thought that feudal structure was banned after the forty-five?'

'They couldn't wipe out centuries of history just like that,' said Flora. 'Clan is family—no government can control our hearts and minds.' She'd heard her father raging about it often enough when he'd been imbibing the whisky. 'So...why Lochmore Castle?'

'The Duke of Lochmore does not care for the place. He and his family have not lived there for years and his heir spends much of his time travelling and so, rather than continue to spend money on its upkeep, he instructed his agent to sell.'

'But none of that explains why you bought a castle to live in. Why? And why Lochmore in particular?'

'Have you finished eating?'

Flora nodded. Lachlan packed up the basket before setting it on the seat opposite them.

'You'd better call your dog,' he said.

Flora opened the door. 'Bandit! Here, boy.'

He streaked across the turf, his short legs pumping, tongue lolling. A flying leap at the doorway and he skidded across the carriage floor like he was on ice before tumbling head over heels to land in a heap at Lachlan's feet. Her husband's mouth thinned. He rapped on the ceiling and the carriage lurched into motion.

'*That* is well behaved?' he commented as Bandit leapt on to Flora's lap, propped his front paws on her chest and licked her ear.

'He is happy to see me.' Flora hugged her pet as he wriggled in ecstasy. 'He'll soon settle down.'

Lachlan raised one brow as Flora persuaded Bandit to curl up on the seat between them.

He leaned back against the squabs and sighed. 'To answer your question, I bought Lochmore because I thought it might gain me acceptance with the Scottish nobility. I was wrong.'

He turned his penetrating gaze upon Flora and a warning shiver trickled down her spine.

'And that is where I come in?' Her voice was barely a whisper.

'It is. With a well-born wife I shall find doors opened to me that would otherwise remain closed.'

Foreboding twisted her stomach as she fondled Bandit's ear, her mind racing. Her one consolation in marrying Mr McNeill had been that she would never again have to face society after the scandal of her almost-betrothal to the Duke of Galkirk. Now, in an awful twist of fate, it seemed the only reason Lachlan had married her was to provide him with an entrée into that society.

'Why do you wish to be accepted by the nobility? Why not socialise with the business classes? These days, many of them are richer than the aristocracy, especially here in Scotland.'

'I seek not only investment, but patronage.' Lachlan leaned forward, propping his forearms on his knees, linking his hands together as he stared at the floor. 'I bought a whisky distillery and invested in new equipment. My whisky is good—a new blend of malt and grain. The business has potential, but I've struggled to get the name accepted. I need influential backers and that's why I need you.'

He twisted his head, his dark eyes intense as he stared at Flora, before lowering his gaze once more to the floor.

'But why buy a castle if you need money for your business? You could afford to sell it for less, perhaps, to gain customers. Or advertise it in the newspapers.'

'It's not that simple. I need introductions to the gentlemen's clubs and hotels in cities such as London, Edinburgh and Glasgow to allow me to increase production, but for that I need patronage. Those establishments are so set in their ways, they need to be persuaded to even *try* a new supplier, let alone make a permanent change.'

He shook his head. 'I *know* I can do better.' The words burst from him. 'I *know* we can produce enough fine-quality whisky to expand the distillery and to supply many more customers, but I just need the opportunity. I need the right doors to open for me.'

Flora frowned at his sudden intensity. 'You make it sound as though it is a matter of life and death.'

'It may be exactly that, for the men and women who rely upon me for work.'

How could Flora possibly understand? She was nineteen years old and even though her family's fortunes had declined over the past years she could still have no concept of what it was like to grow up in absolute poverty, with no choice but to steal to try to ensure your family's survival.

He wanted no further questions. The past was too personal. Too shameful. It belonged in the past. 'As to why Lochmore Castle in particular—it is family legend that there is McNeill blood running in the veins of the Lochmore chiefs. It felt right to have a home with which I share some history, however ancient that link might be.'

And it felt good to put down roots.

'Your clan is linked to the Lochmores? You do know that the McCrieffs and the Lochmores are old enemies?' Her look was almost accusatory.

'Why should that make any difference?'

She huffed in irritation. 'This land we are driving through used to be McCrieff territory until King John Balliol granted possession of it to the Laird of Lochmore.'

'King John Balliol? Never heard of him. How long ago was this?'

'I think…in the thirteenth century. It may have been long ago, but there was enmity between our clans even before that time. Grudges live long in the Highlands and this grudge has never been forgotten. Or forgiven.'

Lachlan suppressed his snort of derision.

'I do not set stock in those ancient feuds and grudges, Flora. I am more troubled by what is happening today… the clearances…the vast injustices in society…the people living in poverty *now*.'

'Well, and so am I.' Her forehead wrinkled. 'I know Highlanders have been forced off their land to make way for sheep, but there are *some* clan chiefs—my father for one— who've worked hard to support their tenants. But then the blight hit again and some tenants emigrated anyway—to America or Canada and a better life.'

Some had gone to Australia, too, and he had seen the poor wretches as they had disembarked after the four-month voyage—lost and confused in a land so far different from their homeland that they might just as well have landed on the moon.

'And those who did not, or could not, take passage went to the cities to search for work, driving down wages and needing shelter where there are already too few houses to go round,' said Lachlan. Glasgow and Edinburgh were already heaving with Irish immigrants following mass starvation and disease in Ireland, caused by the same potato blight now creating havoc in Scotland. 'I do not believe—nay, I know for a fact—that *they* have not gone to a better life.'

And they were right back on the topic he did not wish to discuss. His past. He rubbed his temples.

'Tell me about your brooch, Flora. Why does your father dislike it?'

It helped distract Flora. She touched the brooch again and then she unfastened it and held it out to him.

'He did not dislike it, other than as a wedding ornament. I found it, seven years ago, and…and I like to wear it.'

It sounded like half a tale. Or even less. Lachlan examined the brooch. The workmanship was a little crude to modern eyes—a disc of silver, decorated with the moulded form of a thrift plant, the letters R and A, and a pair of swords that crossed over the centre.

'It looks old—I should have thought a lady such as yourself would wear finer jewellery.' He handed back the brooch.

She bent her head, tutting in exasperation as she struggled to fasten it.

Lachlan reached to help. 'Allow me.'

As their hands touched a distinct tingle chased up his arm, as it had when she had startled him by stroking his hand—a gesture so unexpected he had struggled to know how to react. Was she aware of the intimacy of that touch or had she simply meant to reassure him?

'The catch has always been stiff.'

He felt the tremble of her fingers before she withdrew them to allow him to fasten the brooch to her cloak. He leaned closer to see what he was doing and her soft breath whispered through his hair, sending shivers racing across his scalp. He fought the urge to haul her against him and plunder her mouth, too aware of her innocence and her gentle upbringing to risk frightening her.

'Did nobody miss the brooch, or look for it?'

'No. It had been lost a long time.'

There. It was done. He straightened. 'How would you know how long it had been lost?'

She slanted him a look from those green eyes. 'I went exploring in a forbidden part of the castle.'

She bit her lower lip, staring at him. 'No one but my father was allowed there, but I went anyway. It was thrown aside…discarded among a heap of…' She paused. Then she tilted her chin. 'A heap of old rags.' Her eyes slid from his to Bandit as she fondled his ear.

He really was a disreputable-looking animal—one ear pricked, one drooping; a scruffy, wiry white coat; and those black eye patches that really did give him the look of a bandit. The dog seemed to sense his regard. He raised his head and stared back, almost defiantly, although that seemed almost ridiculously fanciful.

He had enough attitude for himself and his mistress combined. Lachlan broke eye contact first and looked back at Flora, whose attention was still on Bandit. She often seemed wary of speaking her mind, but that tale of defying her father gave him hope she was not as timid as she appeared. He was under no illusions about himself—he'd lived a harsh life, among hard men, and it had shaped the man he had become: self-sufficient and tough. There was no place in his life for a bride easily intimidated, or one who needed to cling to her husband. He had no wish to get too close to anyone, not even his wife.

He had at least diverted her from the subject of his painful, shameful past. Flora need never know about that. He intended to put it firmly behind him. Just as soon as he had tracked down Anna.

It was late afternoon before the carriage turned off the road on to a track that led steadily upwards through ancient woodland of oaks and birches wearing the russet hues of autumn. To their right the land shelved steeply away from the track and Flora caught glimpses of the blue-green waters of a loch, far below.

'That is Loch Arris. We are nearly home.'

'What made you buy Lochmore Castle?' Flora asked on impulse. 'Why not a castle linked to the McNeill clan?'

Lachlan shrugged. 'The McNeills' seat is Barra in the Outer Hebrides but my father never lived there. Lochmore is near enough to Glasgow for me to see to business and, as I said, there is that rumour of that long-ago link between the Lochmores and my branch of the McNeills. It seemed fitting.'

Ahead, Flora could see a gatehouse built of grey stone, with smoke curling from the chimney, next to a square tower that straddled the carriageway.

'Who lives there?'

'Gregor and Brenda Fraser—Gregor is the manager at my distillery. The original outer curtain wall is lower than it once would have been, but I believe the gatehouse and the tower are much as they would have always been.'

The light dimmed as they passed beneath the tower and then brightened as they emerged into what would once, presumably, have been the outer bailey with stables over to the right and what looked like an old chapel to the left. Beyond the stables were a vegetable garden and glasshouses, and the remainder of the ground was grass, dotted with trees and evergreen shrubs.

Craning her neck ahead for a view of her new home, Flora saw another square tower, built of the same grey stone as the gatehouse, but looming four storeys into the sky, its walls punctuated by mullioned windows. They drove through an opening in another low wall.

'This was the inner bailey,' said Lachlan, 'and that is the old keep.' He pointed at the massive stone tower. 'And that—' he gestured out of the opposite carriage window, to their left 'was the great hall, which was remodelled into a ballroom by the current Duke of Lochmore's first wife. She also had a modern wing constructed, to link the keep and the ballroom.'

It was not until the carriage came to a standstill in the

gravelled forecourt and Lachlan handed her from the carriage that Flora truly appreciated the size of the castle and she gasped out loud. Lochmore would swallow Castle McCrieff twice over. Even Bandit seemed overawed and clung close to her.

Three wide stone steps led up to the imposing front door, protected by a portico supported on fluted columns. The newer wing boasted large windows and the ballroom, jutting forward at a right angle, had been modernised by the addition of three sets of glazed French windows that overlooked a narrow terrace and a knot garden.

She gazed back towards the gatehouse and the inner and outer walls. In days gone by they would have stood firm against attack and siege, she knew, and she shivered, grateful such brutal feuds between warring clans were long past. The clans today lived in peace despite the occasional still-rumbling grudge, but the many castles scattered throughout the Highlands—both occupied and in ruins—bore testament to its troubled history.

She became aware of Lachlan's scrutiny.

'Have you never been here before?'

'I have not. I told you, the McCrieffs and the Lochmores are old foes, even though the Lochmores have tried in the past to cool the bad blood between them.' Including the attempt to marry Flora's Aunt Tessa to the current Duke of Lochmore after his first wife died. 'I am amazed my father came here at all—the McCrieffs' memories are long and their grudges are deeply held.'

Lachlan's eyes glinted as he smiled at her. 'I shall remember that, Flora.'

His smile did funny things to her insides, but she soon forgot them as she realised the size of the task facing her: a husband who was a stranger, but who nevertheless imagined she had enough influence to ease his path in society; a huge castle that would no doubt take a mountain of money and effort to maintain; neighbours and workers who might very well resent a McCrieff becoming mistress of Lochmore.

'Are the servants members of the Lochmore Clan?'

'A few are locals who have worked here for years, but I also hired several from Glasgow.'

'Glasgow? But…what will they know about Highland life? And working in a castle?'

He frowned. 'Every one of them is a Highlander, from various clans. They, or their parents before them, were forced to move to the city in order to survive when they were turned off their land. They may not have worked in a castle before, but they are keen to learn and to earn their living. Jobs give people self-respect and they are proud people.' His frown deepened. 'We talked about the plight of the people earlier—why I need my whisky to succeed, for those who rely on me for their living. Starvation and disease are rife in the Highlands now the potato crop has failed again.'

In truth, Flora hadn't fully understood his meaning. She had little idea of what had been happening in the rest of Scotland, outside of the area in which she had grown up. Her father did not believe womenfolk should be concerned with politics. All Flora had known was her family's dwindling fortunes and the loss of several local families as they left to seek a better life elsewhere. She was fortunate. She was not, and never had been, starving.

'I expect the workers to be treated with respect, even though their backgrounds are not the equal of yours.'

She raised her chin, offended. 'I *always* treat the servants well. I am not about to change now.'

His comment stirred her curiosity about his past. She knew nothing about him, other than that his intense stare sometimes made her insides quiver and that his smile was rare but, when it broke, it lit his features and everything around him. A mental image arose of that long-ago day in the tower, when a ray of sun broke through the clouds and glinted off the silver metal of the brooch. She lifted her hand to it, as she had done countless times through the journey, happy that she had managed to keep it safe all these years. As ever, she felt a deep sense of peace as she touched it.

She studied Lachlan, taking in his expensive clothes. His gold fob watch and the signet ring he wore on his right hand. His confidence. He must be very wealthy to afford a place such as Lochmore Castle. And from that thought it was a short hop to realising that her own appearance nowhere near equalled his. In the eyes of the staff she would look nothing like the daughter of a nobleman or the mistress of Lochmore Castle. Her luggage consisted of just one evening gown and one afternoon dress—gowns she'd worn during her brief excursion into Edinburgh society last October. Other than those, she only had her everyday clothing—nothing like the luxurious and lavish trousseau she had once dreamed of. The remainder of her garments from last year were back at home, intended for Aileen who, at seventeen, would soon be expected to catch a suitable husband, with the help of the dowry paid by Lachlan.

'Are you ready?'

Lachlan's gaze swept Flora from head to foot, raising a quiver of awareness in her, but reminding her again of her sorry appearance, clad in a worn velvet cloak and bonnet, both of which had seen better days, with a scruffy wire-haired terrier at her heels. Her husband's expression revealed nothing of his thoughts and she raised her hands to tuck away any stray strands of hair. Did he find her unattractive? Not many men found short, freckled ladies with red hair appealing. If he wasn't already disappointed by his end of the bargain he had struck with her father, he surely would be once he realised how little help she would be in finding patrons for his whisky. The scandal she had caused had been huge. Her parents had whisked her home and she had not shown her face in society since, although she knew from Donald exactly what the gossips were saying, including their speculation that she was no longer an innocent.

She swallowed. She could not avoid this. She was married now and this was her new home. Her new life. She drew in a steadying breath and nodded.

'Then come.' Lachlan swept one arm around. 'Welcome to Lochmore Castle, Lady Flora McNeill. Welcome to your new home.'

Flora took Lachlan's arm—her fingers curling around his hard bicep—and they walked up the front steps and through the door into a spacious, bright entrance hall, a still-subdued Bandit at their heels.

Halfway down the hall, just past a tall stone-dressed archway on the right-hand side, a wide, polished wood staircase carpeted in red and gold swept up from the marble-tiled floor. A huge chandelier hung over the stairwell—luxury indeed, thought Flora, as she pictured the stone staircases of Castle McCrieff, still lit by wall sconces at night.

Footsteps echoed and a tall thin female and a short, wiry man with thinning sandy-coloured hair emerged through the stone archway that gave access to the old keep. They were followed by two footmen. The woman's greying hair was pulled back from her face and a bunch of keys was attached to the belt of her uniform.

'Ah. Allow me to present my wife, Lady Flora. Mrs

Dalgliesh is the Lochmore housekeeper, and Drummond is our butler.'

'May I offer my congratulations on your marriage, Mr McNeill? And welcome to Lochmore, Lady Flora.'

The housekeeper's gentle greeting belied the harshness of her features. What Flora had at first taken for lines of disapproval etched into Mrs Dalgliesh's countenance were, upon closer inspection, lines of sorrow and disappointment. Flora relaxed and smiled at her.

'Thank you, Mrs Dalgliesh.'

Drummond echoed the housekeeper's felicitations before sending the footmen to fetch the luggage.

'I shall leave you to show Lady Flora around the castle and to introduce her to the rest of the staff, Mrs Dalgliesh. I have work to attend to, so I shall be in my study if I am needed.' Lachlan hesitated, then bowed to Flora with a fleeting smile. 'I shall see you at dinner, my dear.'

Flora watched her new husband stride across the hall and disappear through another archway directly opposite the first.

My dear.

He had used no endearments until now. She was not fooled—the endearment was for the servants' edification. She could not help but be disappointed that he chose not to show her around himself.

She stretched her lips into a bright smile.

'Would you show me to my bedchamber first, please, Mrs Dalgliesh?'

Chapter Three

'I have already ordered warm water to be sent up, my lady.' Mrs Dalgliesh spoke over her shoulder as she preceded Flora up the stairs. 'A maid is waiting to unpack your clothes and to assist you. If she pleases you, you may keep her as your personal maid, or you may wish to appoint your own woman, of course.'

The first flight of the staircase angled oddly to accommodate what was clearly the outer wall of a tower. Flora's step faltered as she trailed her fingertips around the curved wall, memories rushing in on her of that long-ago day when she had found her brooch.

Mrs Dalgliesh paused. 'That is Morag's Tower, a part of the old keep,' she said.

'Why is it called Morag's Tower?'

'The Duke of Lochmore's great-aunt Morag lived there, staying on even after the Duke and Duchess moved out. Now, downstairs, the keep consists of the dining room, the morning parlour, the kitchens and it gives access to the new chapel. Not that it's new, actually. It was built in the sixteenth century, but there is an older chapel in the grounds, too. So, the keep has four storeys, with two of the original four corner towers still standing, whereas the modern wing only has two floors. The ground floor of the modern wing has the drawing room, library, billiards room and the master's study, and the passageway leads around to give access to the ballroom, which is closed off most of the time.'

The first-floor landing was bright and spacious with a polished wood balustrade that overlooked the stairwell and that magnificent crystal chandelier. On the far side of the landing was a large window through which Flora could see the portico roof and the castle grounds beyond.

Mrs Dalgliesh pointed left, through a similar archway to the one downstairs, beyond which there stretched a wide corridor. There were doors to both right and left, between which several paintings were displayed.

'The keep end of the gallery leads to guest bedchambers and the back stairs. The second floor has more guest rooms plus a nursery suite and the top floor houses the staff. This way—' she pointed right '—are the master suites.'

'Mr McNeill told me the Duke's wife had this wing built,' said Flora.

'His first wife, yes. It is much newer than the rest of the Castle, but it was all fully refurbished before Mr McNeill moved in.'

The need to know more of the man she had wed warred in Flora's breast against her mother's mantra that one should not encourage servants' gossip. The need to know won.

'It must have taken a great deal of work.'

'It did. The master was fully involved—nothing was too much trouble and he didna stint on expense. If there's one thing I can say about the master, he's no' a stingy man even though he's a man of few words. He works hard and he works long hours, but there are many folks who depend on him. We all appreciate his efforts.'

'Where does the Duke of Lochmore live now, Mrs Dalgliesh?'

'He and the present Duchess live a few miles from here, in a country house not far from Lochmore village. The castle was leased out after Morag died, but the Duke never wanted to move back and decided to sell. I was living in Glasgow when I heard Mr McNeill was hiring.' A shadow crossed her face. 'My husband was already sick when we were turned off our farm by the landlord. He wasna strong enough to face an ocean crossing so we went to the city to find work.'

'Your husband…is he here at Lochmore with you?'

'Aye, that he is. In the kirkyard down in the village.'

'Oh! I—I am very sorry.'

'Don't be. It was the consumption that did for him, but he died happy, knowing I was here and my future was secure. Glasgow was—' She shut her lips firmly, then uttered a mirthless laugh. 'Hark at me, mithering on. You don't want to hear about our woes when you must be exhausted.'

She led the way from the head of the stairs, pausing outside the second door on the left.

'This is the master's bedchamber—his dressing room was the first door we passed,' she said. 'The Duchess's suite is here.'

Mrs Dalgliesh opened the door opposite and flung it wide. Flora stepped over the threshold and gasped. The bedchamber was enormous, the floral wallpaper in shades of green, pale rose and cream, and it was dominated by a large tester bed with rich red hangings that matched the floor-length curtains, but Flora was transfixed by the view of the sea through the trio of tall windows on the wall opposite the door.

'It is *glorious*.'

'It is, but it is not the best of it. Let me show you the rest.' The housekeeper crossed the bedchamber to a door and ushered Flora through. 'This was the Duchess's boudoir—it was designed to take advantage of the sea views.'

Flora crossed to the window as if in a dream. Any detail of the decor or furnishings was lost on her as she drank in the enchanting view. The boudoir was a corner room and, at the outer corner, there was a west-facing bay window, large enough to incorporate a gold and cream upholstered *chaise longue* and a small side table with a vase of flowers. The sun was just starting to set, painting the sky above the horizon with streaks of fiery red, burnt orange, soft yellows and pinks and the reflected colours of that glorious sunset danced and shimmered among white-topped waves as they broke the surface of the indigo sea.

'It feels...' Flora could not put her emotions into words for a moment, she was so overwhelmed. She steadied herself, and gathered her thoughts. 'It feels almost as though I am on a ship,' she said breathily, for there was no land to break the view between the castle and the sea.

She leaned forward to peer at the waves as they crashed against jagged rocks below. In the distance, Flora could see land, presumably one of the many islands—both inhabited and uninhabited—that dotted the west coast.

'It is magnificent.' She would never tire of this majestic view and it awoke in her the urge for music, to start playing the pianoforte again, a joy that had somehow become lost to her over the past year.

'I knew you would like it.' Satisfaction warmed Mrs

Dalgliesh's voice. 'Come. I will show you your dressing room and introduce you to Muriel, the girl I have assigned to help you, before we tour the rest of the castle. I have instructed the staff to assemble in the hall in one hour in order that you may meet them.'

By the time the dinner hour came around, Flora's head was swimming. The sheer size of Lochmore Castle and the luxurious decor near overwhelmed her. Even the servants' quarters in the attic had been refurbished. They were not richly furnished or decorated, but were clean and comfortable—Lachlan was clearly a man who cared about those who worked for him, unlike her father, who took for granted that servants would serve him and be happy to do so regardless of how much he could pay or how spartan their accommodation.

And I am no better. For when have I ever given the servants' comforts more than a fleeting thought?

That realisation shamed her.

She wanted to look her best for her wedding night, so she dressed in her sole evening gown, of sea-green satin with lace flounces, the bodice low off the shoulders with a bertha of lace and with a deep point below the waist and a full skirt. She instructed Muriel, a cheery, round-faced girl, how to dress her hair, with a centre parting and simply braided over her ears. Bandit was still subdued and, rather than leave him on his own, Muriel agreed to take him down to the servants' quarters with her.

Downstairs, Renney, one of the footmen, preceded her to the dining room, in the older part of the castle. Morag's Tower was accessed from the corner of this room and was the only part of the castle Flora had declined to inspect— the empty room and enclosed, tightly spiralling staircase evoking unnerving memories of the day she had ventured up the Great Tower at Castle McCrieff. As she entered the dining room her attention was drawn to Lachlan, who stood by the hearth.

She had forgotten quite how impressive he was—tall and broad-shouldered, dressed in black frock coat and trousers and a blue and red tartan waistcoat, with a white shirt and black cravat, his black hair gleaming in the light cast by the candelabra set at either end of the mantelshelf. He bowed, his expression so grave her immediate reaction was to wonder what she'd done wrong. He held a glass of wine and, before he said anything, he took a long swallow. Her stomach had churned so with nerves she felt sick, but his failure to greet her stirred a touch of temper deep inside.

Did this man have no idea of good manners?

'Good evening, Lachlan.'

Her voice rang across the room and she saw his brows twitch into a frown.

'Good evening, Flora. I trust you are impressed by your new home and situation?'

Impressed? She was, but it was a peculiar question. Boastful, almost. 'Thank you, yes.'

'Then we shall eat.'

Lachlan nodded to Renney, who pulled out a chair at one end of the vast table. Her nerves a-jangle, Flora sat and watched as Lachlan took a chair at the opposite end. All her carefully prepared ideas for conversation and for learning about her husband were for nothing. Unless they shouted at one another down the length of the table, there would be no conversation that evening.

Lachlan hadn't reckoned on feeling quite so off-kilter in the presence of his new bride. She was a lady, born and bred. What did he know about ladies? About how to treat them? When Flora stepped inside the dining room, his mouth had dried and his heart, already racing, appeared to leap into his throat. His hand had trembled as he raised his wineglass to his lips and took in her beauty—her glorious hair, shimmering strands of copper and gold among the red; her long, elegant neck and the creamy smooth skin of her naked shoulders, framed by the wide neckline of her light blue-green gown. The urge to stroke her bare skin...to caress the slope of her exposed shoulders and to trace her delicate collarbone with his tongue...momentarily robbed him of his voice. He marvelled at her tiny waist and could not help wondering what she might look like unclothed.

Would he ever see her fully naked, or would a modest lady like her expect to remain covered in her nightgown and only make love under the cover of darkness?

Before he could gather his wits and greet her, Flora took the initiative, making him feel even more of an uncultured boor as he responded to her greeting and attempted a pleasantry—which had somehow transformed from the harmless question in his head to a clumsy brag upon his lips.

Impressed! Once the word was spoken, though, he could not unsay it.

He knew better than that, even though his life to date had been a million miles from this. After serving four years of his sentence in New South Wales he'd been granted his ticket of leave—which allowed him to work for himself as long as he didn't leave the area—and he had worked tirelessly to not only build a fortune, but also to educate himself in a manner fitting a gentleman, driven by his determination to return to his homeland a successful man.

But what use was that when none of the nobles he had

met so far would permit more than a nodding acquaintance? He knew damned well that Lord Aberwyld had only accepted his offer for Flora because he was desperate. And now the bride he had paid so handsomely for no doubt viewed him with the same contempt as the rest of her class. And she didn't even know the worst of him yet. If she ever discovered the truth of his past, she would despise him even more just like any other decent woman would. Just like Jessica. When she had discovered he was an ex-convict she had made no secret of her disdain and had left him the very next day.

They sat, one at each end of the table for their first meal together as man and wife.

Lachlan finished his mock turtle soup, then picked at his roast venison even though it was delicious, as always, and he noticed that Flora appeared to have little appetite either. They could not even converse because he'd insisted on seating Flora at one end of the dining table—which would hold eighteen—while he sat at the other. He had learned that was the correct seating arrangement but, too late, he wondered if it only applied at formal dinners. Was he a fool, to make things even more awkward between them, or was this the norm for a lady of Flora's class?

She was no doubt nervous of the night to come and, in recollecting that tonight was their wedding night and that his bride was not only a delicate lady but also a virgin, his nerves exploded. He had never thought twice about taking his pleasures before and had even learned a certain skilfulness in increasing his partner's pleasure, but the thought of a man such as he—an ex-convict—taking such liberties with a lady, even though she was his wife, broke him out in a cold sweat.

He tried to quash his burgeoning nerves by draining his wineglass again. Drummond came forward to replenish his glass and Lachlan drank again before signalling to Renney to clear his plate away. At the far end of the table, Flora folded her napkin, placing it beside her plate. Dessert was served and Lachlan was pleased to see his bride partake of the stewed plums and custard with more enthusiasm.

Finally, the interminable meal was done. Lachlan pushed back his chair and waited as Drummond pulled back Flora's chair.

'We will take tea in the drawing room, Drummond.'

He still felt uncomfortable giving orders to servants, but it was important to keep up appearances if he ever hoped to be accepted. He was reconciled to being a master by knowing that without these jobs some, if not all, of his servants would be condemned to scratching a very poor living from the sea—a harsh career for anyone not raised to it—or working up to fourteen hours a day in a noisy, dirty factory in Glasgow.

He paced the length of the table until he reached Flora. Then, quite deliberately, rather than offer his arm, he reached for her hand. It felt dainty and fragile as ever and he felt the quiver of her nerves. He smiled down at her, noting her delicate blush as he folded his fingers around hers.

'Come.'

In the drawing room the tea was soon served and while Flora poured a cup for each of them, Lachlan poured himself a whisky from a decanter set on a silver salver on a side table. He must, somehow, connect with his bride before they retired to bed.

'I like your gown—the green suits your colouring.' And the style accentuated her feminine curves. Desire stirred and blood powered through his veins.

Flora glanced down at herself. 'Thank you,' she said. 'It is my best evening gown, made for me when I attended the Caledonian Rout last year.'

Lachlan knew the annual Rout was taking place now, in Edinburgh, with its races, concerts, balls and other amusements.

'I fear most of my clothes will look outmoded compared to this one,' Flora went on, a hint of apology in her tone, not meeting his eyes, 'but I do have an afternoon dress for if we have visitors.'

He had only meant to compliment her, not remind her of the past. Her father's debts were no different to those of many landowners in the Highlands, a fact that had first been brought home to Lachlan on his return to Scotland via the undercurrent of resentment and envy from the landed gentry when they had realised Lachlan's wealth. It was not only his birth and upbringing that stood in the way of him being accepted.

He cast all thought of business from his mind to focus on his bride.

'Would you care for a dram, Flora?'

He held up his glass and the amber liquid glowed as it swirled, the lead-cut crystal sparkling in the candle-light. Flora looked startled and Lachlan felt his cheeks redden. Had he committed a *faux pas*? Did fine ladies not drink spirits?

'It is my own blend,' he hurried on. 'The whisky we make at the distillery near Ballinorchy, on the shores of Loch Carnmore. I thought you might like to sample it. After all, if you are to help me find patrons, it is fitting you should know the taste.'

Her eyes lit up. Happy that he had asked her? Maybe she was not offended. Perhaps this might be a success after all, if Flora was keen to help him promote Carnmore whisky. He poured a splash into a tumbler and handed it to her.

'It will burn your throat at first,' he warned, 'but give it time. Allow the flavour to come through.'

She tilted the glass, her eyes on his. She drank. Swallowed. Blinked. Coughed, just a little. And, finally, she smiled. 'It is nicer than the malt whisky my father drinks.'

'He gave you whisky to drink?'

Her cheeks dimpled. 'No. He disapproved of females drinking strong spirits. But that just made me want to try it all the more. I was sixteen years of age—it made my eyes water, and I coughed and spluttered so much my mother heard.'

'And was she angry? Did she punish you?'

She stared down into her glass, which she held in both hands, cradled to her chest. The play of candlelight over her décolletage, her shoulders and her pale arms stoked his desire, heating his skin.

'No. She was only scared that he would find out. She never told him.' She tipped up her chin, capturing Lachlan's gaze. 'My father has strong notions of right and wrong. He expects obedience and he can make life unpleasant if his rules are not obeyed.'

'He beat you?'

Lachlan felt again the sting of the lash on board the prison hulk, the *Susan*, and again when he first arrived in Australia.

'At times, yes, but that was only to be expected when we were naughty as children. But if he fell into a rage, the entire household would suffer so we all tried hard not to annoy him. Especially my mother.'

He caught the sudden apprehension in her expression. In time, she would learn that he was not like her father.

'Carnmore Whisky is a milder spirit than the whiskies distilled from malted grains in the old pot stills,' he said. 'We use a Coffey still, mixing malted barley with unmalted grains such as wheat. As it's a continuous process it is cheaper and quicker to produce, but it is still a fine product. I have been experimenting with blending the two types to improve the flavour.'

His cheeks heated at allowing his enthusiasm to carry him away. 'I apologise for boring you with business talk.'

'No!' She touched his forearm. 'I'm not bored. I—I *like* to be involved.'

Now it was her turn to colour and Lachlan felt more comfortable in her presence than at any time since their wedding.

'From where does your father get his whisky?'

'A clansman, Sandy McCrieff. He lives up to the north, further into the Highlands.' Her eyes darkened. 'At least, he did. He could no longer pay the rent, even in whisky, and he left at the start of the summer.'

A familiar story.

Flora handed Lachlan his teacup and they sat side by side on the sofa as they drank. The silence stretched and, as soon as she had finished, Flora stood up and Lachlan immediately shot to his feet. She cast him a nervous smile, but did not meet his eyes.

'I believe I shall retire now. It has been a long day.'

Her cup rattled in its saucer as she went to deposit it on the tea tray and Lachlan followed her with hungry eyes, devouring her curves and the sway of her hips as she moved.

His bride. His wedding night. He grew hard. Painfully so.

'I shall give you time to prepare.' His voice sounded gravelly and he cleared his throat. 'I shall see you in a short while.'

Her cheeks were pale, her freckles clearly visible. She nodded before leaving the room.

Time passed slowly, marked by the tick of the mantel clock. Lachlan paced the room a time or two, then paused by the salver and poured himself another whisky as he tried to gag that insistent inner voice that said he was unworthy. He should have gone with her. That would have helped his nerves. He should have just got on with it. Bedded her. Consummated their marriage. Once they'd been intimate…once she was no longer a virgin…they could both concentrate on what was important. Their future lives together.

But he had not wished to shock her and, although the waiting made *him* more apprehensive, it would be easier for her if she was already in bed when he went to her.

He sighed. Scratched his ear. Drained his glass and, finally, he strode from the room.

Chapter Four

Muriel helped Flora disrobe, unlaced her stays and removed her petticoats before unpinning her hair as she sat
before the mirror on her dressing table. Bandit watched
the proceedings from where he was curled on the foot
of the bed.

'I can manage now, thank you, Muriel.'

Muriel dropped a curtsy. 'If ye're sure, milady? D'ye
want me to take Bandit?'

At his name, the terrier tilted his head and his droopy
ear pricked. Flora scooped him off the bed and hugged
him to her chest.

'No. He can...' Flora scanned the room. Bandit usually
slept in her room, but Lachlan surely wouldn't approve.
'He will sleep in the boudoir. His cushion is already in
there.'

She ignored the wrinkle of Muriel's nose at the mention of the cushion. It *was* a touch smelly, but she was sure
the familiar bed would help him to feel more at home.

'You dinna want me to brush out your hair?'

'No. Thank you.'

Muriel took Bandit and shut him in the boudoir before leaving.

Flora sighed with relief. She needed these few moments alone. Time to prepare, mentally, for what was to come. Her mother had warned her it would hurt, but had also drummed into her that it was her duty to stay silent and to submit to her husband whenever he wished. She had then refused to answer any of Flora's questions, her lips pursed tight in distaste, leaving Flora…anxious.

She knew, from the animals in the fields, what would happen.

She knew, from overhearing maids whispering and giggling in corners, that the act—copulation—could be pleasurable, but that it was not always so. And she knew some of those maids actively pursued the experience.

But all that knowledge was overshadowed by the nights she had heard her father loudly grunting and her mother weeping.

She'd promised herself that her marriage would not mirror that of her parents, but that might be easier said than done when, in the past year, the little confidence she'd had in expressing her views had slowly been leached from her. See what had happened when she had spoken out against the Duke—she'd let down those she loved and made herself an outcast. For certain, had she wed the Duke she would now be fully accepted by those of her own class and her life would be very different. But she would not have been happy. Not with a man such as Galkirk.

The sound of footsteps followed by Lachlan's bed-chamber door opening and closing jolted her from her thoughts. Her heart thudded as she hurriedly stripped off her chemise and pulled on her plain cotton nightgown, buttoning it up to the neck. She pulled a brush hastily through her hair and loosely plaited it as she did every night. Then, after a moment's hesitation, she coiled the plait around her head and covered her hair with a lace-edged cap. A glance in the mirror changed her mind. She tore the cap from her head but then, as her fingers went to the ribbon binding her plait, she hesitated.

Would he think her immodest? She knew so little about her husband. What would he expect of her? The murmur of voices from the adjoining room sent her scurrying for the bed. She burrowed beneath the covers, her hair still plaited. And she waited, fretting that she had no prettier nightgown to wear for her wedding night—a lace-trimmed silk nightgown fastened with satin ribbons rather than plain buttons. But she'd had no opportunity to plan her wedding day, let alone the night. It was a far cry from the wedding she had once dreamed of—the magnificent gown she would wear…how beautiful she would look…how her bridegroom's eyes would light up with love as he watched her walk up the aisle to his side… the splendid trousseau she would bring to her new life— trunk after trunk of fashionable clothes and accessories… the dash she would cut in society, as a nobleman's wife.

All silly girlhood dreams.

Silly and unimportant. I must make the best of what I have.

At least Lachlan McNeill was a handsome man, if somewhat sombre. If only he was not such an unknown quantity.

The door linking their bedchambers opened to reveal Lachlan, clad in a ruby-red brocade dressing gown and a pair of velvet slippers. He paused at the foot of the bed, his gaze slowly travelling the length of her body, outlined under the blankets. His brows twitched into a frown as she pressed into the mattress, trying to minimise her shape, and she forced herself to relax. The last thing she wanted was to annoy him. She trembled, her mouth seeming to shrivel until it was as dry as the herbs dried on racks in the still room at home.

Lachlan's chest swelled as he inhaled. 'I will turn out the lamp.'

When the only light left was the sullen glow of the fire that had been banked for the night, he stripped off his dressing gown. The fire at his back cast his expression in the shade but silhouetted the curve of muscles in his shoulders and arms. His wide torso narrowed to slim hips and his legs were long and well-shaped, but Flora was shocked that he appeared to be completely naked. Did he not wear a nightshirt? He toed off his slippers and approached the bed. She squeezed her eyes shut, but strove to stay relaxed. He was her husband. She must learn to put her trust in him because he now ruled her life.

He slid under the covers and, when she braved a peek at him, she saw he was lying on his back, staring up at the ceiling. She felt no threat from him…maybe he, too, was nervous?

Don't be ridiculous, Flora. He is a man. Why would he be nervous?

But the thought gave her courage and she rolled over to face him.

'Did your mother tell you about…about the marital bed?' The question appeared to grind out between clenched teeth.

'A little.' Flora swallowed. 'I have seen the animals,' she ventured. 'Mother…she told me it would hurt.'

He turned his head on the pillow. 'Only this once. It will not hurt after tonight. You have my word.'

It seemed an odd thing for him to say giving her his word about something as intimate as this, as though it were some kind of business deal, but before she could dwell upon it Lachlan rolled Flora over on to her back.

His warm, hard and very male body half-covered her and she closed her eyes as his mouth descended on hers.

She tried to concentrate on other things, to distract herself from what was happening, but it proved impossible. The slide of his lips on hers was surprisingly pleasant and, when he began to kiss her neck beneath her ear, she felt a giggle bubble inside. She had to clench her jaw to contain it and tensed her body to prevent herself from squirming as her mother's voice echoed in her head: *'A lady must be silent and submit to her husband if she wishes to preserve his respect. Otherwise she is no better than the animals rutting in the field.'*

But it proved impossibly difficult to ignore what Lachlan was doing as his mouth traced her collarbone and his hand stroked down her side to her hip and back again, before he— She failed to stifle her squeak of surprise as his hand closed around her breast and he gently pinched her nipple. It was as though an invisible path lay from her breast to her private place between her legs. She had felt a definite jerk down there. She bit her lip and tensed.

'Relax,' he whispered. 'I will not do anything you do not like. Did that feel nice?'

She dared not answer. It *had* felt good, but what would he think of her if she admitted it? And he clearly took her silence to mean she had disliked it because he released her breast and he was gathering her nightgown, bunching it up, and then his hand was on her naked skin. He stroked her thigh, his touch warm but raising shivers in its wake—and then his fingers were between her legs, moving, and it was all Flora could do to keep still. But then, just as the urge to move near overwhelmed her, he moved on top of her, pushing her legs apart, and she could feel him nudging into her.

'You're ready.'

What did *that* mean?

'I'll be as quick as I can.' Hot breath scorched her ear. 'I hope I don't hurt you too much.'

With one thrust, he filled her. Every muscle in her body went rigid, but there was only the one stab of pain and that soon dulled to a throb. Flora hadn't uttered a sound and she was proud of that, keen to please her new husband. Lachlan started to move then, slowly at first, and, once she became accustomed to the rhythm and to the sensation of being filled, emptied and then filled again, she began to relax and even started to enjoy what was happening. His thrusts quickened, and his breathing, too, and she found her fingers digging into his shoulders, her legs clinging to his hips. She opened her eyes and the sight of him moving above her and the feel of him inside her...*pounding* into her...knowing it was him...it brought a lump to her throat and tears to her eyes.

And then he was done. With one final thrust and a groan, she felt a gush inside her and he withdrew.

Leaving her empty and confused.

They lay side by side, each on their backs, not touching. Lachlan's breaths were harsh in the silence of the bedchamber and Flora tried very hard to suppress her own quickened breathing, so as not to disturb him.

At last, Lachlan moved. But it was not towards her, to take her in his arms and to tell her he was pleased with her, that she had done well—the response she had hoped and longed for. He rolled away from her, throwing the covers back and swung his legs over the side of the bed as he sat on its edge.

'Thank you. I hope you will not be too sore. Next time there will be no pain. Goodnight.'

He stood up, walked to the fireside, grabbed his

dressing gown from the chair, shrugged it on and left the room without another word.

Flora gazed up at the ceiling for a long time, willing herself not to cry.

In the morning, Flora roused from her sleep as Muriel entered her bedchamber and quietly opened the curtains. She sat up, stretched her arms high and yawned, surprised at how rested she felt. The past few days—ever since she had learned she was to marry Lachlan McNeill—had been a time of ever-increasing dread but, now, all she could feel was relief that the worst was over and it had not proved near as bad as she had feared. In fact, there had been a few times—the barest of glimpses only—when she thought that lying with Lachlan might be something less to dread and more to look forward to, shameful though that admission might be.

'Good morning, milady.' Muriel came to the bedside and pulled the pillows high against the headboard. 'I've brought you tea, eggs and toast. And the master ordered water for you to have a bath.'

She cocked her head at a short bark from the next room and went to the door. Bandit scurried across the room and launched himself on to the bed.

'A bath?' Surprise gave way to embarrassment and Flora felt her cheeks redden. She buried her face against Bandit's familiar sturdy body.

'Ah, whisht, milady.' Muriel beamed as she shooed Bandit from the bed and set a loaded tray upon Flora's legs. 'There's nae need for blushing—it was your wedding night and a warm bath will set you right for the day.' She gestured to the window, where Flora could see clouds scudding across a bright sky. 'If the rain stays away, it'll give you the chance to get to know your new home.'

Flora did not know quite what to make of Muriel's forwardness. Mother would never have allowed such familiarity from a servant, but Flora welcomed it…it would be pleasant to have someone to simply talk to. Flora swallowed hard, past sudden emotion that clogged her throat. She was lonely. And she had been for a long time, with Father unforgiving over her failures and Mother and her siblings following his lead, as always. She might have earned their approval at last, by this marriage, but they were not here. Here there were only strangers. Including Lachlan, despite the intimacy of last night.

Muriel could never be a friend as such, but she *could* provide company, with her warm smile and her friendly chatter.

'I should like the opportunity to explore,' said Flora. 'Is…is Mr McNeill at breakfast?'

'Och, bless you, no, milady. He's away off to the distillery, but he'll be back for dinner, he said. He works verra hard. You can ask anyone. It's no wonder he's so rich.' She lowered her voice. 'They do say he made much of his money abroad, milady.'

There was companionable chatter and there was gossip. And the latter needed to be discouraged, no matter how curious Flora was about Lachlan's past.

'Did you work here at the castle before Mr McNeill bought it, Muriel?'

'I did, milady. I was born in Lochmore village. Da's a fisherman and Ma cleans the fish and mends nets, but they wanted better for me, so Ma's sister, who worked for the Duchess, got me a job here as a housemaid when it was leased out and I worked my way up.' The pride in her voice was unmistakable. 'I never dared believe I might be a lady's maid, milady, but I worked hard and here I am.'

Her smile faltered. 'Mrs Dalgliesh says I'm on trial

and if you're not satisfied with me she'll hire a properly trained lady's maid. You *will* tell me what you want, milady, so's I can prove myself?'

'Yes. Of course I shall tell you.'

If only it was as easy to tell Lachlan what I want. The thought came out of nowhere, reminding her just how much the past year had robbed her of her confidence.

Muriel beamed again. 'I'll fetch your bath water, milady,' she said and left the room.

Flora ate her breakfast, pondering the enigmatic man she now called husband, last night never far from her thoughts. The marital act was not what Mother had led her to fear, but she found herself baffled by the entire procedure. Was it acceptable for a lady to actually *enjoy* lying with her husband or not? For there had been moments last night when excitement had seemed to hover just within her reach, but then Lachlan's visit had ended with her feeling…frustrated. And lonely. That word again.

'Thank goodness I have you, Bandit.'

Bandit sat on the end of the bed, head cocked. Flora tore a corner off her buttered toast and threw it to him.

Chapter Five

An hour later, with Bandit at her heels, Flora went downstairs. Renney was in the hall and she smiled at him when he opened the front door for her.

'It's cool out there, milady. Shall I fetch your cloak?'

She was clad in a dove-grey merino-wool morning robe with a blue Paisley shawl around her shoulders and a white lace cap decorated with blue ribbon covering her hair.

'Thank you, Renney, but I just wish to step outside to see what the weather is like.'

It was bright and sunny, with a brisk onshore wind. At least it was dry. For now. Having lived her entire life on the west coast, albeit half a day's journey to the north, Flora knew how quickly the autumnal rains could sweep in. She hugged her shawl closer against the chill, but she lingered, lifting her face to breathe in the familiar salt tang, listening to the crash of waves upon rocks. She had always loved the sound of the sea and here at Lochmore, closer to the shore than Castle McCrieff, it was louder. All-pervading.

'Flora.'

The deep voice, close behind, made her start. Her pulse skittered at Lachlan's stern expression as he clasped her upper arms, ignoring Bandit who danced around his feet.

'You will catch a chill, standing around out here without a cloak.'

Joy bloomed in her chest—he had not left Lochmore to deal with business after all. He was here, with her. There were many things she wanted to say, questions she longed to ask, but the risk of saying the wrong thing kept her silent. Better she should wait until she could determine the true character of this man.

'I was told you would be away at the distillery all day.'

He stilled, his only movement a narrowing of those dark fathomless eyes.

'I was waylaid by a problem,' he said, after a slight pause. 'I am about to leave.' He released her and his hand settled at the small of her back as he urged her indoors. 'I suggest you take someone with you if you wish to wander around out here. The coast can be dangerous—there have been tales of people getting trapped by the tide and there are treacherous currents in the small bay at the mouth of Loch Arris.' He gestured to the north of the castle and the loch Flora had glimpsed through the trees on the journey to the castle the day before.

'I have grown up along this coastline and I well know the dangers,' she said. 'You need not be concerned for my safety.'

They were in the hall now and, at her words, Lachlan's hand slid from her and bowed. 'I stand corrected. But you will nevertheless oblige me by waiting until I am able to show you the safest paths down to the beach and to that bay.'

If she was to avoid becoming a wife who existed merely to obey her husband's every command, she might as well begin now. Her insides quaked, but she gritted her teeth and raised a brow. 'When might that be, do you suppose?'

'Tomorrow. We will do it tomorrow. I must go. I shall see you at dinner.'

He turned on his heel and strode through the door, leaving Flora, again, confused and a little bereft. He was clearly irritated with her. Should she have meekly agreed with what he said and kept her own opinions to herself? Dismay churned her stomach. Her mother always submitted to her father and Flora desperately did not want such a marriage, where she was afraid of even having her own opinions, let alone voicing them, but that seemed to be exactly the type of marriage she would end up with unless, somehow, she summoned her courage to continue speaking out regardless of Lachlan's reactions.

She heaved a silent sigh and went in search of Mrs Dalgliesh to arrange a time to discuss household matters and to speak to the cook about menus. Then she donned sturdy boots, a warm bonnet, gloves and her thick felted cloak and went outside with Bandit to explore. She would compromise for now and obey Lachlan by staying inside the castle grounds, even though the sea was calling to her and she longed to explore the beach.

She walked the narrow paths of the knot garden and marvelled at the skill of the gardeners who had created it before leaving the old inner bailey area and walking along the driveway to the arched gateway under the tower and the adjoining gatehouse. She was curious about Mr and Mrs Fraser, who lived there, but she was disappointed. Nobody came to the door in response to her knock and when she stepped back to look, there was no smoke coming from the chimney.

'Brenda's away to her daughter's cottage in the village, milady. Was there anything you needed?'

An elderly man with a weather-beaten face all but obscured by a full greying beard stood watching her. She recognised him as one of the gardeners she had met the day before. Rab. That was it.

Bandit bounced towards Rab and was rewarded with a scratch behind his ear.

'No. Thank you. Except—' she wouldn't go there, but she couldn't deny her curiosity '—where is the path that leads to the beach?'

He scratched at his chin, his fingers disappearing up to the knuckles in the bushy growth. Flora suppressed a shudder, wondering what might be lurking in there.

'There's a gate over by the old chapel—' he pointed '—if ye're going down to the sand. Or, if you follow the wall around—' he pointed in the other direction, indicating the outer wall as it curved around until it joined the keep '—ye'll find a path and steps down to the cove at the mouth of the loch, but it's treacherous, ye ken—slippery rocks and strong currents that'll pull you under.'

'Thank you. I'll explore that part another day.' She glanced up at the sky. Ominous clouds were massing behind the castle, out to sea. 'It looks like rain.'

'Aye.'

'Before you go—can you tell me how old the knot garden is? I've seen pictures of such gardens in history books, but I can't recall when they originated.'

'Ah.' He reached into his pocket and took out a clay pipe, sticking it between his teeth and sucking on it vigorously, despite it being unlit. 'That'll be young Lord Glenarris.' He removed the pipe, waving it to emphasise his words. 'He found out about it in a book, too. Or was it papers?' He scratched his beard again. 'He's a famous plant hunter now. Goes to other countries...other *continents*...and brings all sorts back with him. Anyways, he found out about the knot garden—it was laid out in the sixteenth century, he said, and he had us make it like it was in them plans he found.'

'Lord Glenarris?'

'The Duke's son. He was born here, at the castle. His mother...' he made the sign of the cross on his chest '... God rest her soul, was His Grace's first wife.'

'Ah. I see. So it was his lordship who restored the garden?'

'Aye. Fascinated, he was, even though he didn't live here for long after his mother died.'

Flora tried to picture the castle as it would have been in the sixteenth century, but failed. The modern wing wouldn't exist, but had the ground between the keep and the great hall been undeveloped, or had there been another building linking the two? She pushed her conjectures from her head. Those clouds were looking very ominous and there was more she wanted to see before going indoors.

'Thank you, Rab.'

Flora nodded and headed next for the stableyard, where she stroked the horses, before wandering along the muddy paths of the vegetable garden, where a few chickens pecked and scratched. They scattered with loud squawks when Bandit tried to make friends. Flora called him to heel, looking around guiltily in case anyone had seen and might report back to Lachlan, but there was nobody there.

Bandit at her heels and keeping one eye on the weather, she hurried across to the opposite side of the outer bailey to the old chapel, as Rab had called it. The door creaked as she opened it and she wrinkled her nose at the dust inside. It was clearly a store, piled high with heavy old-fashioned furniture, and she backed out, closing the door behind her and then, spying a narrow gate, she opened it and saw that it did, indeed, lead to a path down to the beach.

Rain spattered her face. She called Bandit back through the gate, then they ran together for home. By the time they reached shelter, the hem of Flora's gown and her cloak were wet and mud-splattered and she hurried upstairs to her bedchamber where huge raindrops were being blasted against the window by the wind barrelling in from the sea. She hung her gown over a chair, hoping that once the hem was dry the mud would brush out.

It was noon—a whole six hours to fill until Lachlan returned and, even then, would he tell her about his day or was he another such as Father, who believed no woman needed to know about men's business? She sighed and pulled an old gown of apricot striped with dark green from the wardrobe and then rummaged in the chest at the end of the bed for her plaid shawl, the splattering of raindrops on the window making her shivery.

She held the soft wool of the shawl to her cheek as she stared unseeingly at the rain-washed windowpane, the longing for her childhood home—despite the tensions of the past year—welling up inside her, making her throat ache. At least at Castle McCrieff she had been lonely among people she knew. People she had grown up with. Here she was among strangers. She shook out the shawl—the soft greens and blues conjuring the lichen on the stone walls of McCrieff and the blue of the sea on a cloudless winter day—and then swung it around her shoulders, hugging it close. A knock, followed by the door opening, shook her from her reverie. She spun round, alive with the sudden hope that it was Lachlan, returned early from the distillery. Muriel's round, rosy face met Flora's disappointed gaze.

'Luncheon is served, milady.' She bustled across to

snatch Flora's discarded gown from the back of the chair. 'Och, this is wet. I'll take it to the kitchen to dry out and then I'll brush it for ye. It's lucky you came inside when you did or it'd be in a worse state still.'

'Thank you, Muriel. I shall come downstairs now. Is… shall I be expected to eat my luncheon in the dining room?'

The thought of eating alone at that huge table made Flora shiver even more. How had Lachlan borne it, night after night, dining alone in that room? Sympathy stirred even though he did not appear to want her companionship. They'd been as isolated at the dinner table last night as though each of them dined alone.

'Och, no. Mrs Dalgliesh said to serve you in the morning parlour. D'ye ken where that is, or shall I show you?'

'No, I know where it is, thank you. Will you take Bandit to the kitchens and give him something to eat?'

They walked together to the head of the stairs and then Muriel disappeared in the direction of the back stairs, carrying both Flora's gown and a protesting Bandit. The morning parlour was in the old keep, a pleasant southeast–facing room with the ceiling, cornice and frieze and all the woodwork painted white. The walls were papered in lilac and white stripes and the window in its deep embrasure was framed by plain dark green curtains. A maid was waiting to serve her luncheon.

'Thank you, Dolly, but I am content to serve myself. You may go about your duties.'

Dolly curtsied and left the room, leaving Flora to eat in solitary splendour at a round table set before the window, the view across the rainswept forecourt as gloomy as her mood. Was this to be her future? Rattling around this huge castle on her own, with no one to talk to, no one to laugh with, afraid to speak out in case she upset her new husband, about whom she still knew nothing other than he was wealthy and obsessed by his work. The only bright spot on the horizon was the thought of having children. They, surely, would bring light and laughter into her life?

Her hope that she would soon get with child, however, was dashed within hours.

Dinner that evening was, if possible, even more stilted and awkward than the night before. Lachlan said very little and Flora followed his cue.

Dinner over, Lachlan walked Flora to the drawing room, which stood opposite the library. At the end of the corridor between the two was the door to the billiard room, with its comfortable chairs clustered around a fireplace at one end and a billiard table at the other. The corridor then turned a corner beyond which was Lachlan's study and, at the very end, the former great hall, now the ballroom.

Lachlan paused outside the drawing-room door and bowed. 'I have business to attend to in my study. I shall bid you goodnight, Flora.'

He strode off down the corridor and disappeared around the corner in the direction of his study.

Later, before she went upstairs to bed, Flora—her heart beating rapidly—tiptoed along the corridor to the door of Lachlan's study where she hesitated, trying to pluck up the courage to disturb her gruff spouse. But as she paused, holding her breath, she heard the distinct click of billiard balls colliding and the murmur of male voices from the door she had just passed. Fury spiralled through her. She spun on her heel and marched back along the corridor to the stairs.

Muriel was waiting to help her prepare for bed and

Flora strove to keep her emotions lashed down. It would not do for the servants to be told that the mistress was vibrating with fury when she retired to her bed. Bandit seemed to sense her mood, though, for he stayed out of her way. When she was finally alone, Flora worked off some of her energy by pacing the room as Bandit kept one wary eye on her. Gradually she grew calmer.

Calmer, but not calm.

She could not fool herself that Lachlan even liked her very much…he had demonstrated only too clearly that he could not wait to be out of her presence.

She was half-tempted to allow Bandit to sleep on her bed, but she did not want an argument about that to divert her from what she wished to say to her husband.

'Come, Bandit.'

He trotted into the boudoir without a fuss and Flora praised and petted him before closing the door, pleased at how quietly he had accepted his new sleeping arrangements. Then she climbed into her bed and drew the covers up to her chin. No matter how fearful it made her, she would challenge Lachlan when he came to her and ask why he was avoiding her company.

The clock on the mantel ticked quietly on into the night as she waited.

Chapter Six

Gregor Fraser sighted along his cue and hit the white ball. It cannoned first in to Lachlan's cue ball and then into the red which ricocheted off the cushion and arrowed into a corner pocket. He grunted in satisfaction and straightened, eyeing Lachlan.

'Five points. And d'ye care to tell me why you're in here playing billiards with me instead of upstairs with your new bride?' Astute blue eyes peered at Lachlan from beneath shaggy grey brows.

'She needs the time to get used to all this change in her life.' Lachlan turned to a side table and refilled his glass from the decanter. 'I may as well be in here with you as puzzling over those damned ledgers.'

'Those damned ledgers, as ye call them, are the key to making a success of Carnmore Whisky, laddie.' Gregor retrieved the ball from the pocket and replaced it on the table. 'That is your ambition, no?'

Lachlan glared at Gregor, who had already been the manager at the distillery when Lachlan had bought it. They had formed a close bond at their shared ambition for the business and they'd made grand plans, both keen to see the business grow and succeed.

'You know it is,' he growled, at which Gregor cocked

an amused brow. Lachlan bit back his irritation. 'Yes, the ledgers are important, but they fail to command my attention tonight.'

The truth was his mind kept wandering to Flora. What on earth had she made of his boorish behaviour at the dinner table, lost in his own thoughts instead of making light, interesting conversation with his bride?

She will think it is typical of me, after last night.

He cringed at the memory. She had not enjoyed their wedding night, lying under him rigid and unresponsive. When he looked at her, she had been biting her lip with her eyes screwed tight shut. He had closed his own eyes then and simply got on with it.

She is a lady. Why should she enjoy a rutting common ex-convict like me ploughing into her?

'I took you for an intelligent man, Lachlan. Pig-headed, but intelligent. Stubbornness is a useful trait, at times, in business, but not when it comes to women, my friend.' Gregor shot again and missed. He smiled rue-fully. 'And I should know what I'm talking about. I've been married to my Brenda nigh on thirty years now and I've learned problems are never solved by ignoring them. They only get bigger. And ye canna solve a prob-lem when ye are in different rooms.'

Lachlan scowled. At least in business he knew what he was doing, his dogged determination and, yes, stub-bornness having brought him success in Australia. He'd kept his head down and worked hard, rising higher than he'd thought possible, and had returned to Scotland a rich man. He rounded the table, making a show of lining up his shot, his mind racing. Had he given Flora enough of a chance? He had kissed her with his lips closed, wary of shocking her even though he knew other women liked to be kissed more passionately. He had so far forgotten himself as to touch her nipple through her nightgown, but at her first squeak he had whisked his hand away. Had that squeak been a protest, though, or an indication of pleasure? It was easy to be wise with hindsight. At the time he had been too afraid of offending her to relax enough to simply do what came naturally.

Gregor might have a point, but the time to close that gap between them had been at dinner when that physical and mental gulf yawned between them at the table. All day long he had fantasised about Flora—longing to bed her again and to make it better for her, to stroke her silken skin, to breathe in her scent, to decipher the tiny sounds that would escape her lips, to find out if they were signs of pleasure rather than of distaste.

To forget she was a lady born and bred and to make love to her as a woman.

But the minute he saw her again the conviction that he wasn't good enough had gripped him, rendering him clumsy and clueless as they ate in near silence. What did he know of conversation to interest a lady such as Flora? He had spent too much of his life working in the company of rough men, toiling for long, hard hours. He might be a wealthy man now and have no need to labour in the physical sense, but he was no wiser about women—ladies—and how to treat them. Women had been part of his life, but not part of his actual world and, until his pathetic attempt at courtship with Jessica, they had merely provided a service, whether it be sex, or food, or laundry or, as now, as servants and therefore members of his household.

He took his shot and the red object ball dropped into the pocket.

'Three points. And you're wrong, Gregor.' He retrieved the ball and replaced it on the table. 'Flora needs time to settle and to get used to her new situation. I am granting her that time.'

He wanted so badly for Flora to be content. Happy, even. She was a beautiful, desirable woman and his wife, but that very fact made him even more hesitant to bed her simply because he had that right. It might be an impossible dream for a man like him but, deep down, he longed for their lovemaking to be more than lust on his part and obedience on hers. He wanted them to be friends. To understand one another.

Gregor shrugged. 'Well, 'tis your life, laddie. Now, this must be our last game. My Brenda's staying over at our Annie's tonight—her little one is poorly—and she's left me a list of chores to do before I go to bed.'

Gregor and his wife had moved to live in the gatehouse after Lachlan bought the castle. It suited them as their daughter lived with her husband in the nearby village of Lochmore and it was bigger than the cottage near the distillery where they'd lived before.

'I ken better than to risk *her* displeasure,' Gregor added with a wink.

Lachlan laughed although, truthfully, he didn't feel one bit like laughing as he continued to puzzle over how best to connect with a lady who had been brought up with so much and with so many advantages. If she had experienced one-tenth of the hardships of his childhood he would know better how to talk to her.

The only women he had ever really known intimately—in a non-physical sense—had been his mother and his sisters. His heart constricted at the memory. All gone now—Mam, Rose, Taggie, Jenny—losing the battle against poverty one by one, too weak from lack of food to fight the simplest of diseases, until only he and Anna were left. He had returned to Scotland to find his mother had been dead nine years. Anna would have been just fifteen. The shock was still raw, and his guilt at having stayed away for so much longer than he needed to still gnawed at him. He'd searched for Anna ever since, but each and every lead had ended in failure and he still didn't know if she was alive or dead. He refused to give up until he knew for certain and, in sheer desperation before his wedding, he had hired a man to try to track her down.

After Gregor left, having won the game, Lachlan returned to his ledgers until the small hours, still battling the desire to go and bed his new wife despite his best intentions. But he knew that to do so now, after those awkward silences at dinner and after he had clumsily dismissed her in favour of attending to business, would be perilously close to merely slaking his lust.

Flora deserved better than that.

He rotated his shoulders.

Better he concentrate on business and on tracking down Anna until he and Flora got to know one another better.

Dark shadows bruised his wife's eyes the next morning when she entered the morning parlour. Lachlan rose to his feet.

'Good morning, Flora. Did you sleep well?'

'Very well, thank you.'

Dolly filled Flora's cup from the coffee pot and, while Flora was distracted, Lachlan frowned into his own cup. She was lying. She looked as though she hadn't slept a wink. Had she been apprehensive about him coming to her bed? Should he have reassured her that he wouldn't be demanding his conjugal rights for a while?

He, too, had spent a restless night, but he hadn't been

able to escape the self-imposed conviction that—if he went to Flora—he would be using her. Although he was unused to close relationships, he truly wanted them to be friends within their marriage. He wasn't convinced he knew how to build such a partnership, but he hoped spending an hour or so together this morning might help bridge the gap between them.

'As promised, I've set aside a couple of hours to show you around outside the castle grounds,' said Lachlan. 'It is cold, though, so you should wrap up warm.'

She nodded. 'Thank you. I will.'

They met later, in the entrance hall. Her dog was there, bouncing around him, yapping excitedly as though he'd discovered a long-lost friend.

'He likes you,' Flora said, prompting Lachlan to smile at her and a warm feeling to glow inside him.

'Come.' He headed down the inner hallway that led to the ballroom, Bandit trotting ahead.

'Wait!' Flora hurried to his side. 'I thought we were going outside?'

Lachlan grinned. 'We are. It's a secret way down to the beach. I thought you might enjoy going this way rather than using the path down the cliff.'

Her smile was puzzled, but she put her hand in his and followed him through the huge double doors into the ballroom.

'You see the minstrels' gallery in the corner?' He pointed to the quarter-moon balcony high up in one corner.

'Yes.'

'Well, through that door beneath the gallery is a spiral stair to the original kitchens, cellars and tunnels.' He studied her doubtful expression. 'You are not afraid of tunnels, are you, Flora?'

'N-no. I am not keen on spiral stairs, though.'

Her hand trembled in his and his grip tightened.

'I will look after you. Nothing can happen. Come.' He opened the door and felt for the candlestick, matches and sandpaper block that were kept on a ledge just inside. 'There is nothing to fear.'

The candle flame flickered wildly as they descended the tightly spiralling dark stairs to the cellars, Bandit scampering ahead. Lachlan loved the feeling of being needed as Flora clung to his hand.

'Along there...' Lachlan held the candle high, illuminating the wide passage '...are the old kitchens and store rooms. We can explore them another time, perhaps when it is raining. Now. Through here—' he indicated a doorway '—are the tunnels.'

Flora stepped through ahead of Lachlan.

'Can you see that pale light down there?' He shielded the candle flame so she could see.

'I can. Is that daylight?'

'Yes. The tunnel leads to the Sea Gate and the Path to the Sea, where goods used to be delivered by boat. And it was an escape route, should the castle ever fall to a siege in the past. There would have been doors along here once upon a time, to keep attackers at bay, but they have all rotted away by now. I intend to have them replaced, in time.'

He led her by the hand towards that faint patch of daylight. 'We keep straight on.' He indicated a tunnel that branched off. 'Along there, the tunnels lead to the Old Keep. There were dungeons and so forth there in the olden days.'

When Lachlan had bought the castle, he had found old record books and plans—fascinating documents that had satisfied his curiosity about the castle's past. They walked on until they reached a place where their tunnel met another. To their right the brighter aspect showed the way to the Sea Gate.

'Where does that lead?'

Flora pointed to the left, where the tunnel curved away from them into the dark. She shivered, tugging her collar up around her neck. Lachlan put his arm around her and hugged her close.

'Thank you.' She tipped her head back to look up at him and his pulse quickened as he wondered whether he might kiss her. Would she welcome a kiss? 'It's dank and cold down here, isn't it?' she went on before he found the nerve to act on that thought. 'Can you imagine being imprisoned in such a place?'

The memories flooded in, sweeping away any notion of romance.

'What is it? What did I say wrong?' Worry rang in Flora's voice.

'Nothing. You said nothing wrong.' Suddenly, he could not wait to get out of there. 'There's no need to bother with that other tunnel. It's walled off now, but I believe it once led to the crypt under the old chapel. This is the way we go.'

Lachlan turned her to the right, towards the light. The tang of salt air now alleviated the dank smell and their footsteps rang on the rock as the tunnel climbed slightly uphill.

'Careful.'

Flora slipped on the damp, uneven rock underfoot and Lachlan wrapped his arm around her waist. She felt safe, tucked into his side like that. Protected. The tunnel turned a sharp corner and emerged out of the cliff face. The tunnel opening was shielded from prying eyes by a pinnacle of rock jutting up in front. They rounded that pinnacle and stepped on to a path that zigzagged down and around the headland to a low platform of rock just above the surface of the sea.

'That is the Landing Point,' Lachlan said. 'It's where the boats used to land the supplies. And still could, if we had need of it. Was there anything similar at Castle McCrieff?'

'Not like this, although we do have a jetty. Are we going down there?'

'Not today. I thought you would prefer to go on the beach.'

Lachlan pointed to a set of steps that were cut into the rock, providing an easy route to the beach below. Bandit had already reached the sand and was racing around, barking as he ran.

'It looks lovely,' said Flora.

The little bay and its beach were sheltered on one side by a protruding outcrop of rock and, on the far side, by a jumbled pile of boulders.

Flora stared at the pile, then gazed at the cliff above it. 'That must have been quite some event, when the cliff gave way.'

'There is a beach beyond the rockfall, too, but you need to take care not to get caught by the tide. The only way back is over the Devil's Seat...' he pointed to the top of the heap, at a huge flat-topped rock. '...and it is an almost impossible climb from the far side, so I'm told, although it is easy enough from this direction.'

He turned to her, tipped her chin up and captured her gaze, his dark eyes intense.

'That is why I did not want you to explore alone, Flora. I know you are familiar with the coast, but there have been accidents and deaths in the past.'

She willed him to kiss her. To give her some sign that

he found her attractive. But he released her almost immediately and she was left feeling a failure. Her new husband couldn't even summon enough interest to come to her on their second night of marriage...why would he kiss her in broad daylight?

'Follow me.'

He descended the steps and, although he frequently paused to make sure she was coping with the path, he gave no sign that his care was any more than a polite regard for her welfare. Flora followed, her heart heavy.

On the beach, Lachlan dropped Flora's hand and they ploughed through the soft sand side by side, not speaking. For the life of her, Flora could not think what to say or how to draw him out. Better to follow his lead and remain silent, she decided, as they reached the damp sand near the water's edge. To take her mind off her awkwardness, Flora scoured the shoreline for pretty shells and pebbles and anything else washed up by the tide while Bandit splashed in the surf.

'Bandit!'

Her head jerked around at Lachlan's call, in time to see him throw a stick for the terrier. He bounded after it, picked it up, gave it a vigorous shake to kill it and then hared around them in a circle. Lachlan watched Bandit, a smile tugging at the corners of his mouth.

It will be all right. We *will be all right. It will just take time.*

'It is time we returned,' said Lachlan. 'I'm expected at the distillery.'

They plodded back up the beach to the cliff and to the start of the path, Flora sneaking occasional glances at Lachlan, who kept his eyes on the ground in front of them. Then he slid a sideways look at her and his cheeks reddened as their eyes met. He snatched his gaze from hers and returned to contemplating the sand again. Flora took heart from that shared moment. Lachlan seemed as uncomfortable and lost as she did and maybe, therefore, it was as much *her* responsibility to improve their relationship as his. If only she could be braver about speaking out.

I will work on it, she vowed as they continued to trudge through the soft sand, her hand on Lachlan's arm until they reached the path up the cliff.

'We shall return through the chapel gate,' said Lachlan. 'There is no need to face those tunnels or the spiral stairs again.'

He said it with the tone of one doing her a favour.

'I really do not mind going that way,' said Flora. His lips tightened by the merest fraction, but she knew instantly it was the wrong thing to say. She recalled his sudden tension down in the tunnel—maybe he disliked dark, enclosed places? 'But I'm sure Bandit will prefer to stay outdoors and I confess I should like to see where exactly the gate opens into the grounds.'

He didn't need to know she had seen the gate yesterday.

'The steps are wider, too.' He took her hand. 'We can climb them side by side.'

They did so but, again, the uncomfortable silence stretched. She simply had no idea what Lachlan was thinking. Did he begrudge wasting his time with her when he could be working? They entered the castle grounds through the chapel gate and followed the wall around to the inner gate, which was—these days—simply a gap. The carriageway crunched under their feet as they approached the front steps.

'Thank you for showing me the beach, Lachlan.' They

were indoors now and Flora refused to part from her husband in this continuing silence. 'I appreciate it.'

'It was the least I could do after leaving you to your own devices yesterday.' His chest swelled as he drew in a deep breath. One long finger brushed Flora's cheek as his dark gaze fused with hers. 'I—'

He fell silent, stepping back as Renney came to relieve them of their outdoor garments, and Flora cursed the interruption.

'Will you remain for luncheon?' She tried to keep the pleading note from her voice.

'No. I am sorry. I must go.'

He did sound regretful, though. If only she knew more about him, surely their conversations would flow with more ease? She vowed to redouble her efforts to discover more about his past.

Chapter Seven

A week later, a ferry boat docked at the Broomielaw and Lachlan hurried up the gangplank and to the roadside where he hailed a hackney cab. In Argyll Street he pushed open a door beside a bootmaker's and took the stairs two at a time to Tom Delaney's apartment over the shop, where the investigator he had hired both lived and worked. At the top, he rapped on the office door.

'Enter.'

He did. 'Well? What news?'

Delaney's feet were propped up on his desk, crossed at the ankle, his boots immaculately polished. His chair rocked back, balancing on the back legs, and his hands were linked behind his head as he eyed Lachlan.

'I am well aware of the importance of this matter to you, Mr McNeill, but I urge you not to forget the common courtesies in your hurry to get straight to the point.'

Lachlan's face heated. 'I pay you to find my sister, Delaney, not to correct my behaviour.'

'Sure, and don't manners maketh the man?'

Lachlan held the Irishman's gaze, irritated that his red hair and green eyes only reminded him of Flora. Hell— he snatched off his hat and thrust his fingers through his own hair—everything these days brought her to mind and he was at a loss to know how to bridge the chasm that still gaped between them. Her efforts—and he could tell she was trying hard to get to know him—all centred on finding out about his past. A past he was not ready to share with her. He could not believe a lady like Flora could ever accept a man like him—Jessica had only been a farmer's daughter and she had rejected him in a flash.

The only other way he could think to improve his marriage was to take her into his arms and make love to her until she melted in his arms. But the idea he would be using her and the belief she had found their wedding night distasteful had taken hold in his brain and now the longer he stayed away from her bed the harder that short walk between his bedchamber and hers had become. So he ended up doing what he always did—burying himself in his work and ignoring his emotions.

'I've no time for the niceties. What news have you?'

Delaney sighed, shook his head and removed his boots from the desk. His chair tipped forward with a thump on to the square of carpet centred under his desk. Lachlan sat opposite him, his foot tapping out his frustration, gripped by the fear that time was running out.

'If only I'd returned sooner,' he muttered.

'As my old mam used to say, "If ifs and ands were pots and pans we'd all be tinkers".'

Lachlan switched his gaze to Delaney, to find he was being watched by a pair of twinkling green eyes.

'Save me your homespun philosophy, Delaney, and get on with it.'

'Very well.'

Delaney perched a pair of spectacles upon his nose and consulted a document in front of him, his demeanour now one of utter seriousness. Lachlan perked up. For all the lack of progress in tracking down Anna, he was aware there was a shrewd operator beneath the jovial Irish façade. If he had doubted that, he would never have hired him in the first place. The man knew how to get Lachlan's dander up, however, and he rarely failed to do so.

'I have discovered your sister married a...' he consulted the document again '... David McKenzie in June 1843. You have been searching for the wrong name.'

'Married?' Why had he never considered that possibility? Anna was...what? Four and twenty by now? Five years his junior. But he still saw her as a child, the ten-year-old she had been when he last saw her. 'Have you traced them?'

Delaney frowned. 'Yes and no.'

Lachlan quashed his irritation.

'McKenzie was foreman at the cotton factory where Anna worked, but he died under a coal wagon in January forty-six. Your sister worked on at the factory for a few months, but left when she had the baby.'

'A *baby*?'

He felt like he'd been socked on the jaw. *I am an uncle?* This made it even more imperative he found Anna quickly.

'Where are they now?'

'That's just it. No one seems to know. But I'm sure she's no longer in Glasgow.'

'Why would she leave? She was only a year old when my father brought us to Glasgow—it's the only home she's ever known.'

Delaney shrugged. 'I've no idea. All I do know is she fell into debt but, when I probe further, people are quick to clam up. *Very* quick.' He raised his brows to emphasise his point.

Lachlan shot to his feet, shoving his chair aside. 'Take me to them. I'll *make* them give me answers.'

'And how do you plan to do that?' Delaney pointed at Lachlan, then to the chair. 'Force won't work when folk are scared to talk. Sit down, big fella. I've a plan, but I need your go-ahead.'

Lachlan subsided on to the chair. 'Tell me.'

Delaney raised his hand off the desk and rubbed his fingers and thumb together. 'Money. Sure, and does my old mam not always say it makes the world go round? People are scared to talk, but every man has his price. It won't be cheap, mind you, and I'll need compensation for neglecting my other cases—'

'What other cases?' Lachlan eyed the Irishman to whom he paid a weekly retainer. 'Our deal was that you work for me exclusively—'

'And so I do, Mr McNeill. So I do. But, on the days when there is no new information to follow up, why— I'd be a fool to turn down the occasional additional case.' His eyes glinted. 'They're solved in a jiffy. Easy cases, to be sure. Easy money.'

Lachlan sucked in a breath. However reluctant, he knew he must accept Delaney's plan. The man had connections everywhere in Glasgow—both within the vast Irish immigrant community and beyond. He could get answers far more quickly than Lachlan ever could and, besides, he could not afford to neglect his business, or Flora, for the time it would take to get those answers.

'Very well. I shall pay your *reasonable* expenses,' he said. 'Here's one pound to be going on with—' Delaney reached for the proffered banknote, but Lachlan whisked it out of reach. He cocked his head to one side. 'I shall expect a fully itemised list, mind you, Delaney. And regular reports.'

Delaney's green eyes widened. 'But of course, Mr McNeill, sir. I am a businessman. I conduct my affairs with honour.'

'When will you start?'

Delaney shoved back his chair and stood. 'No time like the present, as my old mam used to say.'

They shook hands. Lachlan retained his grip on the other man's hand as he looked him in the eye. 'You write to me the minute you find her, do you hear? I'll come immediately.'

The creases around Delaney's eyes and mouth—the lines that made it appear that he was constantly laughing at Lachlan—softened. 'You have my word, sir. You have my word.'

Lachlan left Delaney's office and took a folded sheet of paper from his inside pocket. Before leaving Lochmore he'd consulted with Gregor's wife, Brenda, about a surprise for Flora. Didn't every woman love to dress well? Brenda helped him compile a list of ready-made gowns, undergarments, fabrics and accessories necessary to provide a complete, up-to-date wardrobe for Flora. That, surely, would make her happy and help reconcile her to her new circumstances? Brenda was a skilled seamstress and would alter any gowns as necessary and make up some new ones.

Flora had been raised in an earl's household and although Lachlan could not yet offer her the status she was used to, he *could* offer her the appearance of status. And he *would* restore her to her rightful place, just as soon as he found—with her help—acceptance among the higher echelons of society.

His campaign would start next weekend, at a house party to which they—along with many in the world of Glasgow commerce and several notable noble families—

had been invited. He scanned the addresses written down for him by Brenda and he hailed a hackney cab.

After several hours consulting with various warehouse and shop assistants—and making arrangement for his purchases to be delivered to Lochmore Castle as soon as possible—Lachlan finally concluded his shopping trip and retired to the hotel where he was to spend the next few nights. He had various meetings scheduled in the coming days, as well as distillery business to attend to, before he could return home on Monday.

Home. The word, even now, sent a thrill through him. That he had a place of his own to call his home seemed something of a miracle, given his past. He finally had a place in the world where he could truly belong. And, with luck, raise a family. He frowned, staring down into the glass of whisky he held—whisky that was far inferior to his own distilled in Carnmore—as he admitted to himself that final ambition might prove hardest of all. He could only hope his gifts for Flora—the proof he wanted her to be happy—would help them, somehow, to connect.

Connect? That word sent a shudder right through him.

Connection meant closeness, meant *sharing.* Which meant revealing thoughts. Revealing *feelings.*

The past fourteen years had taught him that to reveal emotion was to show weakness. To court danger. To risk downfall.

The thought of being completely honest with his wife—an earl's daughter and a lady—and of sharing his past and his innermost feelings terrified him far more than the prospect of seven years' transportation had at the age of fifteen. How could Flora ever accept or understand his past? No. Some things were better left secret.

Nobody back here in Scotland—apart from Anna—knew the truth about his background and that's the way he wanted it to stay.

Well! If he thinks he can buy me like this, he has a lot to learn!

Flora stood, hands on hips, watching with clenched jaw as the footmen carried boxes and packages into her bedchamber and Muriel, with the help of Mrs Dalgliesh and Dolly, opened them, exclaiming in delight as each new garment emerged from the tissue paper in which it had been wrapped.

He did *buy you, though.*

She batted aside that voice of reason. She did not *want* to be reasonable. First he virtually ignored her for a whole week after their wedding, other than that morning when they went down to the beach. He barely spoke to her unless it was about mundane, everyday issues like the weather or the food they had eaten at dinner or some tit-bit of society gossip he had gleaned from the newspapers. As if she could care less about society gossip. She wanted to know about her *husband*. About the man she had married. But he was as much an enigma as he had been the day they met at the altar.

At least he is not a cruel man.

There was that dratted voice of reason again, trying to make excuses for the pathetic man.

He could *have been cruel, for all Father knew or cared when he sold me off!*

A letter from her mother had arrived that morning—exacerbating Flora's homesickness—with a few scraps of news from home and, couched in careful terms, her thanks to Flora for helping to restore the family fortunes. But no talk of a visit and no message from her father.

Not for the first time since her marriage, self-pitying tears scalded behind Flora's eyes, blurring her vision. She gazed unseeingly out of the window until she had herself under control.

What was she to do?

The ocean was restless, mirroring her tossing, tumbling emotions. She wrapped her arms around her waist and swallowed down her feelings. Then she plastered a bright smile on her face and went to help with the unpacking. The servants were excited by the delivery and there was so little of that in their lives she could not bear to dampen their joy.

Her dream that she and Lachlan would, in time, grow closer through the marriage bed seemed doomed. He had not visited her since their wedding night and, although she had tried hard to muster the courage to ask him why, fear of what he might say held her back.

Had she done something wrong? Something to disgust him? There was no one in whom she could confide, no one to ask, even if she dared to speak about such matters. All she knew of the subject was her mother's warnings, with never even a hint that some parts of lying together might feel...well...*nice*. Flora tensed, almost expecting a bolt of lightning to strike her down for even thinking such an outrageous thought.

'Milady?' Drummond stood in the doorway. 'Mrs Fraser is downstairs, asking to speak to you. Shall I tell her you are engaged?'

Mrs Fraser? It took Flora a few seconds to place the name. Fraser—he was Lachlan's manager at the distillery and he and his wife lived in the gatehouse. Mrs Fraser had been away for several days, helping nurse her sick grandson, and Flora had never met her. Lachlan had not even introduced her to Mr Fraser, even though he often called at the castle. Did he imagine Flora would not acknowledge a person of Mr Fraser's class?

Hmmph. If she knew nothing about Lachlan, it seemed he knew even less about her.

She was thrilled to have a caller and she did not give a fig that her neighbour was not her social equal. Flora was lonely and she craved company. A friend.

'Please show her into the drawing room, Drummond. I shall come straight down.'

Drummond disappeared and Flora crossed to her dressing table to tidy her hair, embarrassed at how her heart pitter-pattered at the thought of a visitor, even if it was only Brenda Fraser. She straightened the light shawl around her shoulders—it was pinned at the front with her brooch, which she wore most days. There was something compelling about it—not only that it was a reminder of home but…somehow…fanciful though it might seem… she felt calmer when she wore it. More…*settled,* which was daft, because she was unsettled most of the time but, deep inside her, dwelled a feeling of…rightness. It was something in Lochmore itself, she felt.

Well, it must be, for it is certainly nothing to do with that husband of mine.

With that final, grumpy thought, she went downstairs.

The woman standing in the centre of the drawing room, as though she dared not take a seat, was short, plump and motherly, with kind eyes.

'Lady Flora McNeill, this is Mrs Fraser,' said Drummond.

'Good afternoon, Mrs Fraser. I am pleased to meet you. How is your grandson?'

Mrs Fraser smiled at the mention of her grandson. 'Och, he's on the mend, my lady. I am pleased to meet you, too.'

'Please, sit down. Drummond, please ask Cook to send in refreshments. Will tea suit, Mrs Fraser?'

The visitor's brows lifted. 'That is most gracious of you, my lady.'

'Not at all, Mrs Fraser. I am happy you have visited.'

A light flush coloured Mrs Fraser's cheeks and she bit into her bottom lip.

'Is something troubling you?'

'I…well…' Mrs Fraser shifted in her chair, her hands restless in her lap. 'I didna know whether Mr McNeill mentioned me, milady?'

Flora frowned. 'In what respect, Mrs Fraser? I'm aware you live in the gatehouse, but that is all.'

'Ah.' Silence prevailed, then Mrs Fraser's face split into an unexpected grin. 'Men,' she said. 'They dinna care to talk about their feelings and so forth, do they? They prefer to take action and then they are surprised when we fail to guess the reasoning behind what they do.'

'Has Mr McNeill done something that involves you, Mrs Fraser?' Flora's thoughts flew straight to the numerous boxes being unpacked upstairs.

'Aye. The gowns. I saw the delivery. Mr McNeill asked if I would make any necessary alterations for you, as well as sew a few additional gowns. I used to be a seamstress, you see.'

'I see.' Anger still grumbled deep inside Flora, but Lachlan's failure to apprise his wife of his plan was not Mrs Fraser's fault. 'Not only did my husband not tell me of your part in his plan, Mrs Fraser, he also omitted to mention he had ordered anything for me. The entire delivery took me by surprise.'

Mrs Fraser sipped her tea, eyeing Flora. 'He's a man of few words, I ken. But he has a good heart.'

Flora gave a non-committal response.

'And did he tell you of the invitation?'

Flora was tempted to lie, to cover her humiliation that Mrs Fraser knew more of their lives than she did. But curiosity—and panic at mention of an invitation—persuaded her to answer truthfully.

'He did not. Will you tell me?'

Mrs Fraser, to her credit, looked more discomfited than triumphant.

'Mr McNeill only mentioned you will attend a social gathering next week and you will need enough gowns made ready for then. It was Gregor who told me you have been invited to attend Sir Keith Lawrence's annual weekend gathering.'

Flora's stomach plummeted and then clenched violently. Her parents had attended Sir Keith's gathering at his country mansion near Inveraray in the past. Sir Keith was the grandson of an English earl and had earned his knighthood through his political work. His annual gathering brought together the cream of Highland society, Scottish politicians and various prominent industrialists and businessmen to promote useful connections between those sections of the community. No wonder Lachlan had ordered so many new gowns and accessories. This was what he had married her for. To give him an entrée into society. Little did he realise—

'Are ye quite well, my lady? You've gone verra pale.'

It took effort, but Flora pulled herself together. This was not a subject to discuss with Mrs Fraser, no matter how friendly she was and no matter how much Flora yearned for friendly conversation. She stood up and placed her cup and saucer on the tray.

'If this gathering is next week, then it seems we have no time to waste, Mrs Fraser. Shall we go up and see what needs to be done to prepare me for our visit?'

She would not shirk this duty even though she feared it would be to no avail. Her rejection of Galkirk had created scandal last year and she doubted her peers had forgotten.

Should I warn Lachlan his plans are likely to fail?

She would not.

He did not see fit to warn me about this gathering. I shall go and I shall do my best and at least he will not be able to accuse me of not trying my hardest.

Chapter Eight

On Thursday afternoon, Flora gazed from the carriage window at Sir Keith Lawrence's country estate, Dalbride Castle—a beautiful tower house that blended into the surrounding landscape as though it had been there for centuries, even though she knew it had been built barely fifty years before. Her insides had been a coil of dread ever since Mrs Fraser had told her of Lachlan's plans and now they wound even tighter. The time had come. She intended to try her best and do everything she could to help Lachlan find patrons for Carnmore Whisky because she desperately did not want him to regret marrying her, but she feared he would soon realise the huge error he had made.

He sat by her side, stern and remote, starkly handsome. And a stranger still. She had tried hard to muster the courage to talk to him about this weekend…about his expectations of her…but time and again her courage failed her. The opportunities to exchange any sort of private word with her husband were few and far between—he had been away in Glasgow until Monday and, when he returned, the distillery commanded his attention during the day and at night he poured over the ledgers in his study, checking the estate accounts—urgently completing his week's work before they left for Dalbride.

She was naught but an irrelevance in his life.

Until now.

Bitterness scoured her throat and left a sour taste in her mouth. The only exchange of words about this weekend had been as Lachlan was rushing out to the distillery on Tuesday morning.

'Mrs Fraser has told you about this weekend, I understand?'

Flora had nodded as resentment burned inside her. So he'd spoken to his distillery manager's wife about it since his return from Glasgow, but not to his own wife?

'Good. Good.' He glanced out of the open door, clearly impatient to be gone. 'Are you pleased with your gowns? Have you everything you need?'

She'd wanted to scream at him then. To fly at him and rake her nails down his face. To force him to see her as a person, not just as a wife to parade upon his arm. But she'd merely nodded again.

'Thank you,' she'd said, because that was what he seemed to expect. He'd nodded, looking pleased with himself, before hurrying out to mount his horse.

Thank you! What an utterly pathetic response! But the habit of biting back her true thoughts and feelings was ingrained and nothing so far in her marriage had helped her find the confidence or the courage to fight that habit.

Nausea crowded her throat and she swallowed hard to keep it down. She'd thought they'd have a chance to talk on the journey today, but her courage had failed her again on the ferry as it sailed Loch Fyne—she had convinced herself that anything she said would prompt a row between them—and now Muriel and Murray, Lachlan's valet, were seated with them in the carriage Sir Keith had sent to transport them to the Castle. She fingered the brooch she had pinned to her new mantle of spring-green satin, taking comfort from its familiar shape. She had seen Lachlan's raised brow when he saw it—for in among his purchases for her had been brooches and bracelets, necklaces and earrings—but he said nothing, for which Flora was grateful. Silly for such a simple thing as a brooch to give her comfort, but it did.

They'd arrived and Lachlan—looking virile and hand-some in traditional Highland dress of kilt, sporran, waist-coat and jacket—stepped out and handed Flora from the carriage. As Flora went to take his arm, however, he stayed her. One finger beneath her chin, he tilted her face to him, his expression…yes, serious as ever, but was that a hint of concern?

'Are you well, Flora? You are pale and you have been very quiet.'

I *have been quiet?* She bit back a sudden urge to laugh. Then, amazingly, Lachlan smiled. A rueful smile. Flora stared in wonder.

'I am a fine one to talk.' A muscle leapt in his jaw and a groove appeared between his dark brows. 'I do not know how to talk to you.' His voice was gruff. 'Or what to say. You are a lady. And I…' He tipped his head back a moment, then captured her gaze again, nostrils flaring as he breathed in deeply. 'I have not made our first weeks of marriage easy for you. I shall try to do bet-ter.' Then a smile stretched his lips and lit those sombre eyes. 'Maybe,' he said, 'I might try by asking what it is *you* want?'

She realised then that Mrs Fraser had spoken to him about her and about their marriage because she had said something similar to Flora after she recoiled in horror at one of the fabrics Lachlan had chosen, knowing that the huge pattern in garish colours would swamp her small, curvy frame were it to be made up into a gown.

I dinna ken why the daft man didna simply ask what you'd like, instead of doing it all himself.

'Maybe, another time, I might come shopping with you?' she suggested, feeling very bold.

'I should like that.' He smiled down at her, his gaze sweeping from her head—with her bonnet of dark green crepe decorated with a curled white ostrich feather—to her feet, clad in black satin half-boots with elastic sides. 'Although I must say that shade of green suits you very well. It matches your eyes.'

A blush warmed Flora's cheeks and happiness fluttered in her tummy. 'Thank you.'

Her nerves about this weekend gathering calmed a little—just a few simple, friendly words from her husband and she already felt less alone.

'Come. Let us go in.' Lachlan took her hand and tucked it into the crook of his arm.

Lachlan cursed himself for being all kinds of a stubborn, blind fool. He'd thought he was helping Flora...allowing her the space and time to become accustomed to him, to Lochmore and to her new circumstances. It had taken a few brisk words from Brenda Fraser this morning to make him realise that, far from helping Flora to settle, he had unintentionally made her feel less at home. And now he had brought her here, to parade her in front of all these people, expecting her to act the part of the perfect wife. They were no nearer to actually understanding each other than they had been on their wedding night and he'd realised—but not until they were seated in the carriage and he could not talk to her because Muriel and Murray were sitting right there—that they would no doubt share a bedchamber tonight.

It was a poor excuse, but he'd been so distracted by business and by his worries about Anna that he'd barely even spoken to Flora, let alone begun to bridge the gap between them. He vowed to make more of an effort with her in the future. Perhaps it was good they were to be thrust together without a choice...left to his own devices, how long would it have taken him to pluck up the courage to bed his own wife again? And what kind of a man did that make him?

A coward, that's what.

He continued to be wary of bedding her if she was in any way reluctant but, still, anticipation sent his blood pounding through his veins. But he would never force himself on a woman, wife or not—he'd seen enough of that kind of behaviour on the ship and in the Colonies. He could only hope that the discovery they must share a bed would not come as too much of a shock to Flora, but at least he'd now smoothed things over a little and they would see what the coming night would bring.

A maid showed them to their bedchamber, where there was warm water for them to freshen up.

'Oh!' Flora stopped just over the threshold of the room. 'I—'

Anxious green eyes sought Lachlan's. He smiled reassuringly and a blush washed her cheeks.

'Is everything in order, milady?' asked the maid. 'D'ye not care for your room?'

'Oh. No. It is not that. It is a lovely room. Thank you.'

Muriel and Murray appeared then and, in the kerfuffle, the maid disappeared. A small dressing room led directly off the bedchamber and Lachlan directed Murray to take his bags in there.

'I shall leave you to change your gown,' he said to Flora. 'Let me know when you are ready to go downstairs.'

Lachlan had only his linen to change—Sir Keith had specified traditional Highland dress for the weekend, for the benefit of the English nobles who would be in attendance. Since the Queen and Prince Albert had discovered the delights of Scotland through the novels of Sir Walter Scott, Scotland and all things Scottish had become all the rage with the English upper classes.

Lachlan waited in the dressing room until Muriel knocked. 'Lady Flora is ready, sir.'

Lachlan stopped short at his first sight of Flora—feminine, charming and respectable in a primrose-satin gown with long sleeves and a high neck. She looked gorgeous, but the sheer uncertainty in her eyes wrenched at his heartstrings.

'You look beautiful.'

Her relief was palpable. Her smile tremulous. 'You approve?'

'I do. Very much.'

Their gazes fused. Her huge green eyes appeared to hold a promise...or was that just wishful thinking? His nerves rolled and bucked like a ship in a storm. Would... *could*...Flora accept his past if he were to tell her the truth? Jessica's expression arose in his mind's eye. Not her face—he had long forgotten what she looked like—but he would never forget her scornful expression once she'd discovered the truth.

He swallowed. Hard. Could he ever risk Flora rejecting him like that?

He offered Flora his arm and covered her hand with his, squeezing it gently as her delicate floral scent played havoc with his senses.

Downstairs, the butler showed them into a huge salon, where people sat and stood around, the noise of their chatter deafening. Sir Keith emerged from among his guests, his cheeks ruddy and his eyes bright.

'McNeill! Glad you could make it.' He thrust out his hand and shook Lachlan's with vigour as the smell of whisky curled around them. Sir Keith had already warned Lachlan that the weekend was for indulgence as well as for business. 'And Lady Flora. I don't believe we've met before, have we? I know your father well, of course. Unfortunately, he and your mother could not attend this year.' He bowed and Flora curtsied. 'I had every hope Her Majesty and the Prince might attend, but they have remained in London. Such disquiet, all over Europe, this year.' He lowered his voice. 'Revolution, my dear. The old order under threat. Discord everywhere—the people rising up... France, Germany, Hungary, Poland, not to mention the Chartists—it is of great concern, is it not, McNeill? Business does not thrive where there is uncertainty and we are, first and foremost, businessmen.'

'It *is* a concern, sir.'

The old order... Lachlan stifled his urge to tell Sir Keith exactly what the 'old order' meant to most people— unfairness, injustice, deprivation, starvation. It was going on all around them, yet so many of that same 'old order' appeared oblivious to the reality of it. But he stifled his true feelings. He needed acceptance by these people. He needed their patronage and their help to make a success of his business and to enable him to use his influence to make life better for the poor wretches who had no hope of escaping squalor. Not by revolution—that, he was convinced, merely replaced one over-privileged order with another—but by education and through political debate. He truly believed that to be the only way for long-lasting reform.

'Well, make yourselves at home.' Sir Keith waved one arm expansively. 'No need for formal introductions—I dare say between you both you know most people here. We do not stand on ceremony, so feel free to join in and help yourselves to food and drink. Dinner tonight is early, at six—we have the rare privilege this evening of a private recital by Monsieur Frederic Chopin. I heard him play in Edinburgh at the Hopetoun Rooms a few weeks ago and I managed to prevail upon him and his pupil, Miss Stirling, to stay with me for a few days and to entertain my guests.' He beamed, then leaned closer. 'He is not a well man, however, and he speaks little English, so he has declined to join us for dinner.'

Sir Keith's attention was attracted by more arrivals and he nodded amiably and headed off to greet his guests.

'It will be a treat to hear Monsieur Chopin play.'

'It will indeed.'

'I have some of his sheet music at home and I enjoy playing the pieces. I am sorry to hear he is not well; I wonder what is wrong with him.'

A stout lady standing nearby turned. 'He has the consumption,' she said, all eagerness to be the first to impart the news, 'but he continues to perform and...' Her voice tailed into silence as her gaze slid from Lachlan to Flora. Her lips thinned.

Flora bobbed a curtsy. 'Good afternoon, Lady Barmouth. Might I present my husband, Mr McNeill?'

'Yes. I heard you had wed.'

Lachlan frowned at her ladyship's curt response. She might well disapprove of an earl's daughter marrying a commoner, but there was no excuse for talking to Flora like that. Flora's fingers tightened upon his sleeve as Lady

Barmouth, her chins quivering, fixed Lachlan with a beady glare, then regally inclined her head—all while still managing to look down her nose at both him and Flora.

'*If* you will excuse me?'

Her ladyship strutted across the room to join a cluster of guests by a window and, before long, Lachlan was aware of surreptitious glances in their direction.

'She clearly disapproves of our marriage.' Flora must not think he in any way blamed her for Lady Barmouth's attitude. 'We shall have to hope not everyone shares her view.'

'Yes.' Flora's voice was so quiet, Lachlan had to bend to catch what she said.

'Well. Never mind Lady Badmouth. I doubt she is a whisky drinker in any case and I know for certain she is not a member of any of the gentlemen's clubs I have in my sights.'

Flora's laugh was strained. 'It is Barmouth, not Badmouth.' She soon looked downcast again.

'Well, it is my opinion that Badmouth suits her better. Come, I see some familiar faces from the Glasgow Chamber of Commerce—allow me to introduce you.'

Flora hung back. 'You go and talk to them. I should like to greet some of my old friends first, if you do not mind?'

'Shall I come with you?'

'No, there is no need. Th-they are old friends.'

She could not meet his eyes. Was she ashamed of him? Had Lady Barmouth's reaction caused her to remember their unequal status? 'Y-you go and talk to your business friends.'

Lachlan clenched his teeth. 'Of course. If that is what you prefer. I shall save the introductions until later.' He bowed, then stalked away.

Chapter Nine

Flora watched Lachlan stalk across the room with a sigh of relief. She had vowed to do her best to help Lachlan and his business and here was where she began. But the thought of approaching her former friends within earshot of her husband had sent shivers chasing down her spine. She had told him of her rejection of the Duke of Galkirk, but he clearly had no idea she had been cast as the one at fault. Never mind that Galkirk was a lecher twice her age and that she had not only caught him trying to force his attentions on to a tearful maid but, when Flora had intervened, he had grabbed her and forced a kiss while his hands wandered over her like they were already wed. Never mind that he'd forced her hand to his groin, telling her she'd interrupted his fun and it was therefore her duty to satisfy him.

No. *She* was the one at fault because she should have been honoured by his attentions. Her guilt at letting her family down had weighed her down for a long time. She had married Lachlan to make amends to her father and now it was time to face the rest of society.

She hauled in as deep a breath as possible, given the tightness of her corset, and marched across the room to join three of her erstwhile friends—Cynthia, Mairead and Victoria—and their respective mothers, sitting in a group near to the fireplace.

'Good afternoon.' She smiled brightly and perched on the edge of a vacant chair. 'I am happy to see you all—it has been a long time since we last met.'

Lady Ballinach, Mairead's mother—the highest in precedence of the three mothers—smiled thinly. 'Good afternoon, Lady Flora.'

Oh, dear. Lady *Flora. That is an unpromising start.*

Flora maintained her smile. 'I hear Monsieur Chopin is to give a recital for us this evening. I remember his music is your favourite, Cynthia. You must be eager to hear him play.'

Her friend, tall, slim and blonde, tilted her chin and regarded Flora from beneath half-closed eyelids. 'I doubt tonight's performance will equal that he gave in Edinburgh during the Rout. He played for *two hours. Such* a shame you missed all the fun.' She turned to address Mairead and Victoria. 'Do you remember how we picked the winners in all but one of the races?'

'Oh, yes.' Mairead tinkled a laugh. 'So exciting. And the Campbell ball was such a pleasure.'

A painful lump formed in Flora's throat. Last year had been her first experience of the Caledonian Rout, with its balls, concerts and horse racing. Nobody from her family had attended this October—they were too busy planning her wedding behind her back. She received no encouragement from any of the mothers, who all studiously avoided looking at her. Her heart plummeted as she saw Lachlan watching her, a frown knitting his brow.

'I was married just over two weeks ago,' she blurted out. She knew they would all be aware, but she must, somehow, try to break through the invisible barrier that now appeared to divide her from those she had known since childhood. 'I now live at Lochmore.'

An audible sniff from Victoria's mother, Lady Calvin, revealed that lady's opinion.

A male voice said, 'Castles are so very inconvenient, are they not?'

Flora looked up eagerly, thinking the remark was addressed to her, but it was Victoria's father, Sir James himself, who had spoken, and he was quite clearly speaking to his wife.

'Come, my lady,' he continued, holding out his hand to help his wife to her feet. 'Broforth wishes to consult you on...er...a matter of great importance. Victoria?'

Flora watched miserably as her former friend said, 'Yes, Papa?'

'Come with us, if you please.'

Flora did not miss the smirk Victoria sent in her direction as she stood up. 'Yes, Papa.'

Flora sank her teeth into the inside of her cheek, determined not to show any emotion. She frantically cast around for something to say...anything to encourage the remaining four to talk to her. 'Mr McNeill has refurbished Lochmore. The decor and the furnishings are the very latest in style. You would all be most welcome to visit us.'

She knew she was wasting her breath. Given a choice she would never humble herself like this, offering these arrogant cats further opportunity to snub her, but she had vowed to try and she would not give up yet.

'Mr McNeill,' Lady Ballinach said, haughtily, 'is *not* the sort of person with whom our sort associate.'

At least it was a response. A chance to have a conversation. Maybe one step to forgetting her transgression.

'And yet Sir Keith has invited my husband and me for

the weekend,' said Flora. 'We are guests in his house, as are you.'

'Industrialists and business people,' Cynthia's mother, Lady Finsfield, said with disdain.

'Sir Keith is a businessman, but his grandfather was an earl. It is possible to be both.'

'Breeding is everything,' retorted Lady Finsfield. 'Where has Lachlan McNeill come from? He turned up last year, as brown as a conker... I truly thought him an Arab...and he flashed his money around, expecting to buy his way into favour. He fails to understand the source of *his* fortune is tainted. Come, girls. Let us find guests of our own kind with whom to socialise.'

All four of them swept away, leaving Flora close to tears. She could not sit alone in a group of empty chairs so she gathered her courage and, this time, she approached a group she did not know quite as well, but she knew that some of the people in the mixed group were her parents' friends. In fact... Her spirits revived as she recognised her father's cousin, Robert McCrieff, and his wife, Sarah. Surely they would not snub her?

She soon discovered that they would. She was not greeted as she joined the cluster and, when she ventured an opinion, she was ignored. Her face was flaming hot, the tears burning behind her eyes, but anger also bubbled in her chest. How dare they treat her as though they had never met her before? Blood simmering, she rounded the group until she was behind Sarah and tapped her shoulder.

'Why?' Flora's whisper was fierce. 'Mother must have told you the truth about Galkirk. Why am I an outcast still? It was a year ago.'

Sarah grabbed Flora by the arm and tugged her out of earshot of the group. 'It is not only that, Flora. I am sorry, but you have chosen who you married. There are all sorts of rumours—'

'I did not choose him. Father did. And what rumours? He is a decent man.'

'Do *you* know how he made his money? He turned up in Glasgow, hugely wealthy, and yet nobody knows a thing about him. He might be a *criminal* for all we know.'

Flora looked at Lachlan uncertainly. A criminal? Could that be possible? She wished she knew more about him, but he was still a total mystery to her.

'He is a respectable businessman.' The statement sounded weak, even to her ears. 'He has shares in the Caledonian Railway and a shipbuilding company and he owns a whisky distillery. He is accepted by Sir Keith and by other businessmen. He is even a member of the Glasgow Chamber of Commerce.'

Sarah grimaced. 'They accept him only because of his money. They know no more about his past than we do, according to Sir Keith. But…well, as he says, business is business. Sentiment doesn't come into it.' She touched Flora's hand briefly. 'I am sorry, but Robert owes money to Galkirk. It is hard enough to keep going without flouting his wishes.'

'His *wishes*? You mean that he has ordered you and Robert not to talk to me?'

Sarah could not meet her gaze. 'Not *ordered*, exactly. But he made his expectations clear. I am sorry, Flora. Go and join your husband and his companions and forget about trying to change our minds.'

Our minds. Once upon a time that would have included Flora. Now she was an outcast twice over: through her disgrace in refusing Galkirk and now through her marriage beneath her class.

I would not care a fig for these people's opinions if not for...

She swallowed down her anger, glancing over at Lachlan, deep in animated conversation with two men she did not know. What would he say? What would he think? He had made a bargain with her father...he had paid a sum of money to buy a well-born and well-connected wife who would be an asset to his business. Instead...

He has me. And I cannot do what he wants. I have no influence whatsoever.

Their marriage looked set for a miserable future. She would be drooping in defeat were it not for her stays—even when the body wanted to slump, a lady's undergarments prevented it. All Flora had to remember was to keep her neck long and her chin up and no one would guess how hurt she was. Or how she dreaded her future, having yet again let someone down. Would Lachlan, like her family, decide she was not worth the effort of even talking to? He hadn't spoken to her much this past week—how bad would it be when he realised the extent of her failure?

She cast her eyes around the room in desperation. A group of three younger gentlemen, standing with the Turnbull twins, caught her eye. There were no parents within earshot. She might as well try again. She had danced with them all at Edinburgh last year, in the Assembly Rooms in George Street, before that fateful ball. But she had known them all since childhood, from the various Highland gatherings and social events they had all attended. And they had often visited one another's homes, staying the night due to the distances involved in travelling. She joined them. They cast her a few wary looks, but no one actually snubbed her and she even received a smile from Frances, the prettier of the twins and an unashamed flirt.

'So. You are wed, Flora McCrieff?'

'I am. And it is Flora McNeill now.'

'He looks *very* fierce,' Frances murmured. 'He is handsome enough, I suppose, but *I* should be scared half to death by him.' She sidled closer to Flora. 'Is it true that he *killed* a man for his money?'

Lachlan found his gaze—and his thoughts—continually wandering to his wife, even when the conversation around him grew heated with opposing opinions. The sort of conversation he normally revelled in. Today, however, nothing—not even the thorny subject of wages for their workers—could hold his attention completely.

What is happening?

Flora had looked defiant as she was left alone by the fire by the first group she approached. What had those women said? He feared he knew the answer to that. Their disapproval of the match she had made was obvious. This was *his* fault.

'What say you, McNeill? If we stick together and cut the wages, we'll all benefit.'

That grabbed his attention, even as he noticed Flora approach a different group of guests.

'The workers can barely subsist on what we pay them now,' he growled. 'They can't give you a productive day's work if their stomachs are hollow from lack of food.'

He remembered that feeling all too well. The fear of being hungry again drove him now, but he could never pursue personal profit at the expense of his workers. Many employers, however, saw nothing wrong with hiring workers for the lowest wage possible. They argued it was essential to keep wages low to secure jobs. The argument circled endlessly.

'If the men don't like it they don't have to accept—

plenty more where they came from. It's the law of supply and demand,' said Parker, the owner of a leather factory, with a scowl.

'They are human beings. Not commodities.' This time it was a shipyard owner who spoke up.

At least not all the bosses were of the same mind as Parker. There was a way to go before enough of the employers saw the truth of what Lachlan and other enlightened voices were saying—that men and women needed to earn enough to afford a roof over their heads and enough food on the table. Too many men—greedy men—could see no further than their profit margin and their own lavish lifestyles. They could not grasp that it was to their benefit to have a healthy workforce who could do a full day's work without flagging from lack of energy.

The conversation veered in another direction and Lachlan's gaze, once again, sought Flora. She stood with a younger group of guests—too young to be of any benefit to the distillery—but they were at least talking to her. Judging by the looks cast in his direction, however, he once more appeared to be the topic of conversation. He curbed his impatience. The weekend had just begun. There was plenty of time and by tonight there would several more nobles in attendance, according to Sir Keith, and more opportunity for Flora, and him, to win over patrons for his whisky.

He shifted his position so his wife was no longer in sight and could no longer distract him, and applied his full attention to his companions' conversation.

Lachlan tapped on the door between the dressing room and the bedchamber and Muriel opened it.

'Is your mistress ready?'

'Yes, sir.'

Flora stood by the fire. She turned and Lachlan's breath caught in his throat. He crossed to her and gathered her hands in his.

'That gown,' he breathed, holding her at arm's length and allowing his gaze to lower slowly to the floor and then lift again, taking in every delectable inch of her. The peacock blue complemented the pale skin of her exposed shoulders and arms and her fiery hair was pinned up, with a low comb behind and two long ringlets *à l'anglaise* just touching her shoulder. 'You look beautiful, Flora.'

A light blush coloured her cheeks but, although her lips curved into a smile, her eyes were troubled. Lachlan tipped her face to his.

'What is it?'

She bit her lower lip and his blood surged in response. Without volition, he bent his head and kissed her, his lips moving over hers, his tongue tracing the seam of her mouth, teasing her to open to him. She did. He cautioned himself to go slowly as he took her in his arms, registering the tension in her body. He stroked gentle hands down her back to her waist, and back again, pulling her to him.

He hardened at the first tentative touch of her tongue and grew harder still as her hands slid up his chest to his shoulders and she leaned in to him, murmuring quietly in her throat at the silken glide of their tongues. Lachlan battled the urge to deepen the kiss and pulled back. He gently swept his thumb across her glistening lower lip as joy quietly spread through him. Who would have thought he'd have ended up with such a wife?

'That—' He stopped, his thoughts racing with confusion. 'What is wrong?' He had seen she was troubled in the moment before he kissed her, but he was sure—from her response—that she had enjoyed their kiss. 'Do you not enjoy kissing?'

Flora's huge green eyes were shining, but not with pleasure. Her face was ashen and tears sparkled on her lashes. But she laid her palm against his cheek.

'Yes, I did enjoy it.'

'Then why…?' He passed his thumb very gently beneath her eye, catching a teardrop.

'I am sorry. I do not know…there is no reason… I felt emotional.' She held his gaze as she stroked his jaw. 'Shall we go downstairs? We must not be late for dinner—I am so looking forward to hearing Monsieur Chopin play.'

The music was sublime. The audience in raptures. But poor Chopin looked frail and Lachlan could only admire the strength of his determination to keep on performing when he was so clearly ill. The recital finished, Chopin took his bow to wild applause and was then helped from the room by his pupil, Miss Stirling.

Flora had appeared captivated by the music, but Lachlan was aware of times her hands clenched in her lap and how rapidly her chest rose and fell. And he could not convince himself it was the passion of the music that stirred her emotions—not after her reaction to their kiss and her restraint during dinner. Something was troubling her. Was she ashamed of him? Of the mismatch she had made? Was she anxious about the coming night, when they would share a bed? Whatever it was, she was unlikely to confide in him—they were still strangers after over two weeks of marriage and it was entirely his fault. He had thought he was acting for the best but, given the time again, he would make sure she quickly grew accustomed to their married status.

After the recital, he kept Flora by his side, introducing

her to his industrialist acquaintances and their wives and, gradually, he was relieved to see her cheeks regain their colour and her green eyes their sparkle. The men and the women drifted into two sets and Flora, welcomed into the businessmen's wives' circle, sat with them as the men remained standing, discussing business and politics. A few of the lords present also joined in those discussions, but there was still an undeniable divide between the business and the landed classes and Lachlan again had to curb his frustration that he was no closer than a mere nodding acquaintance with any of these nobly born gentlemen.

In the middle of a discussion about shipbuilding on the Clyde, Lachlan noticed Flora stand up, smiling as she appeared to take her leave of the industrialists' spouses. Pride that she was his wife surged through him.

'What do *you* say, McNeill?'

The question dragged his attention back to the discussion, which had moved on to the merits of various whiskies. But he was distracted, his attention straying to Flora—not only to make sure she was all right, but also because he could not help wondering how soon he could whisk her up to bed without appearing ill-mannered.

Except…he frowned. Flora was like a butterfly that flitted from flower to flower as she moved from one group of guests to the next. He could not, without appearing rude, watch her constantly, but from what he could see none of the groups appeared to welcome her and he could not mistake the slow leach of colour from her cheeks or the white knuckles of her tightly clenched fist. He was on the brink of going to her, to remove her from these people who were clearly upsetting her, when she set her jaw, tipped up her chin and crossed the room with determination in every line of her body.

The woman she approached had arrived late, on her

own—the Countess of Ardhban, Lachlan recalled. He paused, waiting to see what her reception of Flora would be. He didn't have to wait long—the Countess saw Flora walking in her direction, haughtily eyed her from head to toe and then, quite deliberately, she turned her back. On his wife! Fury raged through Lachlan but, before he could even move, Flora rushed from the salon, her head down. A few guests smiled—and one or two even laughed—as they saw her depart.

Lachlan stalked from the room and took the stairs two at a time. Their bedchamber was empty, as was the dressing room. Anxiety wound in his gut. Where did she go? Surely she would not go outside into the dark and cold? He ran down to the entrance hall where a footman, looking anxious, hovered by the front door.

'Have you seen a lady in a blue gown?'

'I have, sir.' The servant's relief was clear. 'I couldna stop her, sir.' He gestured at the door.

'Do not worry.' Lachlan pressed a shilling into the man's hand. 'I rely upon your discretion.'

'Of course, sir.' The footman opened the door for Lachlan, and handed him a lantern, already lit. 'She headed that way, sir.' He pointed in the direction of the stableyard.

The wind was bitingly fierce and rain—never far away in Scotland—lashed down. Lachlan pulled up his collar, bent his head against the onslaught and ran. She would head for cover. She was not stupid.

Unless...

An insidious voice crept into his head, whispering that her distress might drive her into a reckless act. He pushed himself, his legs pumping, breath growing short. A building loomed out of the darkness. The carriage house. If she sought solitude, here was a place she might find it.

He pushed open the door and stepped inside, pulling the door shut behind him as he held the lantern aloft, revealing several carriages.

He listened, alert for any sound. There. A small sniff. Relief wrapped around him, but his heart clenched, knowing that in her distress Flora had not fled to him, her husband. No. She had run from him, too.

Chapter Ten

Flora sat in a corner of the carriage, wrapped in a fur she had found in there. How she wished she could curl up into a tight ball, but her blasted corset made it impossible to do anything but sit straight. Misery squeezed her heart, filling her with despair.

How can I face them again? How can I face Lachlan? I am a failure. Our marriage will be ruined as soon as he knows the truth.

When they had kissed, before dinner, hope had blossomed within her. For a few fleeting, wonderful moments she had forgotten her husband's expectations of her and she had gloried in the possibility of a happy future. A close marriage. Of love growing.

Love!

What did she know of love? If her family had truly loved her, why had they never seemed to value her and why had they sacrificed her future so ruthlessly? She missed them every day, even though the past year had been fraught with the weight of their disapproval. She swallowed past the painful lump that clogged her throat and felt self-pitying tears scald her eyes. Crying wouldn't help. She knew that. But she was alone...there was no one...

The carriage door opened and she clutched the fur rug closer around her, fear pumping her heart as a lantern held aloft illuminated the interior and shone into her eyes. She swiped at them, hoping her tears were invisible to the intruder.

'Flora…?'

A sob escaped her. It was Lachlan. Of all people to find her, he was the best.

And the worst.

The carriage dipped as he climbed inside. He placed the lantern on the floor and sat opposite her, leaning forward, his forearms resting on his thighs.

'Why did you run away?'

'I—' Her emotions overtook her again, throttling her words.

With a muttered exclamation, Lachlan moved to sit next to her and took her in his arms, tucking her head into his chest. His hand rested lightly on her hair and his heart beat reassuringly in her ear as his scent calmed her.

'This is my fault. I've made you an outcast by wedding you. But, please, don't take it to heart so. We will rise above their arrogance, I promise you.'

And the perfect solution dropped into her lap—all she need do was allow Lachlan to believe her failure was his fault and she would never have to reveal her disgrace and that her father was totally aware of her sullied reputation when he struck his bargain with Lachlan.

'No. You do not know the truth.' She hauled in a shaky breath, pulled free of his embrace and swivelled to face him, needing to see his reactions.

'Our marriage is only a part of it. I was the object of gossip long before we wed.' She hung her head. 'Father knew of it—he made a false bargain with you.' She lifted her eyes to his. 'I cannot help you find the patrons you need. Even my own family cannot forgive me.' His features blurred as her eyes filled with tears. 'I am so ashamed. I am sorry, but I can't fulfil your expectations of me.'

'Is it because you refused that Duke?' His brow furrowed. 'How can that make you an object of gossip?'

'He is a *duke*. I am only the daughter of an earl. It was a great honour to be singled out by him.' That is what Father and Mother had told her. 'I humiliated him.'

'*Humiliated?* By refusing his proposal?'

'I caused a scandal.'

The backs of his fingers brushed her face from temple to jaw. 'Tell me.'

Not a demand. A request. But still she hesitated, embarrassed to talk of such things. Even though he was her husband they had only been intimate that one time and there was so much she still had to learn. If she took her courage and confided in him, might it bring them closer? Or would the truth drive a bigger wedge between them? She relived their kiss...the way she had felt—torn, wanting more, wanting *him*, her body softening and preparing for his, and yet full of guilt over her failure to warn him what to expect.

She sensed his strength and his support. He did not seem disappointed or cross with her. Not yet, anyway. And, whatever the result of her confession, there would be relief that the truth was in the open.

'The betrothal was to be announced at a ball held by the Duke's sister during the Caledonian Rout last year. I heard a scream from the library as I passed. I went in. And—' She gulped, the scene imprinted on her memory. 'Galkirk was in there with a maid. He had bent her backwards over a desk, her skirts pushed up, and she was struggling and crying and he...he...' She drew in a steadying breath. 'He was forcing himself on her. I didn't think… I ran to them and pulled him off her. He was f-f-furious.'

Furious barely described his incandescent rage. Spittle had sprayed her face as he yelled at her and the stench of brandy on his breath as he forced a kiss on her had sickened her stomach. She still could not bear the smell of brandy.

'H-he kissed me and tried to force me to touch him. He s-s-said that I had interfered in his fun and I must take the maid's place and as we were to be married in any case there would be no harm done.'

Lachlan's arms were still around her and they tightened, drawing her close.

'I struggled and I managed to scratch his face.' She remembered the satisfaction as all four fingernails raked down his skin. 'He loosened his grip and I shoved him away and ran from the room.' She bit her lip. The next bit was where her view of her world had gone askew. 'I ran into the ballroom and straight to my father. I was in tears.

'And then the Duke walked in, four vivid scratches on his cheek. The room fell silent just as I blurted out that I would not marry Galkirk if he was the last man on earth.' The faces that surrounded her father and their expressions of shock, disbelief and, finally, scorn were imprinted on her memory. 'And Galkirk—he had no shame. He just sneered at Father and said, "You did not tell me you'd raised a hellcat, Aberwyld. The offer is rescinded."'

'You could not have wed such a man, Flora. You did the right thing.'

'But that is not how society sees it. They see me as tainted. And I failed my family—I had no idea how important that match was to them. Nobody told me. They just told me Galkirk had offered for me and that I should be flattered. And then Galkirk refused to deny that he had not…did not…' She hung her head again. 'They all believed I was no longer innocent. That I was soiled.'

Lachlan stroked her hair. 'But *I* know you remained pure, Flora, and I am proud to have a wife with such strength and spirit.'

She relaxed into him, her head on his shoulder.

'I felt so guilty for letting my family down. They all blamed me.'

'And so…when an upstart businessman offered for you, you did not have the strength to refuse? You could not bear to let them down again?'

Flora leaned back against his arm and searched his face. 'It is of no use to pretend that is untrue, but I do not regret our marriage. I… I can only hope you can forgive my father's deceit and that you will not grow to regret our union. And I am ashamed I hadn't the strength to tell you this before but, once we were wed and I realised exactly why you had married me, it was too late and I hoped and prayed that, somehow, everything would work out for the best.'

He searched her eyes, then cupped her chin and lowered his mouth to hers. She melted into his kiss, savouring every slide of his tongue, each gentle caress of his lips.

'I shall not regret it, Flora, and there is no need for you to feel ashamed. I will find another way to increase my whisky business. I have no desire to court narrowminded bigots such as Lady Ardhban.'

'You only say that now because you have heard my story. They had already proved their narrow-mindedness by refusing to accept you and yet still you court their favour.'

She felt him shrug.

'Oh, I always recognised their bigotry. Your story has simply strengthened the case against them. I will find another way.'

'I will help you.' Somehow, she would find a way to prove her worth.

He hugged her to him and dropped a kiss to her forehead. 'There is no need for you to trouble yourself. I have always found a way in the past. I shall do so again.'

She wanted to argue. She longed to help him. For so long her head had brimmed with ideas to help her family and her clan, but no one had paid her any heed and, eventually, she had given up even offering her opinion. That habit, of keeping her ideas and feelings locked inside, was still entrenched so she would not argue with words, but she vowed to show Lachlan through her deeds that her ideas had merit and that she could be of help.

Besides—she snuggled a little closer to him—she did not want words to come between them now, for tonight they would share a bed again. His breathing had quickened and his heart beat erratically in her ear. Her own heart leapt at the thought that, tonight, they would again lie as man and wife. Those few glimpses of pleasure she had felt on their wedding night…she longed to experience them again, to see where they might lead.

Tonight her nightmare had become reality, but Lachlan had not been disappointed with her—he had been supportive. And protective. And kind. She dared to hope that he returned her growing feelings for him.

'Come. Let us return to the house.'

Lachlan's voice sounded a touch gruff, but Flora did not believe he was angry. Maybe, just maybe, he, too, was imagining the night to come and even looking forward to it. He kept his arm around her as they left the carriage house and they hurried back to the house.

'I suggest you go straight on up to bed, Flora. I had better show my face again. I shall say you have retired with a headache.' He tilted her face up, smiled and dropped a kiss on her forehead. 'You are upset. Get some sleep—I shall sleep in the dressing room tonight.'

She had no time to react before Sir Keith and two other gentlemen emerged from the salon.

'McNeill! Just the fellow. Shall you object if I steal him away for a game of whist, Lady Flora? I am persuaded you can spare him for a short time.'

Flora dared not look at Lachlan as she strove to mask her dismay.

'Of course I do not object, Sir Keith. I am sorry for leaving the gathering so early—I have a headache and am about to retire for the night.'

'I shall see you to our room.'

Her chin lifted. 'There is no need, I know the way. I shall bid you all goodnight, gentlemen. Enjoy your game.'

It was not until Muriel had helped Flora disrobe and she was alone with her thoughts that she allowed herself to dwell on all that had happened and her disappointment that Lachlan had chosen to stay away again. So much for her hope that he was beginning to care for her—or was his excuse genuine? Did he believe her so spineless that she needed everything to be perfect before they could be intimate? She didn't understand him. She thumped her pillow in frustration—he now knew the worst of her, but what did *she* know about his past or his family, other than spiteful gossip and innuendo?

She tossed around in the bed, unable to get comfortable as her thoughts raced, Cousin Sarah's jibes about Lachlan circling endlessly. She lay awake for what seemed like hours, but eventually she must have slept because it seemed, all at once, to be light outside.

Lachlan awoke early the next morning, stretching out his stiff limbs to work out the kinks after sleeping in the chair in the dressing room. He'd had a monumental battle to stop himself from joining Flora in the bedchamber next door. But he'd given her his reassurance and had stayed downstairs playing cards until the small hours before— when he could no longer keep his eyes open—retiring quietly to the dressing room.

The desire that had flared within him as he'd comforted Flora in the carriage had shocked him. She had been generous in taking all the blame for being ostracised on to her own shoulders, but he knew much of the fault was his. They were excluded for who he was. Or, more to the point, for who he wasn't. The nobility saw an uncouth businessman lacking the manners and graces of a gentleman and Flora was now tainted by association.

And none of them knows the full truth of my past.

Poor Flora had been so distressed he hadn't wanted to take advantage of her vulnerability. Not here, in a strange place, surrounded by cruel and censorious fools. He would wait until they were home, in familiar surroundings, when Flora wouldn't feel obliged to cling to him as her only safe haven.

Murray came in. If he suspected his master had slept in the chair, he said nothing, but merely asked what Lachlan's plans were for that morning.

'Are you to join the rest of the gentlemen in their pursuit, sir?'

Plans were afoot to stalk the wild deer that Sir Keith encouraged to roam his estate to provide sport for his friends.

The question prompted a decision. 'No. We leave for Lochmore straight after breakfast. I shall ask Sir Keith to provide transport to the ferry. Please instruct Muriel to pack for Lady Flora as well.'

He would not subject Flora to these people for a minute longer than necessary. But that, he realised, as Murray helped him on with his jacket, posed him another dilemma. Just how was he to propel his business forward now?

He tapped on the connecting door and Muriel opened it.

'Thank you, Muriel. Is your mistress ready to go down to breakfast?'

'She is, sir.'

For once, the maid's expression was not cheery but disapproving. He beckoned her through to the dressing room. 'Murray has instructions for you.'

He closed the door behind the maid. Only then did he face Flora. And it was immediately apparent why Muriel had looked daggers at him. Lachlan reached Flora in two strides and gathered her hands in his.

'I have no need to ask whether you slept well.'

He pressed his lips to her hair, then released one hand to nudge a finger beneath her chin, forcing her to meet his gaze. Her eyes were dull, with dark circles beneath, and her freckles were stark against her pale cheeks.

'You have no need to dread the coming days, Flora. You have only to endure breakfast in the company of these people, for we are going home immediately afterwards.'

Her eyes widened. 'Home? But…' She frowned. 'But, what of Carnmore Whisky? How shall we ever persuade anyone to back you?' Hurt, guilt and shame swirled in her eyes. 'I am so sorry. I have let you down.'

His heart cracked. He loved her smile. He wanted to see her happy, not upset and broken like this. Without volition, he gathered her close, nestling her head into his chest as he stroked her hair, instantly hard as her orange blossom scent surrounded him. He shoved his needs and frustration away—Flora needed tenderness and reassurance and, as her husband, it was up to him to provide it even though it did not come naturally to him. She was his responsibility now and he would protect her come what may.

'You have not let me down, Flora. Those people… they are not the sort I want to associate with. I shall find another way.'

She pulled back at that. '*We* shall find another way,' she said.

He smiled down at her. She looked fierce now. Determined. He flicked her nose gently.

'You need worry yourself about it no longer. It is my business and I will find a way. You have the castle to run.' He pressed his lips to her forehead. 'Now let us go and eat our breakfast with our heads high. I shall inform Sir Keith of our departure, but no one else need know until after we've gone.'

They were driven from Dalbride Castle to the dock on Loch Fyne in time to board a steamer for the journey back to Ardrishaig. Lachlan spent the carriage ride propped in the corner with his eyes closed, dredging up ideas, examining them and then rejecting them. He had no idea of his next step. The first full batch of his new blended whisky was even now maturing in oak casks. It would be ready after Christmas and, as yet, he had no market for it. Installing both types of still at the distillery had been a gamble. The malt whisky produced in batches in the old, traditional pot stills was still popular locally—and throughout Scotland—but it was a slow process, producing a low volume of spirit that took more time to mature. Had he been too impatient to invest in the Coffey still?

Once aboard the ferry and steaming down the loch, Lachlan resumed his musings but they were soon interrupted by Flora.

'Will you tell me more about your distillery?'

Lachlan opened his eyes and straightened in his seat. Flora had fixed her earnest gaze upon his face and he felt his mouth twitch.

'Can you read my mind, Flora? How did you know I was thinking about the whisky?'

Her lips pursed as she suppressed a smile. He was pleased to see colour in her cheeks and more sparkle in her eyes.

'You were frowning in ferocious concentration,' she said. 'And your foot has been tapping ever since we left the Castle. You cannot wait to get home and to get on with business, can you?'

He laughed at that. 'I am that transparent, am I? I shall have to take care how I behave in future if you are not to guess all my secrets.'

'Secrets, Lachlan?' Her laugh was light, but sounded strained. 'What secrets?'

Chapter Eleven

Lachlan swallowed down his dismay. 'None for you to worry about, Flora. Now, about the whisky.' Of the two subjects, that was by far the least prickly. There was no reason not to tell her about the dilemma facing his business.

'When I moved to Lochmore I decided to set up a business I could be more involved with. I have investments in Glasgow, but it's not the same as running a business and, besides, they provide employment in the city. I wanted a business nearer to Lochmore to provide jobs in the area to help stop people crowding into the cities to find work or having to emigrate. I found out that much of the local economy around Lochmore is linked to the Glenarris Distillery, which was established nearly thirty years ago by the present Duke of Lochmore, although he doesn't own it now. It provides work for local people, alongside fishing and farming, and, as a result, this area has not suffered as badly economically as some other areas of the Highlands.'

'I think my grandfather used to own part of Glenarris Distillery, but my father sold his share after Grandfather died. Is that the distillery you bought?'

'No, but it sparked the idea. I found another small distillery about an hour's ride from the castle, in the village of Ballinorchy by Loch Carnmore, and I bought it from the previous owner's widow. I've set up a construction company to build cottages for the additional workers we'll need if my plans to expand succeed. My dream is to build Ballinorchy into a prosperous town.'

'That is a brave ambition.'

'I suppose it is. Ballinorchy is close to Loch Fyne, where the steamers from Glasgow to Ardrishaig pass regularly, so I should be able to ship the whisky straight into Glasgow and from there by rail to Edinburgh and even into England. To London.'

'But you need customers.'

'I need customers.'

The crux of the matter. He needed someone with influence to take a chance on him. On his whisky.

'But…whisky is popular. I don't understand why there is difficulty selling it.'

'It's new,' he said. 'The whisky you are familiar with… the malt whisky…that has been produced in the Highlands for years. It's made from malted barley, in batches, in pot stills.'

Flora nodded.

'There is a different sort of still available now—a Coffey still, with two columns. It still uses some malted barley, but that is mixed with cheaper, unmalted grains and it produces a higher-proof spirit, more quickly and in far greater quantities because it is a continuous process. The grain whisky has a blander, smoother taste than the malt and currently much of what is produced here in the north goes to gin manufacturers where they add all sorts of spices.'

'So why not just sell your whisky to the gin distillers?'

'Because I have found that by blending malt whisky with grain whisky the resulting spirit is far more palatable to southern palates. It is smoother and gentler—not such an acquired taste as the smoky malts. There will be a market for it in London, I am sure, and I see an opportunity to bring some of the wealth from England into Scotland. Fresh money will increase living standards and wages. It must be a good thing.'

'Well, I think it sounds like a splendid idea.' She smiled up at him. 'I shall do all I can to help, Lachlan.'

At that moment, he had never felt so well understood or appreciated. His heart twitched as he saw both pride and tenderness in her eyes. There was hope for them in that look, he was sure.

'We are nearing the Canal,' he said. 'It won't be long until we're home.'

And he couldn't wait to finally give Flora the wedding night she deserved. He would forget all his worries about not being good enough for her—they would be a man and a woman. Husband and wife.

'Did you know this is called the Royal Route since the Queen and Prince Albert sailed along the Canal last year?' Flora said. 'They stopped one night at Castle Mc-Crieff during their trip. It was before…before…'

'Before Galkirk?'

She nodded, a faraway look on her face. 'They love Scotland and last year they decided to holiday in the Highlands. So they sailed up the Crinan Canal—just as we are about to do now—and met the royal yacht, the *Victoria and Albert*, at Crinan.'

'I remember the excitement,' said Lachlan, drily.

Flora frowned. 'You do not approve of the Queen?'

He shrugged. 'I have no feelings about her one way or the other. What?'—at her look of horror—'You are shocked? You think that a disloyal comment? But she is nothing to me...she is so far removed from my life, and from yours, that I do not understand her and, if she were to know of my existence, she would not understand me. We would,' he added, with a smile, 'hold each other in healthy disregard.'

And he could never forget that it was Her Majesty's court that had sentenced a fifteen-year-old boy to seven years' transportation for the theft of a loaf of bread to feed his starving family. Desolation washed through him, guilt in its wake. His family, all gone. Everyone he had ever loved had died and then he had let down Ma and Anna by getting caught. He'd abandoned them. He battened down those emotions. Dwelling on the past wouldn't change it.

'Tell me how the Royal party came to visit Castle McCrieff.'

'My father received a letter informing him that the Queen would honour us by coming ashore to dine with us.'

'And was the visit a success?'

The ferry docked, and Lachlan helped Flora across the gangway to the landing stage.

'My father grumbled that it near ruined him.' They walked arm in arm to the *Sunbeam*, the horse-drawn track boat waiting to transport them along the canal to Crinan. 'But only after they had left,' she added with a mischievous smile. 'Their entourage was huge and we had to accommodate and cater for them all. My mother was thrilled, but my father hoped never to be so honoured ever again.'

Lachlan laughed. 'And did you meet their Majesties?'

Flora nodded. 'Although all I did was curtsy. They both smiled very graciously. I was most surprised, though. Do you know the Queen is only five feet tall?

Even shorter than me. The Prince is very handsome and dashing, with his moustache and his whiskers.'

Something very like jealousy twisted in Lachlan's chest. *No. Nonsense.* It could only be possessiveness... irritation that *his* wife should say that about another man, be he a prince or a pauper.

They boarded the *Sunbeam*, ready for the nine-mile journey to Crinan, a port on the Sound of Jura. Then it would be another carriage journey home, to Lochmore Castle.

He could not wait until they were home.

Drummond met them at the door of the castle, a letter in his hand.

'It arrived yesterday, after you left, sir,' he said. 'It says Urgent on the envelope.'

'Thank you, Drummond. Pay the driver, will you, please?' he said as he broke the seal.

He read the contents, then scanned them again. Finally! Delaney had a positive lead on Anna. Every fibre of his being tensed with the need to act. Finally, he would find her.

'What is it?' Flora had also stopped and was looking back at him with concern.

'Nothing,' he said. 'A business matter I must deal with.' He raised his voice, shouting to the driver of the hired carriage who had brought them home and was about to drive away. 'Hie!'

The driver reined in and looked back.

'Wait, please! Murray?'

The valet was carrying his portmanteau up the stairs. 'Yes, sir?'

'Pack another bag for me, will you? Hurry, please. I must go to Glasgow immediately.'

'Glasgow?' Flora's face dropped. 'Now?'

He brushed her cheek, regret humming through him. 'I am sorry. I shall write and let you know when to expect me home again.'

He was too much on edge to offer her further reassurance. He strode across to the coachman.

'I must return to Crinan immediately. Please wait.'

The man tipped his hat. 'Very good, sir.'

Flora was waiting where he left her. Still. Expressionless.

He cursed having to go now, when they had finally been getting closer. When he had made plans for tonight. But she would still be here when he returned and then he vowed he would be a better and more attentive husband to her.

Flora sat at the grand piano in the drawing room, her fingers stumbling over the trickier passages in Chopin's *Nocturne Opus 9 No. 2.*

'Grrr!'

She growled her frustration under her breath. She'd already intercepted too many pitying glances from the servants since Lachlan's hasty departure three days before and she had no wish to add to their gossip. Her emotions lurched from hope—*See how kind he was that night! Look how he trusted me with his hopes and ambitions for the distillery!*—to despair.

However kind he had been, and however much he'd seemed to enjoy their kisses, he'd still not come to her bed that night. And no sooner had they arrived home than he could not wait to leave her again. A scrawled note had arrived yesterday to announce his return today and although she had scanned the words for some hint of a personal message for her—some intimation that he had missed her, or was looking forward to seeing her again—she could find none. The note had been for the entirely practical purpose of ensuring the carriage would meet the track boat at Crinan the following afternoon.

She stared blindly across the room, her fingers pressed to her mouth. What would her future be? She had never felt so…unnecessary. And that, she thought with a low, self-deprecating laugh, was quite something after that final year at Castle McCrieff, with a family who only seemed to notice her when they had something to criticise.

Maybe it is me? Maybe I am so easy to overlook that it is all I should expect?

Her hand slid to her chest and she caressed her brooch. As ever, it improved her spirits. She stared at the music in front of her, questioning whether she really had the heart to conquer this piece. She hauled in a deep breath, turned the sheets back to the start and settled herself, her fingers poised above the keys.

As the music flowed her thoughts wandered yet again to Lachlan. Her husband. Except…he was barely even that, was he? One time they had shared the marriage bed. *Once!* She did not expect miracles. She did not expect him to love her. But she *had* expected that a man—a *husband*— would take advantage of, and enjoy, his conjugal rights. How would she ever get with child? A baby would at least give her the hope of joy and love in her future.

She had seen the letter summoning him to Glasgow with her own eyes, so it had not been merely an excuse to leave Lochmore. He *had* been summoned.

But by whom?

She hadn't read that letter. He'd put it in his pocket and taken it with him. It could have been from a woman. Did he have a mistress? Was that why he had no interest in bedding Flora? She tried to banish that suspicion from her mind. Mrs Fraser had told her how focused Lachlan was on business and that he was often from home. She mustn't jump to conclusions. Distracted, her fingers faltered and she grimaced as she fumbled the music and played the wrong chord.

'Ahem!'

She started. Drummond stood at the door.

'Her Grace, the Duchess of Lochmore, has called, my lady.'

Flora shot to her feet. A visitor! Her initial rush of pleasure soon fled. A duchess. She must know about Flora's disgrace. And she was a Lochmore—how would she feel seeing a McCrieff as mistress here?

Flora's stomach jittered, but her voice remained steady. 'Thank you, Drummond. Please invite the Duchess to join me—'

'Oh, dear.' The well-modulated voice was very English and apologetic but, somehow, it appeared to contain suppressed laughter. 'I do hope you will forgive my disregard of the rules governing formal visits, Lady Flora, but I simply could not help myself in case I was denied. This was always one of my favourite rooms and when I heard you playing, I could not resist following poor Drummond, even though he, quite correctly, showed me into the morning parlour first.'

The Duchess approached Flora, smiling, with her hand outstretched. She was a petite woman and somewhat plain at first glance, but that initial impression was quickly overridden by her intelligent expression and her keenly observant grey-eyed stare. As if in a dream, Flora proffered her own hand. The Duchess was not wearing gloves and her slim hands were cool as she clasped Flora's hand between both of hers.

'I have been away visiting family so please forgive me

for not calling upon you sooner, Lady Flora—or might I call you Flora? And I am Joane. I really cannot take to all the pomp and circumstance that goes with being wed to a duke!'

'Er...yes. Of course. Thank you.' Flora's senses reeled. She looked for Drummond and rallied her thoughts by concentrating on the mundane. 'Please ask Cook to send up a tea tray, Drummond.'

Flora's unexpected—and unusual—visitor crossed to the window to gaze out over the ocean. She was nothing like any other high-ranking noble Flora had ever met.

'It is the only thing I miss about living in this dank and draughty place,' said Joane, with a sigh. 'The view and the sunsets. Although—' she turned abruptly '—you have done wonders with the castle. It is very...' she cast her eye around the room '...*modern*.'

Flora could not decide whether that meant the Duchess approved or disapproved of the changes. 'My husband must claim the credit, for he had the entire castle refurbished before we were married.'

'Yes. I gather nothing but the most up-to-date attire and furnishings will satisfy Mr McNeill. I guess he believes that is what is expected of a gentleman.'

Flora bristled at the insinuation that Lachlan was not a gentleman—even though she still knew nothing of his origins—but Joane forestalled her.

'That is not a criticism, but an observation, my dear. I am aware he bought the castle in the belief that it would make him more acceptable to society—but you and I know it is never quite that simple. Appearances are not everything in that world, are they?'

'*That* world?'

Joane cocked her head to one side. '*Our* world, then, if you like, although I fear I have never quite slotted comfortably into the rarefied world of high society.' She smiled with a hint of apology. 'I am sorry. Forthrightness is a bad habit of mine. My husband, Benneit, complains that I treat every new face as an instant friend. But the fault is his…he always encouraged me to be more open and honest about my thoughts and feelings and now I am so used to speaking my mind that I do so without thought. And, after all, who will dare to correct a duchess?'

Her grey eyes twinkled with suppressed laughter, drawing an answering smile from Flora. There was no hesitation in her heart. She sensed no hostility in Joane, even though their clans were old enemies, and her comments reassured Flora that, whatever else the reason for this visit, it was not to censure or criticise. She was here for a neighbourly visit and Flora dared to hope she had found a new friend.

'Shall we sit? We might as well enjoy the view while we talk.' They settled a pair of chairs by the window. 'I hope your family are well?'

'Thank you, they are indeed. Well, the girls are. We have three—Lily, Violet and Marguerite—but Jamie, our son, is overseas and I have not seen him for a while. He is a botanist and he travels the world seeking new plants. He has found several new species for the Botanic Gardens in Glasgow.'

'You must be very proud of him. And what lovely names you gave your daughters. Especially Marguerite— it is unusual.'

Joane smiled. 'We named her after a French lady who married Benneit's ancestor, Ewan Lochmore, to become the Countess of Glenarris. That was before the Lochmores were elevated to dukes. Not that either Benneit or Jamie care for such privilege, of course. They would far rather be adventurers than aristocrats and landowners.' She smiled ruefully. 'Benneit is in South America with Jamie now.' She sighed then, her features settling into sorrowful lines. 'It is so far away and it feels so very long since I saw him.'

'Do you not like to travel, too? Could you not have gone with them?'

'I could have, but Marguerite was with child—her first, you know—and I could not bring myself to travel so far away and for so long in case she had need of me.' She smiled. 'Our first granddaughter—born nine months ago. Our other grandchildren are all boys, so little Louisa is very, very special.'

'I am sure she is. The Duke has been gone a long time.'

'He has indeed.' Joane sighed again. 'But he should return early in the New Year. I miss him terribly, but we both knew that if he did not take this chance to travel with Jamie he would soon be too old. He is over sixty now and, although he is still healthy, we are too aware that old age will eventually take its toll on us both—for I am but a few years behind him.'

It was hard to believe the woman opposite Flora would ever be anything but full of vitality. Her elegance, her unlined skin and her light brown hair, streaked with silver but still glossy with health—all suggested a woman a decade younger. Flora wondered if the Duke, too, still looked youthful for his age.

A maid entered with the tea tray and a cake stand loaded with fruit cake and shortbread and poured tea for Flora and her visitor who had, it seemed, run out of conversation. The distant look in her great grey eyes suggested that thoughts of her faraway husband prompted her silence. Suddenly, though, she looked up.

'I hesitated over whether or not to come here in person,' she said.

'Why should you hesitate?'

'Oh, you know—that silly ancient feud between the Lochmores and the McCrieffs. I did not know if you might feel, shall we say, a little antagonistic toward me and my husband?'

'No! Why should I? That was all in the past.'

'There was that matter of the expectations between your Aunt Tessa and Benneit—the union that was intended to cement kinship between the clans.'

Of course! Joane's husband was the very Lochmore Aunt Tessa had refused to marry, before Flora was even born.

'It is true my father has never forgiven my aunt—they have not spoken since.' She felt a fleeting sympathy for her father, so thwarted in his plans and ambitions.

Will Father ever truly forgive me either? Two dukes rejected—one by his sister, one by his daughter.

'I know Tessa deeply regrets that rift, but neither she nor Benneit care to dwell on the past.'

'You know my aunt?' Flora leaned forward. 'I have never met her.'

'Oh, yes, indeed—she and her husband have been our good friends for a long time.'

She sipped her tea while Flora wondered about her aunt and if she might ask Joane to introduce them. Joane placed her cup in its saucer, picked up her reticule and withdrew a card, which she handed to Flora.

'I have brought an invitation for you and your husband.'

Chapter Twelve

Flora puzzled over the names on the card. 'Mr and Mrs William Anderson?' She had never heard Lachlan mention the name and she was almost certain there had been no Mr and Mrs Anderson at Sir Keith's house party. 'Is this…?' She raised her eyes to Joane's smiling face, barely able to conceal her sudden hope. 'Is Mrs Anderson my aunt?'

'She is. She and your uncle live in Partick, just outside Glasgow, not far from Marguerite and her husband. Tessa and William are hosting a soirée next week and she tasked me with persuading you to attend. So, you see, you cannot possibly refuse, for I shall have to bear the blame for it.'

Flora's heart sank.

'I do not think we should accept.' Clearly the Duchess had no idea she was such an outcast in society. Flora fingered her brooch as she confessed that Tessa's guests and friends would be unlikely to welcome her company.

'But why ever not?' Joane's eyebrows shot up. 'What could they possibly have against you?'

Flora told her about Galkirk and her disgrace.

'Galkirk?' Joane snorted. 'That old goat? I wouldn't

allow any of my daughters within a mile of him. I wonder at your parents even considering such a match for you.'

Flora stared at her visitor in astonishment. Then, in a bid to leave no fault or black mark on her character unexposed, she also told Joane of her recent experience at Sir Keith's house party and of her failure to help Lachlan find patrons for his whisky.

'And that is the sole reason he married me,' she concluded. Misery wrapped around her heart. 'To help introduce him to well-born patrons and I cannot even manage that.'

No wonder he is constantly away on business. I failed as a daughter and now I am failing as a wife.

Joane patted Flora's hand. 'You are mistaken if you expect our friends to be the same as those fools, Flora. Benneit and I...' She paused, considering, and Flora felt the weight of her great, grey-eyed stare. 'Well,' she at last continued, 'I suppose you might call us unconventional. He never aspired to be the Duke and he disappointed his father in almost every way imaginable. And Tessa, do not forget, bore her fair share of ostracism after her family disowned her. They thoroughly disapproved of her eventual choice of husband, too—Tessa was sent to live in Glasgow with her maternal aunt and she fell in love with and married an English marine engineer who had moved to the city to work in the shipbuilding industry. He had lodgings in the house next door. You can imagine how furious her father and brother were at her choice, but she was over twenty-one and they could not stop her.

'Do say you'll accept, Flora. I promise you won't feel uncomfortable and you will not be ostracised—there are many within our circle who will empathise with your experience. And—as an added incentive—we may contrive to find some patrons for Lachlan's whisky yet.' She grinned and extended her hand. 'What do you say?'

Flora could hardly believe her ears. Her heart, from feeling a leaden weight within her chest ever since their return from Dalbride Castle, now soared. She reached out and Joane closed her fingers around Flora's hand in a gentle squeeze. Tears sprang unbidden to Flora's eyes and she screwed them shut. If only her own mother had been so understanding…so supportive… Guilt at even thinking such a thing scoured her throat. She should honour her own mother, not criticise her. And Flora, better than anyone, knew what a hard man her father could be— Mother never went against him in anything. She swallowed down her emotions and opened her eyes, to see Joane's eyes riveted to her chest. To her brooch.

'Where did you get that brooch? It is quite distinctive.'

'Um… I found it at home… I mean, at my family home, not here. Why?'

A groove slashed between Joane's eyebrows. 'I'm not sure. It looks familiar… I have seen one like it before, but I cannot think where.' She met Flora's puzzled gaze and laughed, shaking her head. 'Never mind. I am sure it will come to me. Now, what about Tessa's invitation? Do say you'll persuade your husband to accept.'

Flora smiled, excitement speeding her pulse. 'Yes. I would love to meet my aunt and I'll do my very best to persuade Lachlan to accept.'

Their conversation turned to the people they were likely to meet, their wider family connections and how Flora might help Lachlan secure support for his whisky. Joane did not plan to attend the event, but she undertook to write to Tessa and ask her to help by making appropriate introductions at the soirée and she also promised to write to introduce Flora to friends who were prominent in London society.

After Joane left, Flora—her head buzzing with ideas and opportunities—went upstairs to her boudoir and sat at her writing desk to list all the names mentioned and how they were linked to various establishments in London and larger English towns as well as in Glasgow and Edinburgh. She was determined to impress Lachlan with her ideas, burying deep her nerves at putting herself forward and, even worse, at making any demands on her inscrutable husband. How would he respond to Aunt Tessa's invitation? And, even more worrying, how would Flora respond if Lachlan flatly refused to go? Instead of agonising over his response and her possible reactions, she focused all her attention on her plans, refusing to allow her thoughts to slide away to start fretting over *What ifs*...

By the time Lachlan arrived home early that evening, Flora was so full of enthusiasm for her ideas she even forgot to be annoyed with him for disappearing yet again on business. Bandit, too, appeared to catch her mood, for he would not settle, constantly running to the door and whining, and they both rushed out of the house at the first sound of carriage wheels.

'Good evening, Flora.' Lachlan stared down at her, his mouth set in a grim line.

'Did...did you manage to solve your problem, Lachlan?'

He frowned. 'Problem?' His frown deepened into a scowl. 'What makes you ask that?'

Flora tensed. 'I—I just meant...you were called away...an urgent business matter. I hope all is now well?'

His brows lifted and his expression softened, but he still failed to smile. Flora's heart sank. She seemed doomed to dwell in a perpetual state of anxiety when it came to dealing with her husband. It was a stark contrast to her earlier elation.

'I dealt with the matter at hand, although I shall have to return to Glasgow again shortly.' He bent to give Bandit a quick pat. 'It is an ongoing situation.' A fine but needle-sharp rain started to blow in on the strengthening wind as they went indoors. 'I shall go upstairs and change and by then dinner will be ready, so I shall see you in the dining room.'

Dismissed. Again. It was as though he couldn't get out of her company fast enough. The rapport between them after the disaster of Sir Keith's house party seemed a hurtful illusion. Nothing had changed.

Flora waited impatiently for Lachlan to join her for dinner. She had thought about ordering Drummond to set her place next to Lachlan's, but she was not quite brave enough for such a bold step. Instead, they ate dinner in near silence but, when Flora rose to leave Lachlan to his cigar and whisky, she seized her courage in both hands.

'Would you join me in the drawing room when you leave the table, Lachlan? There is a matter I should like to discuss.'

She quailed as his dark, unfathomable gaze settled on her. A frown stitched the skin between his brows.

'If you wish it, of course I shall.'

He bowed and, dismissed yet again, Flora went to the drawing room, where she sat at the pianoforte to amuse herself while she waited for Lachlan.

'If you howl again at my playing, Bandit, I shall banish you to the kitchen,' she warned the terrier.

Before Joane's arrival, Bandit had disgraced himself by trying to join in the music. The resulting cacophony had hurt Flora's ears. Fortunately, this was a softer piece and Bandit settled on the rug by the fire. Lost in music, Flora did not notice Lachlan come into the drawing room and it was not until she finished a piece that the sound of clapping alerted her to his presence sat upon the sofa.

'Oh!' Her cheeks burned. 'How long have you been there?'

'Long enough to appreciate your skill.'

She bent her head, staring unseeingly at the keys as she strove to assemble her thoughts. All her well-reasoned ideas and suggestions had scrambled in her brain and she barely knew where to start.

'Monsieur Chopin is a hard act to follow,' she said. 'I wish I had one-tenth of his ability.'

'Do not put yourself down. You play well—I presume you had lessons?'

The question surprised her. 'But of course.' Playing an instrument was one of the accomplishments expected of a young lady. She wondered if Lachlan had sisters. Or brothers, even. She dared not ask…his brows lowered at her response to his question and she could not fathom out why.

'You are very fortunate in your upbringing.' He stared down at his hands, clasped together between his knees. 'You were sheltered from reality and you wanted for nothing. You despair now at your family's seeming indifference and your isolation from your former friends, but there are very much worse things in this world.'

Flora dared not speak. Her upbringing was not her fault and there were, no doubt, much worse things that could happen, but she had no experience of such and she feared saying the wrong thing.

His chest expanded as he inhaled, then he pinned her with his dark eyes. 'What did you wish to speak to me about? I have work to do.'

'Work?'

The word came out as a squeak. She wanted to protest. He had been gone for days and he had come home only to desert her for his ledgers?

He raised one brow. A surge of anger took Flora unawares and, before she could plan how to phrase her request, she blurted out, 'The Duchess paid me a visit. She knows my Aunt Tessa and she brought us an invitation.'

She shoved back the piano stool, sprang to her feet and marched to the mantelpiece, conscious the whole way of that dark gaze following her. She grabbed the invitation and stalked over to Lachlan, thrusting it beneath his nose. He took it, reading it in silence as Flora stood nervously before him.

'Joane said Aunt Tessa has well-connected friends... people who will not care about my disgrace.'

'Joane?'

'The Duchess.'

Lachlan rubbed his scratchy, stubble-covered jaw, weariness coursing through his entire body.

She calls a duchess she has only just met by her forename?

As if it was the most normal thing in the world. Well, no doubt it was for a young lady who couldn't imagine growing up without piano lessons, but it merely served to widen the gulf between his world and hers. When he thought about his family's experience and what Anna might even now be suffering... He pushed his sister from his thoughts. Time enough to think about her when he was alone. First, he must deal with whatever Flora had planned—the stubborn set of her chin told him she would not allow herself to be fobbed off. At least this Duchess hadn't snubbed her.

Suddenly, Flora dropped to her knees before him, and gazed up at him, beseechingly and, as if to lend weight to her plea, Bandit leapt on to the sofa and fixed his own eyes on Lachlan.

'Joane has offered to write letters of introduction to some of those who will be attending the soirée—gentlemen she thinks will be able to help us. And she will also write to some of her friends with influence in Edinburgh and London society to ask if they would sample our whisky.'

Our whisky. He liked the sound of that. Emotion swirled in the depths of her green eyes—he could see the importance of this to her. He could not...*would* not...deny her. Not when it was obvious how much it mattered—perhaps it would help to make up for him being such a poor husband to her. He really did want to make her happy, but there was just so much demanding his attention right now...

She put her hand on his knee and, despite his utter exhaustion, his groin tightened in response. How he longed to bed her again. She'd been on his mind the entire time he'd been with Delaney in Edinburgh searching for Anna, who had moved there just over a year ago. When the trail petered out, Lachlan returned to Glasgow, leaving Delaney to continue his enquiries. He blessed the railways that had transformed travel in the years he had been in Australia. It was so convenient and so speedy, even though the disadvantage was that the railways made it easier for someone like Anna to travel to strange towns. And to disappear.

His heart ached with the not knowing of what had become of his sister and her child.

They were the only family he had left and now he was failing them like he'd failed the rest.

Racked with guilt, he stared down into Flora's sweet face, with its freckles and its soft pink lips and he felt nothing but disgust. For himself—an urchin from the gutter, daring to believe himself worthy of such a perfect lady. She would surely reject him if she knew the truth, exactly as Jessica had done. If he could only find Anna and the bairn and put things right, maybe he could begin to believe in himself again and he could become the husband Flora deserved.

When he bedded her again, he wanted it to be special. Meaningful. Not just a physical coupling—such as their wedding night, which he knew she had not enjoyed—but more…he could not describe what he wanted. He had neither the vocabulary nor the experience. But it needed to be more…*special*. And that needed time and energy he couldn't spare at the moment. His mind was clouded by his constant fear about what had become of Anna and Flora deserved his total attention.

It could have been so different if that message hadn't sent him hotfoot to Glasgow the instant they returned from Dalbride Manor. It was almost as though the Fates were conspiring against him.

'Lachlan?' Her eyes were anxious now, awaiting his response, and Bandit nudged his wet nose against his hand.

'Your aunt…will she not blame you for your rejection of that Duke like those others did?'

Flora's eyes crinkled with a mischievous grin. 'No, for she is estranged from my father for the same reason— she refused the Duke of Lochmore. *Please*, Lachlan. Do say we might go. I have never met her and it will make up for not having my family nearby.'

Family. How could he deny Flora when he craved the same for himself?

Bandit was on his feet, his head cocked to one side, stubby tail wagging furiously. If he didn't know better, Lachlan would swear that dog knew what they were talking about.

'Yes, we shall go.'

Flora beamed. 'Wait a minute.' She jumped to her feet and hurried once again to the mantelpiece.

Lachlan took the opportunity to check the date on the invitation, idly scratching Bandit's head as he did so. Only three days hence. That would give him ample time to consult with Gregor about the distillery before they left for Glasgow. And, with any luck, Delaney might have some more news for him by then. His stomach clenched. Anna had been alive twelve months ago, but a lot could happen in a year to a mother and child in their precarious position. All he wanted was to find her and to bring her home. To look after her, as was his duty as her brother.

Flora handed him a sheet of paper and sat next to him. It was a list of names of people, hotels, clubs and businesses.

'These are some of the names Joane mentioned,' she said. 'And... I had another idea.' Her cheeks washed with pink. 'You may think it a silly notion, but I overheard Mr Burns at Dalbride Manor. He was talking about the steamer service he and his brother run to the Hebrides and the food and drink served on board. And I know there are companies that run cruises to the Highlands and Islands for the English tourists. And I remember you said the English palate isn't accustomed to the traditional malt whiskies, so I thought we could approach some of those steamer operators and offer to supply Carnmore Whisky for their passengers.'

She bit her lip as Lachlan thought over the idea. He took her hand then and raised it to his lips.

'I think it a splendid idea,' he said. 'In fact, I wonder

why I did not think of it—I was aware of the growing popularity of those boat trips and people certainly like to drink when they are at leisure.'

A ball of excitement lodged under his ribcage—the feeling he always got when a great business prospect occurred to him. Except, this time, it had occurred to his wife. His respect for her grew—she'd led such a sheltered, privileged life and yet she had identified an opportunity within the growing tourism industry, which had mushroomed with the Queen's enthusiasm for all things Scottish. Ever since he had discovered in himself a talent for business, as a young man of nineteen awarded a ticket of leave, he had recognised the importance of sniffing out a new trend and getting in early. That habit had served him very well but, this time, he had been beaten at his own game by his wife.

He smiled at Flora and pressed his lips to her soft cheek, breathing in her unique scent. He jumped to his feet before he lost himself in her. He had no time to lose if they were to go to Glasgow for her aunt's soirée. He must work on his ledgers tonight and then he would have two clear days to deal with matters at the distillery before returning to Glasgow.

'I shall bid you goodnight, my dear. I have a busy day at the distillery tomorrow so I'm unlikely to see you at breakfast and I shall leave it to you to instruct Murray and Muriel to pack for our trip to Glasgow on Thursday.'

Flora watched as Lachlan strode from the room. What could she do to keep her husband's attention? She'd seen his desire as his eyes darkened, but it was almost as though he were fighting against it. But why? She didn't understand him. The delight she'd felt at his response to her idea slowly leached from her, leaving her deflated. For almost the first time in her life a man had listened to one of her ideas, considered it and found merit in it. Her father had never really given her a chance to voice her suggestions—ridiculing her ideas before she'd had the chance to explain them in any detail. It had left her resentful...he had always paid far more attention to her brother Donald's ludicrous, unworkable money-generating schemes than he did to hers. He'd dismissed out of hand her suggestion of refurbishing the apartment Queen Victoria and Prince Albert had slept in last year and advertising it to the English tourists who loved to explore the romance and the beauty of the Highlands.

Hmmph. Donald's schemes fail and he gets nothing but praise, and my sisters get respectable dowries to enable them to marry well, whereas I...

She reined back her grumbling thoughts and took in her surroundings: the drawing room, furnished in the latest style; the floor, fully carpeted; the beautiful pianoforte, such a Godsend to her; a blazing fire in the grate; the valuable ornaments dotted around the room; the floral wallpaper of various colours on a crimson background; the luxurious crimson floor-length curtains and pelmet...how could she doubt she was better off than her brother and her sisters? Lachlan might not be the most attentive husband in the world, but he was hard-working and he had at least appreciated her idea. He'd even praised it—quite the novelty for a woman who was more used to being ignored by her father and her brother. Father could not believe that a mere female could have any idea worth considering and Donald had always been jealous.

With any luck she might also secure a patron for Carnmore Whisky and prove herself even further. If she could not have the satisfaction of a close marriage, at least she could enjoy the satisfaction of helping her husband to build his business empire.

Chapter Thirteen

Flora clutched Lachlan's arm as he opened the wrought-iron gate to a small but modern double-fronted sandstone villa, set back from the road in Partick, a village to the west of Glasgow. Large bay windows set either side of the wide front door gave the house a pleasing symmetry, as did the chimneys from which smoke curled lazily, there being no wind.

They had arrived at her aunt's house early for, the day after Lachlan had returned home, Flora had received a letter from her aunt, begging them to arrive an hour before the start of their soirée.

For I long for nothing more than to sit quietly and get to know my dear niece, and I fear I shall be too tempted to neglect our other guests for you. Please say you will come.

And Lachlan—even though he was so busy—had agreed. They had set forth early that morning and steamed up the Clyde on the *Pioneer* before taking a hackney to the Tontine Hotel on the Trongate. Muriel had accompanied them, but not Murray as Lachlan would manage without his valet. Flora had been disappointed, but not surprised, to discover that Lachlan had reserved two bedchambers for their visit. Her hopes of understanding her husband diminished with each passing day—he seemed content for them to be friends rather than lovers. He was constantly distracted and, when he forgot to blank his expression, she could see how anxious he was. But what about? Was it the success of Carnmore Whisky that worried him or was there something else on his mind?

'Are you nervous?' Lachlan patted Flora's hand. 'Your aunt would not have invited us if she did not wish to get to know you. Besides...'

She glanced up at him as he paused. He met her gaze and humour glinted in his dark eyes.

'Besides, you have me here to protect you and, if all else fails, you can always make a run for it again.'

His mouth twitched and Flora laughed, giving his arm a gentle slap. 'I suppose I deserve that. I shall not run away, but I cannot help worrying she won't like me.'

A maid opened the door in response to Lachlan's knock.

'Mr McNeill and Lady Flora McNeill,' he said.

Flora glowed with pride. Lachlan was so handsome in his black suit, his red and ivory waistcoat and his black silk top hat, his appearance the epitome of a prosperous gentleman and she realised, with a start, that she wouldn't swap him for any number of dukes. If only... She swallowed past the lump that lodged in her throat. If only they were closer, as a man and wife ought to be.

The hall had a polished wooden floor and painted panelling on the walls but, before Flora could take in much more of their surroundings, a trim lady dressed in a blue shot-silk gown bustled towards them, her hands outstretched, her gaze fixed upon Flora. Flora only needed to see her red hair—a little faded by age—and green eyes to know this was her Aunt Tessa.

'Flora!' She was enveloped in a scented hug. 'Oh, this is such a joy!'

Flora instinctively hugged her in return as a tiny sniffle reached her ears. Tessa held Flora's shoulders and looked her up and down. Her eyes were moist and her mouth trembled a little before she controlled her emotions.

'I am so thrilled you are here.' She released Flora and smiled at Lachlan. 'And this, I presume, is your husband? Well, that settles it. You and I are definitely alike—we like the tall, dark, handsome fellows, do we not?'

She winked at Flora and then tiptoed up to kiss Lachlan on the cheek. Flora stared, open-mouthed. Her aunt dared to be openly affectionate to a nephew she had only just met and yet Flora hesitated to act upon such impulse, even though Lachlan was her husband. Never in her entire life had she seen her parents behave so spontaneously.

Lachlan raised Tessa's hand to his lips. 'And *I* see that not only good taste but also beauty runs in the McCrieff family, Mrs Anderson.' He frowned. 'Or...should I call you Lady Tessa?'

'A charmer, too!' Tessa's eyes twinkled. 'And it's Mrs Anderson, or plain old Tessa to friends and family.' She shot a rueful smile at Flora. 'I haven't used that courtesy title since my marriage. I almost forgot it existed!'

Lachlan handed her a bottle. 'I have taken the liberty of bringing you a bottle of whisky from my distillery at Carnmore. I shall be interested to hear your verdict upon it.'

Tessa laughed. 'And an opportunist to boot! I like him, Niece.' She linked her arm through Flora's. 'Come on in. I cannot wait for you to meet my William.'

William was, indeed, tall, dark and handsome, with serious grey eyes. He seemed every bit as fond of his wife as she was of him and neither of them hesitated to show it.

'And let us not be formal,' said Tessa, once the men had shaken hands and William had gravely bent to kiss Flora's cheek. 'No aunt and uncle, please. We are Tessa and William, and I do hope we shall be good friends.

'Come, let William pour you both a drink and we can chat until our other guests arrive. William?'

'My dear?'

'Lachlan has brought us a bottle of his whisky. Would you be good enough to pour me a wee dram? I am curious to sample it, having heard about the grand plans he has to expand his distillery.'

Tessa led them into a light, airy drawing room with a carved marble chimneypiece and pale blue and silver striped wallpaper. She guided Flora to a large mahogany sofa upholstered in blue and dressed with colourful tasselled cushions. As they chatted—Flora answering Tessa's many questions about her old home and her brother's family—Flora couldn't help overhearing snatches of Lachlan's conversation with William.

'William is an engineer,' said Tessa. 'He works for Robert Napier and Sons—they designed and built some of the first ships to be constructed of iron instead of wood. It is hard to imagine such a heavy ship staying afloat, is it not? But they do—they have been most successful and William says that is the future of shipping—huge vessels powered by steam to carry goods all over the Empire.'

Her voice rang with pride.

'You clearly don't regret not marrying the Duke.'

'Benneit?' Tessa laughed. 'Not in the slightest. I was

sent in disgrace to live with my Aunt Isobel and before long a handsome young engineer came to live next door and stole my heart.'

Her hand rose to her chest and a quiet sigh escaped her and, at that very moment, Flora heard Lachlan say, 'I have but recently returned from Edinburgh—'

'I used to find excuses to linger on the doorstep, hoping to see him as he returned home from work, and before long we were in love. So, no, I have no regrets, other than being estranged from my brother and not knowing my nieces and nephew.'

Tessa's comment drowned out whatever else Lachlan said and Flora murmured an appropriate response even as she wondered what he had been doing in Edinburgh. He had been called away to Glasgow by that letter. He'd never mentioned business interests in Edinburgh before. What else did he keep from her? She turned and stared at his profile as he concentrated on what William was saying.

Who are you?

He'd shown he could be charming to women when he chose to be—flirting and teasing, as he had with Aunt Tessa and with some of the other ladies at Sir Keith's house party...those who would speak to him. Even Brenda Fraser, who was old enough to be his mother, got that certain look on her face when she spoke of him—the look that declared that she thoroughly approved of him. But with Flora he all too often seemed self-conscious and stiff—except for the few occasions when he seemed to forget himself. And allowed himself to relax. And revealed more of the real man she sensed was hidden inside him. It was almost as though he feared offending her.

Either that or he simply didn't care what she thought of him.

Does he see no reason to make an effort with me because I am already his wife?

That thought gave her more pain than she expected and she quickly quashed it. She didn't want to believe that because it would mean any effort she made to get closer to him was doomed to failure. She pasted her smile in place and concentrated on the names of the people she would meet that evening as Tessa told her about the expected guests. Upon hearing that there would be owners of shipping and ferry companies among them, Flora confided her idea to Tessa.

'Well, Carnmore Whisky certainly has our approval,' said Tessa. 'William will always prefer a single malt but, for my part, I liked the smoother taste. I will make sure to introduce you to anyone I think might be able to help your expansion.' Her sharp eyes roamed Flora's face. She took her hand. 'You are apprehensive, but there is no need. Our friends will not judge you. Joane wrote to me about what happened with Galkirk and, if it comforts you, I believe you did the right thing. He is thoroughly unpleasant with an unshakeable belief in his own superiority merely because of an accident of birth. Your Lachlan is much more suitable…' She hesitated, then continued with determination, 'Although, forgive me, but you do seem rather…stiff…with one another. You have not quarrelled, have you?'

Flora shook her head.

'Did you not know him very well before you wed?'

Flora's cheeks burned. 'I did not know him at all. We met for the first time at the altar.'

'What?' Tessa clapped her hand over her mouth, her eyes huge. She lowered her voice. 'Do you mean to tell me your father married you off to a complete *stranger*?'

Flora nodded. Tessa's eyes searched hers. 'Are you

happy? Is he kind to you? Oh, dear God, child…whatever was that brother of mine *thinking*?' She leaned closer even as the unmistakable sound of new arrivals filtered into the room from the hallway. 'If ever you need a place to stay, my dear, you will come to me, won't you? I mean, he seems nice enough, but—'

'It is all right, Aun— Tessa. I promise you. H-he is nice. I j-just don't know him very well yet.'

'I should think not! Now, I have my duties as hostess, Flora, but…please write to me. Let me know if anything is troubling you. You *promise*?'

'I promise.'

And, with that, the room was suddenly crowded with an influx of people and Tessa was gone.

The evening proved an enlightenment for Flora. The people she met were nothing like the members of Scottish society she had known from childhood. Nor were they the serious, business-focused men and their quiet but supportive wives that she had met at Sir Keith's house party. *These* people were a mixture of writers and engineers, journalists and scientists, poets and politicians, musicians and manufacturers, and they discussed every subject under the sun—both serious and frivolous—with much laughter and waving of hands, agreeing and disagreeing in a stimulating debate. And the one thread that seemed to bind these people together was the dream of making things better. Of helping the poor to rise. Not of revolution, such as had been occurring all over Europe in the past year—revolutions that Flora, to her shame, had never even heard of until recently—but through political and social reform.

And Lachlan joined in the cut and thrust of debate and she could see the respect dawning in others' eyes. Pride swelled her heart. She knew, from when their own conversation had veered towards the issue of poverty and inequality, that he felt passionately about the subject but here, tonight, his fervour shone bright and her determination to learn more about her husband grew.

'He is quite the orator once he starts, is he not?' Tessa slipped her arm around Flora and hugged her. 'I like him,' she whispered into Flora's ear. 'And I am relieved to be able to say that.'

Flora smiled. 'Thank you. I like him, too.'

Tessa laughed out loud. 'Well, that is a most welcome piece of news, my love.'

A smiling Lachlan looked around at that moment and, as his gaze met Flora's, he stilled. Then he was walking towards her, still smiling, his gaze never leaving her face and she recognised it as the smile of a man interested in a woman. Intent. She felt her cheeks heat and her stomach tumble with nerves. With heat. With anticipation.

'I shall see you later,' murmured Tessa and she moved away as Lachlan stopped in front of Flora.

Her heart beat erratically as his dark eyes roamed her face, then settled on her lips. He dipped his head and his hand sought hers.

'Are you enjoying yourself?' His breath tickled her ear and the sensitive skin of her neck.

'Yes. Thank you. Everybody has been very kind.'

How she wished she could say something clever— something to grab his attention—as these other people seemed to do quite effortlessly.

'I am...' He coughed, his gaze sliding from hers to settle somewhere beyond her left ear. His cheeks flagged a dull red. 'I am proud to be here with you, Flora.' His gaze touched hers again, for a second, before skittering away. 'Very proud,' he added gruffly.

Heat kindled inside her and her heartbeat picked up speed. Not only at the compliment, but at the realisation—and it was an eye-opener—that Lachlan was embarrassed. Uncertain. Her taciturn husband—the self-assured businessman—was shy. Of her. A small piece of the puzzle of their marriage slotted into place. All this time she had felt inadequate and she had not realised that he, maybe, felt the same uncertainties that she did. It was so unexpected. He was ten years older than her. Much more experienced. He was a man. Why would he feel that way about *her*?

She touched his sleeve. 'And I am proud to be here with you, too, Lachlan. As your wife.'

His jaw tightened, but a smile flickered around his lips.

'Come and join our discussions.' His voice was husky as he placed his hand at the small of her back.

She hung back. 'I do not know enough about politics and so forth to join in. I am not clever enough.'

'You *are* clever enough. You just lack experience. You need not venture an opinion but, by listening to the arguments, you will begin to form your own beliefs. And then, before long, you will be eager to voice your opinions.'

The idea was a revelation—that the men here in this room might value a lady's opinion. Admittedly, looking around, she could see that the gentlemen still dominated the conversation but, when a lady spoke, they did her the courtesy of listening and agreeing or disagreeing based on the merits of what she said, not dismissing her ideas merely because of her sex. Flora could still never imagine being bold enough to voice her thoughts on such serious subjects, but she allowed Lachlan, his hand settled supportively at the small of her back, to guide her to the nearest group where she listened diligently to the conversation. Occasionally she was lost but, for the most part, she understood the subject—the formation of burghs to enable areas to raise taxes and to help them retain their independence from the City of Glasgow.

'Flora?' Tessa was beside her, accompanied by a tall, fair-haired gentleman. He looked a similar age to Lachlan, but he sported a luxuriant growth of side whiskers that made him look a decade older. 'Might I introduce Lord Andrew Smillie?'

Flora smiled as his lordship bowed. 'I am pleased to meet you. You are Lord Rannoch's son?' She knew of the family, but had never met any of them.

'I am. The youngest of four, so I shall never accede to the title.' He grinned. 'I don't envy my eldest brother *that* honour, not in the least. And you are Aberwyld's daughter?'

'Yes.' Flora watched him closely, but saw no hint of scorn in his clear blue eyes.

'Andrew has just been telling me about his new business venture, Flora. I think you might be interested. Oh! It seems I am needed.' Tessa waved back at William, who had beckoned her over. 'I shall leave you two to talk.'

'You are in business?'

'I am.' Lord Andrew's blue eyes crinkled into a smile. 'Steamships. It's a newish company, running regular cruises up the west coast and to the Hebrides. The tourist industry is growing so fast and these boat cruises are all the rage, you know, in England. Demand last summer grew week by week and, by this summer, I plan to double the number of ships.'

'And are you seeking suppliers of food and drink for your steamships?'

'Indeed. I have already sampled your husband's new blended whisky and I found it very pleasant.' He leaned a little closer to her and lowered his voice. 'I have never been a great whisky lover myself, although it is sacrilege for a Highlander to admit such a thing, of course.'

Lachlan couldn't stop watching as Flora laughed up at the tall, blond, aristocratic-looking gentleman. His teeth were clenched so hard his jaw hurt. Then she caught Lachlan's eye and she smiled at him, beckoning.

He struggled to wipe the scowl from his face as he joined them and Flora introduced them.

Lord Andrew Smillie. I knew *he was an aristocrat.*

'Lord Andrew is interested in Carnmore Whisky, Lachlan,' Flora continued. 'For his tourist ships.'

And Lachlan felt instant shame at his unwarranted jealous reaction.

'We won't be sailing again until the spring,' Smillie was saying, 'but, in the meantime, we offer Sunday excursions along the Clyde and out of the city for the workers. They are very popular, too—it's an opportunity for the workers to breathe fresh air, away from the smoke and the grime of the city. Of course, the very poorest cannot afford such trips, but we must hope to slowly change all that.'

'I wonder what they will make of the new blended whisky,' said Lachlan.

'To be honest—' Lord Andrew winked '—I don't believe they will care if they can buy it cheaper than malt and it'll make a change from gin. Drinking,' he added, 'appears to be something of a national pastime, does it not? I cannot believe it is good for their health, but the poor wretches must have some pleasure in their lives, after all.' He glanced across at the clock on the mantelpiece. 'Now, I apologise, but I must take my leave of you.

My wife is indisposed and could not accompany me this evening and I promised not to be gone too long.

'I'm pleased to have met you both.' He took out a card and handed it to Lachlan. 'That is my office address. Call in some time over the next couple of weeks and we'll talk terms.'

Lachlan and Flora smiled at one another in delight when he left, although Lachlan felt even guiltier about his initial boorish reaction. Thank God he was used to hiding his feelings.

The hackney that had brought them to Partick returned to collect them at the prearranged time and Flora hugged and kissed Tessa and then William, her beaming smile filling Lachlan with joy.

'And next time you stay in Glasgow, you will stay with us,' said William.

'Thank you. I hope you will both visit us at Lochmore, too,' said Flora.

'That would be delightful.'

The horse and carriage set off at a smart trot and Lachlan turned to Flora. The sparkle in her eyes and the sheer happiness of her smile mirrored his own triumphant joy.

'*What* an evening!'

He grabbed her gloved hand and brought it to his lips. He craved the heat and the taste and the scent of her skin and he unbuttoned her glove and pushed back the cuff before pressing his lips and then his tongue to the delicate skin of her inner wrist, feeling her pulse leap and stutter. He wanted more… He took each finger of her glove between his teeth, one by one, and tugged until the glove slid off and dropped unheeded to the floor.

'You were splendid, Flora. Thank you.' He kissed

her palm and then leaned into her touch as she cupped his face.

'It was you who was splendid, Lachlan. I—I told you before. I am very proud of you.'

Her shyness tore at his heartstrings. He cradled her jaw, turning her face to his and their lips met in an explosion of passion. He gathered her into his arms…on to his lap…kissing her as though his life depended upon it. She wriggled closer as his arms tightened around her. She tasted so sweet…so damned sensual as her tongue tangled with his…all this time of staying away from her bed…telling himself he wanted no distractions…persuading himself he was doing the right thing for her… he cursed himself as all kinds of a fool.

He angled his head, deepening the kiss, a groan of need vibrating in his throat. Her breasts were solidly encased by her tightly laced corset and high-necked gown and he groaned again, this time in frustration. He skimmed his hand down to her hem and found her ankle. He caressed the delicate bones, growing almost painfully hard as his hand trailed higher, stroking her silk-encased calf and behind her knee as he explored her mouth. Her hands were in his hair, her fingers on his scalp, her breathy sighs driving him wild.

He sensed the hackney slow and he wrenched his mouth from hers.

'Enough!'

She leaned back, her eyes wide and wary. He swallowed down his frustration and gently lifted her from his lap and sat her on the seat next to him, willing his body back under control. A glance out of the window confirmed they were on the Trongate.

Lachlan stretched his lips into a smile he did not feel. 'I am not so uncouth that I will ravish my own wife in a hackney. Especially not here.' He gestured at the window.

Flora looked and gasped. 'Our hotel.'

'Yes.'

The concierge trod down the front steps and opened the carriage door, holding aloft an umbrella to shelter them from the rain that was just starting to fall. Lachlan pressed a coin into the man's hand, paid the driver and took Flora's hand. Her bare hand. He frowned.

'Wait!'

He soon found the discarded glove on the carriage floor and he handed it to Flora, who blushed bright red as she pulled it back on. He bit back a grin. He would soon have that off again. They would go straight to her room. He would dismiss Muriel and he would play the part of lady's maid himself—unlacing her, unpinning her hair, brushing it out to fall like liquid fire around her white shoulders. He wrenched his imagination back into line, for he was growing hard once again just thinking about the night to come.

A tall figure stepped from the shadows. 'Mr McNeill, sir.'

Lachlan's gut clenched. 'Delaney.'

He moved Flora to place himself between her and the investigator.

He had written to Delaney in Edinburgh to let him know they would be in Glasgow for a few days in case... He hauled in a breath. He could not hear what Delaney had to report here. Not in front of Flora.

'Give me a minute, Delaney. I'll be back shortly.' He took Flora by the elbow. 'Come, my dear.'

Inside, he steered her towards the stairs.

'Who was that man, Lachlan? What does he want with you? Can it not wait until morning?'

He hated the fear in her voice, but he couldn't explain. Not when the question of whether Anna might be alive or dead weighed down upon him like a huge black cloud.

'It is nothing to worry about, Flora, I promise you. But I do need to talk to him tonight.'

Muriel was waiting in Flora's bedchamber, to his relief.

'I shall see you later.'

He kissed Flora's cheek, ignored her hurt look and headed back downstairs, his stomach churning. Delaney waited, leaning on his cane, his hat tilted at a rakish angle.

'Well?'

'Not here.'

Delaney grasped his arm and steered him across the road, into a side street and into a tavern. He commandeered a table in the corner and, at his signal, a servant brought a bottle of whisky and two glasses.

'I found her.'

Delaney poured them both a dram. He downed his drink in one swallow, then pushed a piece of paper across the table. An address was written on it.

'She's alive, then?' Lachlan's voice sounded rough and he knocked back his own drink. 'Is she well? And the bairn?'

Delaney nodded. 'Well enough. I haven't spoken to her, but I've seen them both.' He hooked his hand around the back of his neck and grimaced. 'You might not like what I found out.'

'Tell me.'

'She's a whore.'

The air whooshed from Lachlan's lungs. His baby sister? A whore? He battened down his emotions. He needed to keep a clear head. He needed facts.

'Why Edinburgh?'

Delaney shrugged. 'Why not?' Lachlan saw sympathy in the other man's eyes as he continued, 'She's not alone in following that path. She needed to survive and she had a baby to support.' He leaned on his forearms, lacing his fingers. 'Does this change your intentions?'

'No.' He didn't need to think about it. 'It makes no difference. She's still my sister. They are still my family.'

It was his fault she'd been reduced to this.

I will care for them from now on. They'll want for nothing.

'I'm pleased to hear it.' Delaney scratched his jaw. 'It might make it easier to know that it looks like she was forced into that life. She was in debt and her debt was sold to an Edinburgh pimp called Hopkins.'

Lachlan scowled at him. 'Why did you not say so at the start?'

Delaney shrugged. 'Because I can't be sure I've been told the truth and I was curious to know if you would still take her in, were you to find her only to discover she had willingly chosen such a life.'

Lachlan grunted. He understood Delany's reasoning, but he objected to being manipulated like that.

'When will you go?'

'As soon as I can. In the morning.'

'And what will you tell your wife? *Very* pretty, by the way.'

Lachlan's scowl deepened. 'So glad you approve! I shan't tell her a thing. Not until I've spoken to Anna.'

How would Flora react to Anna coming home to Lochmore with them? Maybe she need never know about her past? He thrust that problem aside. The first thing—the most important thing—was to see Anna.

'Do you need me to go with you?'

'No. There's no need. I'll go on the first train. Send your bill and I'll settle up.'

He shoved back his chair and the two men left the tavern together and walked back up to the Trongate.

They shook hands on the corner.

'Good luck,' said Delaney and he sauntered off down the street, swinging his cane.

Lachlan watched him go and then stood, irresolute, gazing at the hotel over the street. The rain had stopped. He tugged his collar up against the cold and began to walk. A passing hackney slowed, but he waved it on. He had a lot of thinking to do.

Chapter Fourteen

When Flora awoke early the next morning she was filled with a strange sense of foreboding. She opened her eyes and took in the unfamiliar bedchamber. She turned her head on her pillow, and saw that the other half of the double bed lay undisturbed, the pillow plump and the bedcovers smooth. The events of the previous evening burst upon her with the suddenness of a clap of thunder: the soirée; the joy of meeting Tessa and William; the euphoria of working together with Lachlan to secure success with Lord Andrew; her growing confidence; the kiss on the way home and the heat and anticipation that built between them. Finally, she had thought, they would become a real couple. Even when Lachlan had gone back downstairs to talk to that man she had never imagined—not for one minute—that it would prevent him from coming to her. From keeping his word. *I shall see you later*, he had said. And why would she not believe him? She'd prepared for bed and she had waited for him. And waited. And finally, gathering her courage, she had crept along the corridor to his door and tapped before opening it.

Only to be greeted by an empty room and both his coat and hat still missing.

The same defeat and dismay she had felt last night churned her stomach again as she remembered creeping back to her own bedchamber and into bed, careful to keep to her own side so that when Lachlan eventually returned, he would feel welcome and would know that she was expecting him.

Except he never came.

She sat up, anger supplanting every other emotion and, in a fit of rebellion, she flung herself across the other side of the bed, hitting the pillow and rucking up the sheets and blankets. The sound of the door opening sent her pulse rocketing, but it was only Muriel.

'Ye're awake early, my lady,' she said. 'Would you like me to bring your breakfast to your room?'

'No, thank you, Muriel. I shall breakfast with Mr Mc-Neill.'

The maid bit her lip. 'The master is nearly finished his breakfast, my lady. He said there's been a change of plan and you and I are to go home to Lochmore.'

Flora stared. 'And what will Mr McNeill be doing as we travel home?'

'He said something about the early train to Edinburgh, my lady.'

The rebellion that had awoken inside Flora erupted anew. She leapt out of bed and poured the remainder of last night's water into the basin on the washstand, oblivious to its chill as she splashed her face. She snatched up the towel to dry herself.

'Help me dress, Muriel. Quickly now.'

She refused to be left wondering what she had done wrong, scared to speak out in case it angered her husband. *She* was angry now. With him. And she refused to be sent back to Lochmore in a state of ignorance, while he... Lurid images cavorted through her mind. She thrust them aside. While he did whatever it was he intended to do in Edinburgh.

She stormed from the room, straight into Lachlan, who had one hand raised ready to knock on her door. He grabbed her by her shoulders to steady her.

'I am coming with you.'

'I am...*what* did you say?'

'I wish to come with you to Edinburgh.' She would set out her demands while her blood was up. This was no time for delicate diplomacy—if she gave him any opportunity to naysay her, she might lose her nerve entirely. 'If you have meetings to attend, I shall be perfectly happy visiting the warehouses and shopping.'

His brows snapped together. 'My time will be fully occupied by business,' he growled as he spun her around and urged her back inside her bedchamber. 'Muriel—give us five minutes will you, please?'

Muriel scurried from the room, casting an apologetic glance at Flora as she passed. But Flora was too fired up to need her maid for moral support. She strutted to the window, then whirled around to face her husband. There was a look of something like panic in Lachlan's dark eyes and suspicions swirled through Flora. He was hiding something from her. What, if not business, was it that so preoccupied her husband? Could Cousin Sarah have been right and he was involved in something criminal? Or could it be another woman keeping him from her bed? He had bedded her once in three and a half weeks of marriage, and had spent much of the time away from home, despite his declared priority of building up the whisky business. *Could* he have a mistress? How mortifying, if that was the case. She didn't want to believe it but, if not another woman, what on earth could it be?

She folded her arms across her chest and waited, her lips pursed.

'You will be bored.'

'I have only travelled on a train once before,' she countered. They had travelled from Glasgow to Edinburgh by train last year to attend the Caledonian Rout last October. 'I should like to do so again. In fact, I cannot imagine anything I would rather do today.'

Lachlan consulted his pocket watch, swept a hand through his hair and paced across the room and back again, halting in front of her. Towering over her.

'You have not even eaten yet. Nor are your clothes packed. The train leaves in half an hour.'

'I am not hungry and Muriel will pack my bag in no time, I assure you.'

She raised her brows at him. He sighed. Loudly. It was a very male, very put-upon sigh.

'Do not blame me if you are bored,' he snapped before striding from the room.

Flora smiled in triumph and followed him to the door to summon Muriel.

'God preserve me from stubborn women,' she heard Lachlan mutter as he entered his own bedchamber.

The train was waiting when they arrived at Queen Street Station. Lachlan handed Flora into a carriage and pure excitement coursed through her as the train pulled away from the platform and steadily built up speed.

'How fast can trains go?' She gazed with awe as the countryside flashed past.

'Almost forty miles per hour on level stretches of track, I believe.'

'So fast! It is almost unbelievable, is it not?'

She sensed that her husband wanted to remain angry

with her for her defiance, but she could not bottle up her excitement. After several morose responses to her comments Lachlan told her about the efforts to join the Scottish railways to the English network. The number of companies involved in developing the early railway lines meant many tracks in Scotland had to be relaid because they had—rather short-sightedly—been laid in different gauges.

On arrival at Edinburgh's General Station, they took a hackney to Douglas's Hotel on St Andrew Square where Lachlan reserved a private parlour.

'I need to go out immediately,' Lachlan announced as he escorted Flora to the parlour. 'I shall arrange for refreshments to be served and I shan't be very long. A couple of hours at the most.'

As soon as Lachlan quit the room, Flora turned to Muriel. No longer would she timidly accept whatever treatment was meted out to her.

'Can I trust you to keep a secret?'

The maid nodded.

'I intend to follow Mr McNeill. There is something I do not understand about my husband and it is burning inside me here.' She placed the flat of her hand to her midriff. 'I must know the truth, for only then can I decide how to deal with it.'

'Milady...' Muriel's eyes were huge in her round face '...are you sure you should? If the master catches you he will be so angry...with the both of us.'

The guilt she felt at embroiling Muriel in her affairs was not enough to change Flora's mind. 'We will ensure he does not see us, Muriel and, if the worst comes to the worst, I shall say I gave you a direct order. Come, now. We must make haste if we are not to lose him.'

Muriel peered from the door and then beckoned Flora. They hurried to the front door, through which they could see Lachlan climbing into a hackney. As it drew away from the kerb, they exited the hotel.

The concierge touched the brim of his hat. 'Hackney, my lady?'

'Yes, please.'

He hailed a passing carriage.

'Where to, my lady?'

'Please instruct the driver to follow that cab.'

The concierge's eyebrows rose and Flora fumbled in her bag for a coin, which she pressed into his palm.

'My husband need not know, need he?'

He touched the brim of his hat again. 'No, my lady,' he said before helping her into the carriage.

Flora's heart sank as Lachlan's hackney headed south, away from the New Town, with its streets laid out in a rigidly structured gridiron plan and its white sandstone Georgian buildings, across Princes Street and into the medieval herringbone street pattern and dark granite buildings of the Old Town. If Lachlan was heading for one of those narrow alleys, Flora would never find the courage to follow him on foot.

Luck was with her, however. Lachlan's hackney finally halted in a narrow but accessible street just off Cowgate. Flora's hackney stopped on the wider thoroughfare, from where Flora had a clear view of Lachlan as he climbed from his cab. He consulted a piece of paper and then stood looking up at the upper windows of a tall building with dull, grimy windows. The slump of his shoulders made him look, somehow, defeated and concern softened some of Flora's anger. Her suspicions, so believable earlier, now seemed ludicrous. If he had a mistress, she would not live in such a place.

As Lachlan hesitated, a woman emerged from the house. On seeing Lachlan, she approached him and rubbed up against him, her lips to his ear, her hand on his arm. He jerked away, shaking his head. She shrugged and walked away.

Flora reached for the handle of the carriage door.

'Don't get out, milady. This is no place for decent women.'

Flora felt queasy. She knew exactly what Muriel meant and she knew exactly what that woman had been offering Lachlan, but she felt strongly that he was in need of her support…whatever his reason for being here.

She wavered too long, however, and the delay was enough for Lachlan to disappear inside the house. She could not follow him inside—too afraid of what she might find and what she might see. Her heart quailed as she took in their surroundings and the people, including barefooted children, so very many of whom were scrawny and grubby and dressed in ill-fitting and ragged clothing. Did people really live in such conditions? She felt shame she had not realised quite how poor some people in the cities were and she understood better the zeal with which Tessa and William's guests had debated the need for reform.

She turned to Muriel. 'I shall wait here until Mr McNeill comes out.'

Lachlan trod up the creaking bare boards of the stairs, his emotions battened tightly in place. When he'd entered the dim hallway a bald man with a battered nose and accompanied by an offensive cloud of body odour had emerged from a back room and barred Lachlan's way, holding out his hand for cash. Reluctantly, Lachlan paid up and asked for Catriona—the name by which Anna was known here, according to Delaney.

After one touch, he avoided the banister, the sticky surface giving him the urge to wash his hands thoroughly. How far he had come since his days on the convict ship and in the colony in New South Wales—there had been no place for fastidiousness then. For the first time he wondered whether Anna had been any better off than he. Yes, he had been incarcerated and transported, but had she really had any better or easier choices?

The air was thick with the stench of smoke from coal fires, stale cooking smells and other odours he did not care to identify. As he passed each landing, noises he would rather not hear—the grunts and the groans of sexual activity—filtered from behind the closed doors despite it being mid-morning. He passed a man descending the staircase—a respectably dressed merchant type, who ducked his head to the side so Lachlan could not see his features even as his hands busied themselves refastening his trousers.

Nausea clogged Lachlan's throat, but he swallowed it down and continued to climb. A new sound penetrated his consciousness. That of a child sobbing. He quickened his step.

He recognised her the second he entered the room—it was as though his mother stood before him. His sister turned from the small pallet on the floor, upon which lay a small, still whimpering child, and her mouth fell open as their eyes clashed.

'Anna!'

With two strides, he reached her and wrapped her trembling body in his arms. She was so thin. Her shoulders bony knobs, her arms like sticks.

'Thank God I've found you. I've been searching everywhere.'

'Lachy!' His name ended on a muffled sob. She pushed his chest and Lachlan released her.

'I thought you were dead.' Her brown eyes swam with tears, tearing at his heart as he took in her dull hair and skin.

'And I feared *you* were dead! Pack your belongings. You're coming home with me. You and the bairn.'

Deep lines bracketed her downturned mouth as she shook her head in defeat. 'Hopkins won't let me go. Not until I've paid what I owe him.'

'Is that him downstairs? How much? I'll pay whatever it takes.'

She laughed then, bitterly. 'Aye, that's him. But you can't pay him enough. It's never enough. I thought I could work off my debts, but the interest piles up and then the interest on the interest.' She turned away. 'I thought nothing could be worse than ending up in the poorhouse. I was wrong.'

Guilt layered upon guilt. He could have saved her. He should have returned immediately. He hung his head. 'I let you down. I am sorry.'

'No!' She spun to face him and it was the first sign of the sparky sister he remembered from their childhood. 'You didna let me down.' She swung back to the pallet, scooped up the child and returned to Lachlan. '*Life* let me down. The fact I am a woman let me down. Circumstances let me down. But not you, Lachy.' Her hand rose to touch his face. 'I ken better than anyone what you sacrificed for me and Ma.'

'I should've come home sooner. But I'm here now and you're coming home with me.'

She buried her face into the angle between the child's neck and shoulder. 'He willna let me go.' Her voice was muffled. The child squirmed and let out a grumble.

'Hush, Davy.' She kissed his cheek before looking up at Lachlan. 'Hopkins threatened to get rid of him if he makes a noise. It puts off the…the…' She shrugged hopelessly.

'Davy? He's a lad, then? How old is he?'

'He'll be three next April. I named him after his poor da. How did ye find us, Lachy?'

Lachlan cupped her cheek. 'I hired a detective who tracked you down—it was he who discovered you were married.'

'Aye, that I was, to the foreman at the cotton factory where I worked. We had a good life until he was killed in an accident, three months before Davy was born.'

She slumped on to the bed, Davy still clamped in her arms. He lay quiet and listless, as though the energy to even move was beyond him.

'I couldna go out to work, not with a newborn. I took in some sewing, but could never earn enough and I got into debt. But I tried to keep going… I did try!' She turned tragic eyes to Lachlan. 'If I'd gone to the poorhouse, they'd have taken Davy from me… I couldna bear that, Lachy. I *couldna*. But I got deeper in debt and we would have been on the streets but this…this *woman* I knew—for she was no friend to me—told me Hopkins would help me. She said he'd pay off my debts and give me a job in Edinburgh, where I could start again.' She stared around her in disgust. 'I was a fool.'

Her bitterness tore at Lachlan again. 'You were desperate, Anna.'

She hunched one shoulder. 'It makes no difference now. Once I was under his control, my shame was complete.' She stared at Lachlan. 'You look prosperous, Brother. I am a fallen woman. There is no hope for me, but…here.' She surged to her feet and thrust Davy into

Lachlan's arms. 'Take him. *Please.* It is not too late for him.'

'No! A bairn belongs with his mother. You will both come with me—it is not too late for either of you.' Lachlan freed one arm to hug Anna. 'It is never too late.'

She pulled back and stared up at him, hope dawning in her eyes.

'Could ye help me get away, Lachy? I go out most afternoons to run errands for Hopkins. He lets me take Davy for the fresh air.' Her eyes sheened. 'That's what Ma used to say, even when she was so ill. "Get ye outdoors and breathe some fresh air."' Her laugh choked off into a sob. 'Never mind that the air outside was filthier than the air inside that room we called home.'

Lachlan's heart ached at the memory of his mother. All she had wanted was to return to their croft in her beloved Highlands. His father had longed for the same. But they had been turned off with nothing and their home burnt behind them. And they had both died, in poverty, in Glasgow. The familiar anger rose inside him at the injustices in the world.

'I'll do more than help you to leave here, Anna. You will come home with me. Now. Both of you.'

She backed away from him, shaking her head, fear in her eyes. 'No. Not now. Hopkins...you don't know what he's capable of, Lachy. I canna risk Davy getting hurt.'

Lachlan could see the sense—if they went downstairs together, Hopkins would hear them and be ready for them. He'd do nothing to put Anna or Davy in harm's way. Not now he'd found them.

'Very well. I'll wait for you on the corner of Cowgate. You'll come home with me—there's plenty of room for you both at...at my home.' He could not bring himself to admit he lived in a castle and had been living there for the past year while his little sister had been in hell. 'And there is fresh air and countryside for young Davy to run around in and grow strong.'

Davy had grown heavy in his arms and a glance showed the child's eyes were closed, his breathing soft. Lachlan put him back on to the pallet and, as he straightened, Flora's image arose in his mind's eye. There would be explanations required. She had demonstrated her stubborn streak this morning, but he prayed she'd understand why he hadn't been honest with her from the start. The thought of admitting the truth of his past to his beautiful wife was almost enough to unman him. How could he bear it if the dawning affection he had glimpsed in those lovely green eyes changed to scorn?

'And you, Lachy? Have you bairns of your own? A wife?' Anna laughed that bitter laugh again. 'No, of course not, for no decent woman would have a creature like me in her home.'

'Don't say such things.' Lachlan clasped her shoulders and shook her, but gently, because she was so slender, so delicate, he feared she might snap. 'I do have a wife—we have been wed less than a month, but you will leave Flora to me.' He couldn't help but add, 'She is the eldest daughter of the Earl of Aberwyld.'

'A *laird's* daughter? She willna want the likes of me sullying her home, Lachy.'

'You are my sister and Flora will accept you...she has a good heart.'

'She must have if she's lowered herself to marry a lad from the slums and an ex-convict.'

'Ah.' He grimaced. 'She doesn't know.'

Anna's eyes widened. '*None* of it?'

'No. And I shall only tell her enough for now to explain about you, Anna, so I'd be obliged if you'd keep the conviction and the transportation to yourself.' Jessica's reaction still haunted him. 'She has no need to know about that.'

'And do ye mean to tell her, Lachy? Ever?'

He said, with more confidence than he felt, 'When the time is right, I shall tell her. She will understand.'

The sound of footsteps clumping up the stairs reminded him of where they were.

'What time will you go out?'

'Around three. I bring him back a pie from the pie shop. And gin.'

'I'll be in a hackney. Don't bring anything to arouse his suspicions. You will go out as usual and simply not return. He'll have no idea where you have gone. You and Davy will be safe. I promise.'

He kissed her forehead.

'I must go. I was told I have half an hour and I don't want to give Hopkins any reason to remember me.' Fortunately, the earlier footsteps had gone straight past Anna's door and a door had opened and closed further down the corridor. The murmur of voices—male and female—could be heard distinctly through the walls, as could the slap and the sudden cry. Anna paled at the sounds, but said nothing.

Lachlan forced her to look up at him. 'Three o'clock,' he said. 'I *will* be there. If you do not come, I shall come looking for you.'

'I will be there, Lachlan. I promise.'

Chapter Fifteen

Flora sat in the hackney and watched life continuing in the street outside, a deep shame growing inside her—not because she felt any responsibility for the state in which these people lived, crowded into slums and living, clearly, without hope—but because she had not known. Nothing in her life had prepared her for such sights. Her family had endured a gradual decline of prosperity, but to compare their circumstances with that of the people in the street outside was to compare the stunning sapphire and diamond brooch given to the Queen by Prince Albert on the eve of their marriage—and which Flora had seen when the Queen visited Castle McCrieff—to Flora's silver brooch.

She could not bring herself to leave the carriage. She simply did not dare to go inside that house and search for her husband.

Eventually the house door opened again and Lachlan emerged, stepping out on to the pavement. He halted, his head down. A moment later, he swiped one hand across his eyes and that movement spurred Flora into action. She thrust some coins at Muriel.

'Take the hackney back to the hotel and wait for me there. And tell *no one* where we have been.'

She pushed open the carriage door, but Muriel grabbed her arm.

'Milady! Ye canna go out there. It isna safe.'

Flora shook free of her grasp and climbed awkwardly from the vehicle.

'I shall be with my husband. No harm will come to me, Muriel. Now do as I say. Go!' Poor Muriel's face was as pale as Flora had ever seen it. 'You may wait there until you see I have reached his side. But then you must go.'

'Very well, milady.'

Flora kept her gaze firmly fixed on Lachlan as she hurried across Cowgate and into the road where he stood, holding her skirts clear of the filth that soiled the street. He was still standing on the same spot when she reached him. She put her hand on his arm and he jerked it away, spinning to face her.

'What…? *Flora?*'

His dark eyes were rimmed pink and some deep emotion swirled in their depths—more emotion than she had ever seen in her normally impassive husband. A spark of jealousy ignited in her belly. Why could he not show such emotion for her? She was his wife…surely she deserved…? She hauled in a deep breath. No longer would she remain silent and swallow down her fears.

'I should like an explanation.' She propped her hands on her hips even as her old doubts and fears tried to batter their way to the surface. She quashed them ruthlessly. What she really wanted to know was why he did not bed her, but she settled for asking, 'What are you doing here?'

He clasped her elbow and began to walk down the street. She had to scurry to keep up with his long strides.

'What are *you* doing here, more to the point?'

She swallowed. 'I followed you.'

He stopped dead. He stared at her, his eyes still haunted.

'Why?'

Flora bit her lip. Noticed his gaze drop to her mouth and his sudden intake of breath. Whatever else was going on here, she recognised his desire for her. His kisses and caresses last night were proof enough of that—so what was so crucial as to keep him from her bed and to bring him here, in secret?

His shoulders slumped again, and his gaze slid from her face to linger on her chest. 'You are not wearing your brooch,' he said.

Flora frowned at such an inconsequential remark. 'I left it at home. At Lochmore.' It had seemed a symbolic gesture—a new beginning for them both. All of that seemed unimportant now. Childish, even. This—standing here with her husband in a filthy, overcrowded street—*this* was important. But she needed to understand. '*Please*, Lachlan. I am… I am *worried* about you. You are upset. Please. Allow me to help.'

He heaved in a deep breath, then choked out a cough. 'Urgghh! I shouldn't have done that! Come. This place stinks. It is no place for a lady. Let us get out of here.' He popped one finger beneath her chin and bent a serious look upon her. 'I will tell you. I must. Matters have come to a head and you will have to know. But not here. Let us go back to the hotel—although I must return here by three o'clock.'

Back at the hotel, Flora crossed their private parlour, stripping off her gloves and then removing her hat before facing Lachlan with a lift of her brows. He gestured for her to sit on the small sofa and he then folded himself into an armchair.

'Why did you visit that house?' she demanded when he seemed reluctant to begin. 'Who is Delaney? And where did you disappear to last night? Do you have a—?' She leapt to her feet and took a turn around the room. 'Do you have a *woman* there? A—a *mistress*? Is—is that why you do not want me?'

A huge, painful lump formed in her throat. This was it. His answer could destroy all her hopes for their future.

Lachlan surged to his feet, grabbing her upper arms. 'No! I do want you. How can you doubt it? I just—' He thrust his hand through his hair, staring at her with such pain in his eyes she believed him. 'I have been preoccupied. I know. And I'm sorry.' He hauled in a deep breath. 'Delaney is an investigator. He came to the Tontine last night to tell me he'd found someone I have been searching for.'

'Who?'

'My sister. Anna.'

'Your *sister*? I was not even aware you had a sister. What is she doing in...?' Flora's voice trailed into silence as the implication hit her. 'Your sister...she lives *there*? But...is she a...?' She could not bring herself to utter the word.

'A prostitute. Yes. And it is my fault.'

The words hung bitterly in the air. Flora sat again and then patted the sofa beside her. 'Please. Tell me about her.' She couldn't get the picture of that street...that house... out of her mind. Surely no one would choose to live in such a place?

Lachlan began to talk, telling her about his own past and his sister, Anna, five years his junior.

'Ma and Da were tenants of a Highland farm. It was a hard life, but they were happy until they were turned off to make way for sheep and relocated to a croft, just a handful of acres, on the west coast. Da was expected to boost our income with fishing and kelp working, but the year before, the Government removed the duty on cheaper, imported kelp and the industry collapsed. I was four when we left our farm. My sister, Rose, was just a year old.

'My parents struggled to keep going for three years, but then hunger drove Da to seek work in Glasgow. By then Anna and Taggie had been born so there were six of us to house and feed. Da found work in a saw mill and Ma worked at home as a handloom weaver.'

His words, at first halting and cracked with emotion, now sped up and disgust at how his family and thousands of others had been treated rang through his words.

'My sister Jenny was born two years later and died within months. We were hungry. All the time. Da...he died when I was eleven. An accident at work. And from having little, we had less and inside a year both Rose and Taggie had gone.'

He dropped his face into his hands and Flora could see the muscles at the side of his jaw clench as he fought his emotion.

'I found a job at a carpet factory but then I... I...' A frown creased his forehead and he scrubbed both hands through his hair. 'I went overseas. I—I wanted to make something of myself...and that was impossible in Glasgow. I should have come home sooner... I didn't know...' His head dropped into his hands again. 'Ma died five years later. Anna was working in a cotton factory and she married the foreman, but she got with child and then he died.' His voice hardened. 'After the babe was born she couldn't earn enough and she got into debt. She was promised a job and somewhere to live in Edinburgh, but it wasn't until she got here that she discovered the truth and by then she was trapped by her debts.

'Just one year ago!' The words burst savagely from his lips. 'Not long after I returned to Scotland! I searched and searched for her, but everyone I knew had gone. I didn't know she had married. I was searching for the wrong name.'

Shocked by his story, Flora held back her urge to pepper him with questions. The immediate problem was to save his sister from the situation she was trapped in and Flora found herself more grateful than ever before for her marriage to Lachlan. She had never appreciated how circumstances could change a life so dramatically and she realised how fortunate she had been in her family life and childhood, although it had not always seemed that way to her. And without Lachlan's money providing dowries, her father would be unable to demand decent settlements for her sisters and, if widowed, either one of them might find herself on that slow slide into genteel poverty that was the fear of every well-born woman. Women had so little power. No rights. No choice. The injustice of life burned inside her.

For the first time, Flora had an inkling of the strain upon her father who, to his credit, had never followed other lairds along the route of evicting tenants and replacing them with sheep in order to replenish their own coffers. The English landlords had begun that cruel practice, but some clan chiefs, to their shame, had followed suit when they had seen the profits to be made. She was proud her father was not one of them. He might be a hard man, but he had needed to be.

There were good men in the world—even men who held power over others. It was just a shame there were not more of them with a sense of social responsibility like Lachlan. He was wealthy, but she could see, more than ever, that he *cared*.

She tore her thoughts from the wider issues to focus on the matter in hand. She hardly dared to ask. 'And her child?'

Lachlan turned bleak eyes on her. 'He lives there with her. In the room where she...where she is forced...'

Again, he hid his face so she could not see the extent of his anguish. Flora put her arm around him and he started at her touch.

'How old is he?'

'He'll be three in the spring.'

Flora stood. 'We cannot leave them there. They must come home with us.'

He stared up at her. 'Think about what you are saying, Flora. She—she is a fallen woman.'

His words said one thing, but she could see the hope in his eyes. 'Would you object to your sister living at Lochmore Castle, Lachlan?'

'No. Of course not. But you...'

'What about me?'

He jumped to his feet. 'You are a lady! Is it not bad enough you find out you are married to a man who was raised in the Glasgow slums?'

She took his hands, swallowing back her doubts about welcoming a woman with such a troubled past into her home.

'Lachlan. You are my husband and you are a good man. It is not your fault your family ended up in such straitened circumstances and I do not care where you were raised. I care only for the man you are now—honest, compassionate, hardworking. Anna and her son are our family and they are welcome in our home.'

Lachlan closed his fingers around Flora's, basking in the glow of her praise. Not only was his wife beautiful on the outside, she was beautiful inside as well. And she had said she cared for him. Him! His heart cracked a little and he felt warmth infuse his chest. She was kind, generous and understanding despite having led such a sheltered life. Her expression had revealed her horror as he had confessed his early life—but it was not horror that he had been poor. It was horror at the circumstances that had led to his family's downfall. She did not know the worst of it, however. She didn't know about his criminal past—that he was not the honest man she had just declared him to be—and she didn't know about the punishment that had rebounded so harshly upon his mother and his sister. The shame and guilt at having let his family down so badly still made him squirm.

'Thank you.'

He raised her hands and pressed his lips first to one, then the other. Her intake of breath sounded loud in the silent room. He turned her hands over then, kissing her palms and her inner wrist, feeling her pulse jump under his lips.

'You are more generous than I dared to hope.'

She frowned. 'I wonder if I would have understood so readily had I not seen with my own eyes where your sister lives. And I am horrified that a decent family can be sucked down into such straits by the actions of one greedy landlord. It makes me wonder...'

He waited, while she obviously struggled with internal thoughts.

'It does make me grateful that you married me. *My* sisters will now face a more secure future, thanks to you.'

Her words startled him. 'I do not believe your sisters would have been reduced to such dire circumstances as Anna—they would have your father and your brother to support them.'

'That is true.' She shuddered. 'It has made me very aware, though, of the vulnerability of members of my own sex, should they fall on hard times. It is difficult enough for the men, I know. But a woman, with a child? What made Anna come to Edinburgh?'

Anger boiled inside Lachlan. 'I think she was guilty only of naivety. She believed there would be a job waiting for her in Edinburgh. And so there was, only it was not the job she expected and—put yourself in her shoes—she was in a strange city where she knew no one and had a child to support. She had no money to return to Glasgow. Hopkins gave her no choice.'

Flora placed her hand against his chest. 'What will you do? He must be punished for what he has done.'

Lachlan heaved a sigh. 'I must go. I promised to meet Anna at three. My priority must be to get her and the bairn away without a fuss...much as I should like to go there and to—' He stopped speaking, aware that his fists had clenched and his words were clipped. 'I doubt the authorities would take action even if I did report him. He is just one of many such men who prey upon the weak and the desperate.'

'Maybe...'

Her fingers played with the buttons of his waistcoat and his body reacted, despite the seriousness of their discussion. Once Anna and Davy were safe at Lochmore, he could concentrate on his marriage at long last. He wanted nothing more than for Flora to be happy as his wife, but he'd made a poor start. The way he felt about her, though...the look he sometimes saw in her eyes... they gave him hope. Such hope.

'Maybe,' she continued, apparently oblivious to the effect she was having upon him, 'the best revenge will be to help prevent women falling prey to such men in the first place.'

'Maybe. But there are many women, too, who choose to follow that path for themselves.'

Her nose wrinkled. 'I cannot imagine any woman choosing to lie with a stranger for money.' Then her face washed bright red and she raised stricken eyes to his. 'Is that what *I* did? Only, somehow, my choice is legitimised because we said our vows first?'

'No!' He hugged her to him, relishing the way her body fitted into his. 'Do not say that. Marriage is different. Of course it is. Only…' he tipped her chin up and smiled ruefully '…only you appear to have bagged a poor bargain in me.' He lowered his mouth to hers and kissed her tenderly. 'I promise I shall make it up to you, Flora. I have been distracted by business and by my search for Anna, but I shall change.'

She grinned at him, then tiptoed up to brush her lips over his. 'Do not make promises you cannot keep, Husband. You will, I have no doubt, still find yourself distracted by business matters. But I have proved I can help now, so it is a shared interest. Now…' she stepped back '…go and fetch your sister and your nephew. I shall wait here to meet them.'

Anna and Davy were rescued without drama. The street corner was busy with people going about their business, but—and Lachlan had noticed this before—no one looked at anyone else, almost as though they feared attracting attention of any sort. Nobody gave the hackney cab a second glance as they waited. After a few minutes, he spied Anna hurrying towards him, Davy clutched to her chest, her face drawn with worry. She wore a shabby but respectable dress with a shawl around her shoulders and looked just like any other young mother, although his heart still clenched at the sharpness of her cheekbones and the dark shadows beneath her eyes. He leapt from the hackney, took the child from her arms and helped her inside.

Lachlan climbed in and slammed the door and the carriage immediately set off.

'Did you have any trouble getting away?'

Anna shook her head, but her ashen skin and fearful expression spoke for themselves. Back at the hotel, he escorted Anna, carrying Davy, inside and straight to the parlour. Anxiety twisted his stomach as he opened the door. It was so important that his wife and his sister got along—what would happen if they loathed one another on sight? Flora had said all the right things about Anna and Davy being welcome at Lochmore, but would that translate into reality or was he expecting too much of his young aristocratic wife?

Flora crossed the room with a welcoming smile. Before he even had the chance to introduce the two, Flora was speaking.

'I am Flora. I am so pleased to meet you—I am only sorry it has taken Lachlan so long to find you and your little one.'

Anna frowned at Lachlan. 'You have told her the truth?'

'Yes.' Had he done right or wrong? It was impossible to tell from Anna's closed expression. 'We both understand that it was not...'

He couldn't think how to finish what he had started. To cover his discomfort he took Davy from his sister's arms, hugging him close. The little boy accepted his embrace passively, as though nothing could spark any interest in him, and Lachlan vowed there and then to ignite the joy of childhood for him.

Flora flicked a glance at him. 'Come,' she said to Anna. 'Warm yourself by the fire. Please don't feel uncomfortable about what you were forced into, or what you had to do to survive and to support your child. No one but us will know, unless you choose to tell them.'

Anna slumped into a chair and buried her face in her hands. Lachlan moved, intending to comfort her, but Flora shook her head at him.

'And this is Davy?' She ruffled his wispy brown curls. 'What a lovely boy. I can see you will have a fine time living at Lochmore.'

Davy hid his face against Lachlan's chest as Anna watched Flora warily.

Flora smiled at her, anxious to put her at ease. 'He will soon get used to us, I'm certain. Are you hungry? I am sure Davy must be—my brother never seemed satisfied when he was growing up...he always had room for more food. I asked for sandwiches and coffee to be served when you arrived.'

Lachlan felt out of his depth. His emotions churned his insides and he was almost afraid to open his mouth and say anything in case they burst forth uncontrollably. He felt that, if he once started to speak of his feelings, he might never be able to stop. He had learned as a youth that to reveal emotion was a sign of weakness, one that was instantly taken advantage of by stronger, tougher men. The habit was so far ingrained that the thought of exposing his innermost thoughts and feelings reduced him to a state of terror.

The conversation as they ate was stilted. Anna was clearly overwhelmed and Davy remained mute as Flora did her best to fill the silence.

'You will need clothes, for you and Davy.' Lachlan finally found something to say.

'Oh!' Anna looked down at herself. 'But I—'

'Yes, indeed.' Flora leapt to her feet. 'We can go shopping. We can buy you a few ready-made gowns for your immediate needs, then we can buy some suitable fabric to make you more.' She clapped her hands together, beaming. 'It will be—'

'No!' Anna wrapped her arms around her waist. 'I canna go out. I canna risk—' She choked off on a sob. 'I *cannot*.'

That surge of emotion from his sister somehow spurred Lachlan into action. He might be useless at talking about what his brimming heart felt, but he *could* protect her from more distress.

'The only place we are all going is to the station,' he said, standing up. 'The sooner you and Davy are away from Edinburgh, the happier I shall be. We are going home.'

Chapter Sixteen

Lachlan placed a protective hand on his sister's shoulder as he spoke and she smiled up at him, her dark eyes wide in her narrow, clever face. Flora tried hard to ignore the squirm of jealousy in her gut. They were all family now, but it did seem harsh that she must now share Lachlan just as they seemed to be growing closer. She quashed her instinctive condemnation of Anna's past as a prostitute. Yes, her sister-in-law had been forced into that life, but Flora was finding it hard to instantly change her natural bias despite her assurance to Lachlan. She vowed to work hard to overcome her prejudice and to hide any doubts from Anna.

'And Anna's new clothes?'

'We shall shop for them in Glasgow. After all, I know exactly where to go for them, don't I, Flora?' He winked at her and that shared gesture reassured her somewhat. 'If you instruct Muriel to pack our bags, we shall leave for the station and catch the first train to Glasgow.'

The train journey from Edinburgh back to Glasgow gave Flora an opportunity to learn more about Lachlan's past as he and Anna reminisced about their childhood and their family. The more she heard, the more she realised just how privileged she had always been. Although she tried to join in the conversation she could not help but feel excluded when her childhood experiences were so vastly different from theirs. But she had one advantage over Anna, she realised, as her eyes clashed with Lachlan's in yet another smoulderingly intense look, full of promise and excitement that sent her pulse racing and washed heat across her skin. Only when Anna noticed one of their exchanges and looked uncomfortable did Flora cease to play and instead she stared resolutely out of the window.

Once back at the Tontine Hotel, Lachlan impressed Flora with his decisiveness, his forethought and his attention to detail. It was the first time she had really observed him in action—this must be why he was so well respected by the business community. He ordered baths for both Anna and Davy; he sent out for a modiste to attend them at the hotel and to bring a selection of clothing suitable for his sister and nephew; he purchased enough garments for their immediate needs and charged the modiste with selecting and purchasing suitable fabrics for making additional gowns and forwarding them on to Lochmore.

Anna was mistrustful of everyone other than Lachlan, including, it seemed, Flora. She refused to let Davy out of her sight, either with Flora or with Muriel.

'He doesna care for strangers,' she said.

Flora bit back her retort that she wouldn't be a stranger for long if they were coming to live with her and Lachlan. When she mentioned his sister's spikiness, Lachlan asked her to be patient.

'She's been through a terrible ordeal.' He cupped her cheek and she turned to press her lips to his palm, her heart brimming with joy. 'She's bound to be wary at first. Give her time. Hopkins used threats against Davy to force her to do as she was told. She's bound to be overprotective.'

As time ticked by, Anna became more and more agitated. She wouldn't rest. She wouldn't let Davy out of her sight, settling him down to sleep on the sofa instead of allowing Muriel to put him to bed. The child had barely said two words and it was clear he would need much care and attention to help him overcome the trauma of the past year.

'What if he's found out where I've gone?' Anna said for the umpteenth time. 'What if he comes after us? He'll take Davy. I couldna bear to—'

Lachlan hugged her, exchanging an anxious look with Flora over the top of Anna's head. 'Hush. You'll wake the wee lad and frighten him. I'm here. I won't let Hopkins near either of you. I'll kill him if he shows his face.'

'But what if he comes for us in the night, Lachy? I'm scared.'

Pity for Anna's distress battled with irritation at the way she clung to Lachlan. Flora knew the jealousy that churned her stomach was irrational—this was Lachlan's little sister, for goodness sake. She'd been through a terrible time and Lachlan was bound to be protective.

'He can't possibly know where you've gone, Anna,' she said.

Anna shook her head. 'There's eyes and ears everywhere. I lived in Glasgow all my life. Someone might recognise me.'

Lachlan sighed at that. 'I'll write to the investigator who found you and instruct him to go to Edinburgh tomorrow and pay off Hopkins. He'll never bother you again.'

He crossed to a small writing desk in the private parlour where they were gathered. They had dined in private, too, Lachlan having decreed that the fewer people who saw them together the less speculation there would be.

'In the meantime,' said Flora, making a huge effort at magnanimity, 'perhaps it will set Anna's mind at rest if you stay with her and Davy tonight, Lachlan? I'm sure the hotel could provide a truckle bed.'

Lachlan flashed her a grateful smile. 'The *Pioneer* leaves at six in the morning.' He gathered the sleeping Davy into his arms. 'We should retire early and try to sleep.' He caught Flora's eye. 'Thank you for your understanding.'

Flora spent a restless night, her sleep disturbed by images of the miserable people and mean streets she had seen and by the ideas flashing through her thoughts... ideas and dreams of, somehow, making a difference. She lay awake at one point, making plans. But could she persuade Lachlan to take them seriously?

It was still dark—a cloudless sky spangled by stars— as they all huddled, shivering, on the dock ready to board the *Pioneer*, the steamer to Ardrishaig. Both Anna and Davy were now smartly attired, as befitted the sister and nephew of a successful businessman and Muriel— already in a fair way to being besotted by Davy—had promised faithfully to keep to herself the reality of where they had been living, although she was unaware of the full truth of Anna's past.

'Ye live in a *castle*?' Anna hung back as Lachlan and Flora descended from the hired carriage that transported them to Lochmore from Crinan.

Flora waited in the forecourt as Lachlan helped Anna out of the vehicle.

'We do.' Pride rang in Lachlan's voice. 'Welcome to your new home. I told you... I'm a wealthy man these days.'

'Considering your past, Lachy, I have to wonder how you came to be such a rich man.'

It was said in a teasing voice, but Lachlan's curt rejoinder cut through the air. 'I work hard.'

Flora puzzled over Lachlan's response as they all trooped inside. Was there something he hadn't told her? Mrs Dalgliesh met them in the hallway and Lachlan introduced Anna and Davy, whose brown eyes were huge as he gazed around.

'My sister and nephew will be making their home with us here at the castle,' he said. 'Will you show her to a suitable bedchamber? And the nursery wing must be made ready for Master Davy and one of the maids assigned to help care for him.'

'Anna. Please allow me to show you upstairs,' said Flora. 'I'm sure you'd prefer to choose your own bedchamber. I shall let you know as soon as Mrs McKenzie has decided her preference, Mrs Dalgliesh, and could you ask Cook to send refreshments to the drawing room in about half an hour? It is a while yet before dinner.'

'I canna put you to that trouble, Lady Flora.'

'It's no trouble, Anna. And we are sisters now. Please call me Flora.' She smiled down at Davy, clinging to his mother's skirt, and tousled his hair. 'Or Auntie Flora to you.'

'Thank you... Flora.' Anna sounded almost unbelieving and Flora realised it would take time for the other woman to feel comfortable with her.

'I'll leave you in Flora's hands, then, Anna,' said Lachlan. 'I'm sorry, but I really must check if there is anything in my study that requires my immediate attention. I shall see you in the drawing room in half an hour.'

Lachlan strode away, leaving the two women and Davy together.

It was hard work, conversing with her sister-in-law as they climbed the stairs. All Flora got in return for her efforts were monosyllables. She was beginning to think Anna would never say more than *Yes* or *No* to her until they went into the Yellow Room.

'I like this one,' Anna said. 'It is a happy colour. But it is very grand.'

'It's yours for as long as you wish.'

'Could…?' Anna fell silent.

'Could…?'

'I dinna want Davy to be upstairs.' Flora had explained to Anna where the nursery was. 'He's used to being with me.'

Her dark eyes pleaded with Flora.

'He can sleep in the next room for now,' said Flora. 'He can move upstairs to the nursery later, once you've both settled here.'

Anna crossed to the window and stared out, her arms wrapped around her body.

'Anna? Is there something wrong?'

'It is so…*empty* here.' Flora could see her tension from across the room. 'So big. So wild.' She faced Flora and the words burst from her in a rush. 'How do you stand it, being out here all alone?'

'I am used to it, I suppose. I grew up in a similar place.'

And even I have been lonely here. How much worse for Anna, who grew up in a bustling city?

Anna glanced out of the window again and shivered.

'I am sure you will get used to Lochmore.'

Anna's expression and the stubborn set to her mouth revealed her doubts. Flora prayed Anna would settle at Lochmore for at least a while now she knew how important Lachlan's family were to him.

'Come, let us go down for a cup of tea and I shall instruct Mrs Dagliesh to have these two rooms made ready.'

Davy was bouncing on the bed and, seizing her chance, Flora swung him up into her arms. 'Come along, Davy. Come with Auntie Flora and you shall have some cake.' The sooner he became accustomed to them all the better and, if he was happy, hopefully that would help Anna settle.

As they reached the drawing room, Lachlan approached from the direction of his study, Bandit at his heels.

Fickle hound! He spends more time with Lachlan than with me!

Davy stiffened in her arms and began to squirm. Her arms were tired—he was heavier than he looked—and Flora put him down.

'Doggy!'

It was the first word Flora had heard him speak. Bandit had stopped dead, staring at Davy, his head tipped to one side. Then, with a happy *Yip* he bounced towards them, stiff-legged, stubby tail wagging furiously. Flora held herself ready to snatch up either Davy or Bandit should the child get frightened, but relaxed as he giggled and chased the terrier in a large circle.

'*That* introduction went well.' Lachlan grinned. 'Bandit will make a good friend for Davy. Until he has a cousin or two to play with.'

The intent in his gaze sent a shiver of anticipation up Flora's spine, but Anna still had that stubborn look on her face.

* * *

Later, after they'd had their refreshments—Davy having to be forcibly prevented from feeding the entire cake to Bandit—Lachlan amazed Flora by stripping off his jacket and settling on the fireside rug with Davy. Bandit barked deliriously, dashing in circles as Davy ended up in a wriggling heap being tickled. Her heart swelled. He would make a wonderful father. Oh, how she longed—

'He was a good brother to us younger ones.' Anna's attention was on Lachlan and Davy and Flora strained to catch her words over Davy's giggles. 'Family was everything to him until he got—' Her mouth snapped shut and she went red.

'Until he got…?'

Anna shook her head. 'Nothing. He went overseas. We missed him, Ma and me.'

Flora puzzled over what Anna stopped herself saying. That was the second time her sister-in-law had seemed to let slip about some big secret in Lachlan's past. She'd thought he'd told her everything. About his childhood. About the family's struggles. Their poverty. Maybe she should have questioned him more closely about why he had left Scotland at a time when his mother and sister must have needed him, but the priority had been to rescue Anna and the moment had passed. Maybe she would ask him about it when they were alone.

The feeling that there was something she did not understand—some secret she was not party to—unsettled her. Rather than sit there stewing about it, she decided to keep busy.

'If you will excuse me, I must consult with Cook on tomorrow's menus.'

After speaking to Cook, she hesitated over whether to

return to the drawing room, but decided to leave Lachlan and Anna to talk undisturbed. Anna still seemed wary of Flora, but Flora hoped they would eventually become friends.

Upstairs, Muriel helped her disrobe. She pulled her dressing robe on over her chemise, went through to her boudoir and crossed to the window bay. The weather had, for once, remained fine all day. The afternoon was drawing to a close and Flora gazed across the ocean at the sun as it sank towards the horizon, painting the sky with blush pink, the colour deepening by the second and reflected in the gently rippling silver sea. In a short time, she knew, a rainbow of colours would appear, painting the sky with a vibrant palette as the day reached its end and darkness descended. She wrapped her arms around her waist, a shiver chasing across her skin as she wondered what the coming days would bring.

'You are pleased with your bedchamber, Anna? And with the nursery suite for Davy?'

Lachlan propped his shoulders against the mantelshelf and watched as his nephew dozed in Anna's arms, his heart swelling with joy that he had found them and brought them home.

'They're verra nice. For the time being.'

His gaze snapped to Anna's face. 'What do you mean, for the time being?'

'Lachy…' Anna lay Davy on the sofa and came to Lachlan. 'I'm grateful you helped us escape and that you're paying off that bastard Hopkins. But…' she swept her arm in a wide arc '…we canna stay here for ever.'

'But I—'

'We dinna need to talk about it now.' She patted his cheek. 'We'll stay a few weeks at least.'

'But I *want* you to stay.'

She smiled at that. 'Ye haven't changed, Brother. Ye always did want your own way. And Lady Flora seems welcoming, but I canna help but worry...well. Never mind that now. We'll talk again. I'm bone weary. I'm going to lie down.' She scooped Davy into her arms. 'Will ye open the door for us, please?'

He crossed to the door as if in a dream as all his plans teetered on a knife's edge. Anna paused on her way from the room.

'Dinna look so worried, Lachy. I promise I'll not sneak away in the night.' She leaned closer and whispered, 'And if ye'll take my advice, you'll tell that wife of yours about Australia before she finds out some other way. I'll not deliberately let it slip, but I hardly ken how to speak to a lady like her without also watching my tongue over your secrets.'

He watched her carry Davy up the stairs.

'Drummond?'

'Sir?'

'Where is Lady Flora?'

'She is resting in her room, sir.'

He returned to the drawing room and paced. All he wanted was to forget his shameful past and atone for his guilt by taking care of his sister and nephew. Was that really too much to ask? He needed her and Davy here, where he knew they were safe—surely she'd see the sense of that in time? She just needed time to adjust.

But Anna was right about one thing. It *was* time to confess everything to Flora. He'd been a fool to think he could hide something as big as that from her. He shoved his fingers through his hair, frustration bubbling through him.

He didn't want to tell *anyone* about his criminal past, dammit, let alone humble himself in front of his wife.

All he wanted was to forget the horror, the fear and the shame. The shame most of all. The fear of her reaction to the truth hung over him like a dark cloud. Jessica had deserted him as soon as she learned the truth…what if he lost Flora, too? Could she really fully accept him once she knew the worst or would she reject him? They had grown closer in the past few days and he had revelled in it. But to glimpse the joy that lay within his grasp only to see it slip away…that would be more than he could bear.

Life had taught him that to display emotion was to reveal a weakness others would exploit and he'd learned to keep his cards close to his chest. Flora, though, had found the courage to change—to speak her mind and to demand answers from him when, in the first weeks of their marriage, she had suppressed her own opinions and needs. She had found that strength from within and that gave him hope that, maybe, he, too, could change. The difference in her was astounding. From the young bride afraid of speaking her mind she was now a woman who could take the reality of the slums of Edinburgh in her stride, not to mention a sister-in-law who had been a prostitute. And now he was about to present her with a bigger challenge—a husband who had been a convict. As if their match hadn't already been unequal enough, with an earl's daughter wed to a boy from the slums.

He paused by the window. There would be a glorious sunset tonight. Nature was so uncomplicated. Unlike people. It followed its own path and rhythm, rolling on regardless. He eased his shoulders in a circle, wishing he could shake off this feeling of impending doom.

He could put it off no longer.

Flora's bedchamber door was ajar and, peering in, he saw Muriel busying herself folding and putting away clothing. Flora was nowhere to be seen.

'Where is Lady Flora?'

'She is in her boudoir, sir.'

This conversation needed no audience. 'Leave that for now, Muriel, if you please. Go down to the kitchen and... and...have a cup of tea. Tell Mrs Dalgliesh I said so.'

Chapter Seventeen

Lachlan didn't allow himself to hesitate at the door.

'It will be a glorious sunset this evening, Muriel. I—oh!' Flora's hand splayed against her chest. She had changed out of her dress into a silken robe secured around her waist with a tie belt. 'Is there something amiss?' She came to him, her words breathless, eyes filled with concern.

'No. There is nothing amiss.' He was captivated by her. There was no artifice to his wife: her honesty and her kindness shone. He wrenched his gaze from hers and looked beyond, out of the window. 'You are right. It *is* a glorious sunset.'

'I am pleased you are here to share it with me, Lachlan.'

Her smile was shy and it tugged at his heartstrings. How could he sully her pure spirit with the sordid truth of his life? And yet she already knew so much and she had accepted it. And she continued to accept him. Would she really reject him for stealing a loaf of bread and for suffering the consequences? Now he was with her, he had confidence in her generosity. The hesitation, then, was his own cowardice—he was afraid of owning up to his past and exposing his shame.

Honesty. Openness. *Sharing.*

All words he feared. All traits he must henceforth embrace.

'As am I, Flora. Come, let's watch the sun set together.'

They sat side by side on the *chaise longue* and he took her hand, lacing his fingers through hers. Her shy sideways glance set his heart racing with its innocent promise. Would she continue to look at him like that once she knew?

'I am sorry I wasn't honest with you about my search for Anna from the beginning, Flora. I know how hard it must be for you to accept her into your home.'

She laced her fingers through his. 'I confess I sometimes struggle to accept what Anna has been, despite knowing she was forced into such a life. But then I remember Galkirk and how *I* was cast as the offender even though I was the victim, and how it would have been infinitely worse had he succeeded in forcing himself on me and that reminds me to put aside my...my...natural aversion.' She pressed their clasped hands to her heart. 'I swear I will try to be a friend to her and that I will keep trying.'

He lifted her hand to his lips. 'I am humbled by your generosity of spirit.'

Her thoughtfulness and her reasoning gave him the belief that she would not instantly condemn him, but would try to understand.

'There is something about my past I must tell you, Flora. Anna knows and it is unfair on you both to expect her to keep it secret. It is time for there to be no further secrets between us.'

The colours outside were deepening into streaks of red, burnt orange, violet and indigo as the sun began to slip below the gently rippling sea. Unexpectedly, Flora leaned into him and nudged him with her head. He put his arm around her. 'Tell me, Lachlan. I am listening.'

And it was easier when he could not see her face and there were no changes of expression to distract him. He brought their joined hands on to his thigh and covered them with his free hand.

'I did not choose to go overseas. I was sent. By the courts. To Australia. When I was fifteen years old.'

She tensed and a tiny sound of distress escaped her. 'You were transported? Why?'

'I stole a loaf of bread.'

Flora's fingers tightened on his. 'A judge sent you to the other side of the world for stealing a *loaf of bread*?' She shifted to face him. 'I was afraid you were going to confess to much worse.' She reached to caress his face. 'Poor, poor boy,' she whispered.

His throat ached and his eyes burned and blurred but, now that he had started, he could not stop. He told her how he was sent to London, to be incarcerated on the *Susan* until she had her full load of convicts, about the desperate conditions on board, where one wrong look or careless word could get a man, or boy, beaten or even killed. He heard a quiet sob or two as he talked, but he did not stop. It must all be told now. No more secrets. He told her of the horror of the voyage; the number of convicts—men, women and children—who perished from disease and deprivation; the unforgiving climate of New South Wales and the backbreaking work and harsh punishments that were the lot of many convicts.

'I was lucky. Because of my youth I was assigned to private employment.' That had been harsh, too, but he would not distress her with the details. 'After four years I was granted a ticket of leave, which allowed me to start working for myself as long as I didn't leave the area. By the time I'd served my sentence three years later, I'd seen the opportunity to make money—not only for my passage home, but enough to set me up for a new life in Scotland. My pride drove me to come home a successful man, but now... I cannot forgive myself for not returning as soon as I had enough money put by for the passage.'

Flora smoothed his hair. 'But you *did* come home. You were not selfish enough to stay out there for ever, enjoying your good fortune, when you could have done so.'

'If I had returned sooner, I would have seen my mother before she died.'

The reality hit him, making him gasp with the pain. Although that was the truth, he had never allowed himself to think it in so many words. His selfish determination to make his fortune had robbed him of the chance to say goodbye to his beloved mother.

'I might have *saved* her, simply by being here and bringing in another wage.'

'Lachlan...' Flora brushed his cheek with tender fingers, comforting. He closed his eyes. 'You were trying to make amends, the only way you knew how. You couldn't know what was happening to your mother and Anna and it was admirable that you wanted to prove yourself. You broke the law. You stole. And, yes, I know you were desperate and that you did it for your family, but it is still the law and you were ashamed of the label that hung over you. Thief. Convict.'

Lachlan stiffened, opening his eyes. The vista in front of them was constantly changing—the colours darkening as the sun slowly sank deeper and twilight advanced.

Thief. Convict.

She was right, but those words, from *her* lips, pained him.

'I am still ashamed.' The words tore from him. He

risked a look at her. All he could see was compassion in those beautiful green eyes. He hung his head. 'So very ashamed. You deserve better than a boy from the slums and an ex-convict. You should be married to a duke; you should be a duchess.'

Before he realised what was happening, Flora was on her knees on the sofa, embracing him, her body warm and pliant, her soft cheek pressed to his.

'No!' She hugged him close. 'No. I had that chance… to marry a duke and do you know what? He is not half the man you are. *I* am not ashamed of you. You were driven to extremes and you have paid your price. You are a good man and you have made a success of your life. I am proud of you and I am proud to be your wife.'

He turned his head. Her gaze lowered to his mouth and then she tentatively touched her lips to his. A groan tore from his throat. He shifted towards her, framed her face with his hands and he kissed her again. Properly. Her lips softened beneath his and he teased with the tip of his tongue until they opened and he could lose himself in her lush warmth. He pulled her on to his lap. She threaded her fingers through his hair and he groaned again. Then he detected moisture against his cheek and, a moment later, tasted saltiness on his lips. He stilled. Pulled away.

'What is wrong?'

A tear rolled down each of her cheeks. She shook her head.

'Flora?' He blotted the tears with his thumbs. 'Why the tears?'

'They are happy tears.' She visibly swallowed. 'I feel emotional.'

She blushed, but she held his gaze and he saw the effort it took for her to do so. He frowned, unable to understand the concept of happy tears—surely it was a contradiction?

'About?'

'This. Us. Is it wrong to be so happy that we are closer than ever? Although...' She bit her lip. 'You do not think me...*forward*...because I like kissing you?'

Lachlan stared, then burst out laughing. '*Forward?* Flora! I am your husband!'

She pouted. And shoved at his shoulder. 'I *know* that. But my mother warned me—'

He put his hand across her mouth. Her eyes widened above it. This was his fault. He'd been too afraid of the secrets between them and had kept his distance to protect himself against the rejection he'd been sure would come. In protecting himself he'd confused his adorable wife.

'Your mother was wrong. Forget whatever nonsense she told you.'

She dragged his hand away. 'You are not...*disgusted*?'

'Sweetheart. No! You could never disgust me. I love kissing you and it makes me happy that you enjoy kissing me. And, later, we will do other things that give us *both* pleasure. We are married.' He pinched her chin. 'It is allowed.'

She searched his eyes, a tiny frown stitched between her brows. Then she smiled. 'Then kiss me again, Husband. I need the practice.'

He'd called her sweetheart! Flora hugged that knowledge to herself as she hurried down the stairs to the dining room. She was late. Lachlan's fault, with his wonderful kisses and caresses—the time to dress for dinner had passed without them even noticing.

Lachlan had been reluctant to leave her, but in the end had torn himself away, saying, 'We cannot neglect Anna on her first evening, but—' and his voice had deepened, his eyes darkening '—we will have all night together. Would you like that?'

She had nodded, happiness flooding every fibre of her being as pure anticipation sent the blood humming through her veins. When he had realised she was crying, he had been so tender with her and she had taken her courage in both hands and forced herself to ask the question that had troubled her ever since their wedding night—whether it was wrong for a lady to find pleasure in marital relations? And he had reassured her. She could not wait for dinner to be over and bedtime to arrive.

She walked into the dining room and halted, taking in the scene. Lachlan, as usual, sat at the head of the table. He had risen to his feet as she entered. Her place, as usual, was set at the opposite end from him. And poor Anna sat marooned in the centre of one of the long sides. With her newfound confidence, Flora walked forward.

'Good evening,' she said. She kept walking until she stood next to Lachlan. 'Do you think,' she murmured, 'that we might sit closer together when it is just family to dine?'

Lachlan frowned, surveying the table. 'But…is this not correct?'

'Yes, at a formal meal. But we are family, are we not?' Their eyes met and they shared a smile. 'It is not very comfortable to sit where we cannot talk with ease and your poor sister looks totally lost. May we move to sit closer to you?'

'Of course, if that is your wish. Drummond?'

The butler stepped forward.

'Please move the ladies' setting to either side of mine.'

Once the dishes were served, Lachlan dismissed the servants and Flora seized her opportunity.

'Will you tell us about your time in Australia, Lachlan? How did you rise from prisoner to successful businessman?'

'I was sent to work for a farmer when I first arrived—I was deemed too young to be put to hard labour. He was a harsh man, but I worked hard and I kept my eyes open and I learned a lot. When I became a ticket holder I left him and went to work for James Glover, himself a freed convict, who owned a few thousand acres of land in the west of the territory. He'd been transported to Australia when he was fourteen, but he'd married and stayed there. He lost his wife and son the year before I went to work for him. He was a hard taskmaster, but an astute businessman and, again, I learned a lot. He said I reminded him of his Robbie and I think he saw something of himself in me, too, and before long I was virtually running the place for him.

'I got my certificate of freedom in forty-one, but Glover begged me to say, offering me a higher wage. And then, one day, I stumbled across an outcrop of copper ore—I'd seen copper in rocks before, but this...even *I* could tell it was a rich deposit. It wasn't on Glover's land although it was close, but I couldn't afford to buy the land outright so Glover and I went into partnership.'

As Lachlan talked and they all ate, Flora could see Anna becoming more and more engrossed in his story.

'The assay results were good and once we dug out the surface ore we began mining underground where there was a rich seam of copper. There were good profits and, although home was always in my thoughts, I stayed on. Glover's health started to fail and he relied on me more and more to run both the mine and the farm.'

He stared down at the table and Flora put her hand over his. 'I'm sure that was a comfort to him, Lachlan.'

'Oh, aye, I stayed for entirely selfless reasons,' he said bitterly. 'All I could see was my fortune mounting up, but I would trade it all to have seen Ma again. And to have saved you, Anna.'

'What happened to the old man?' asked Anna.

'He died. And then I discovered he'd left me his share of the mine plus a sum of money. I sold the mine, moved to Sydney and began investing in businesses, and I discovered a talent for it.' He smiled mirthlessly. 'Am I not the lucky one?'

'Do you feel *guilty* that he left you the mine, Lachlan?' Flora could see from the look he slanted her that he did. 'You should not—Mr Glover would not have discovered it on his own so he benefitted as well. And you said yourself you were running the farm and the mine for him. Surely you deserved some reward?'

His expression said he disagreed and Flora cast around for a change of subject.

'How old were you when Lachlan was sent to Australia, Anna?'

Anna jerked her attention to Flora. 'Ten.' She stared, almost defiantly, across the table at Flora.

'That must have been very hard for you and your mother.'

'We did well enough. I got a job in the cotton factory when she fell ill. I was twelve by then—old enough to earn a wage and handloom weavers were earning hardly anything by then anyway, only a few shillings a week. We managed for three years before she died.'

Her voice rang with pride and Flora felt a glimmer of respect for this woman who had such a hard start to life.

At the end of the meal, Lachlan refused his customary whisky and cigar and instead accompanied the ladies to the drawing room. At the door to the room, Anna looked from Lachlan and Flora and back again.

'I am tired,' she said. 'If ye have nae objections, I'm for my bed.' She stared across at the staircase. 'I'm not keen on leaving Davy alone much longer, ye ken.'

'Tilly is watching him.' Mrs Dalgliesh had assigned one of the kitchen maids, with experience of caring for younger siblings, to help with Davy. 'She will take good care of him, Anna, but by all means retire now if that is your wish. You do not need to ask permission…this is your home now.'

Anna bent an unfathomable look upon Flora. 'Aye. Well. For the time being. Goodnight.'

She headed for the stairs, leaving Flora and Lachlan alone. Flora's pulse tripped and then started to hammer. Surely, tonight, he would come to her? His dark eyes travelled over her face and down her body, leaving fiery shivers in their wake.

'And what about you, Flora? Are you ready for your bed? Or would you prefer to read or to play cards?'

'I should prefer to retire, too, if you don't mind, Lachlan?'

Chapter Eighteen

Outside Flora's bedchamber, Lachlan carried her hand to his lips.

'I shall see you in a short while, my dear.'

It sounded so formal. Was this really how married couples behaved? Where was the passion? He felt it, she knew. He had kissed her with passion earlier. And she had kissed him back. She searched his face. It was impassive, but she saw the fire banked in his eyes and she knew the passion was there, tightly controlled. And she sensed the air between them shimmering with…uncertainty. And she knew, in that instant, that his hesitancy had nothing to do with how he felt about her and everything to do with being unsure of himself. *He* was afraid of doing something wrong. And in that moment, she saw she must be brave enough to show him when she enjoyed his lovemaking.

A short time later, after Muriel had left her, Lachlan entered Flora's bedchamber through the connecting door, clad in his dressing gown, his bare feet pushed into his slippers. Flora sat in bed, watching him but, as he went to douse the lamps, she said, 'Please. Leave them.'

She would not allow this to be a repeat of their first

night together, conducted in silence in the dark. She wanted to learn…about him…about what he liked…and about what she liked. She felt her face fire red, but she forced herself to say, 'I should like to see you.'

Surprise and then pure happiness shone in his expression. His dark eyes, always intense, glowed with an inner fire. He smiled, his teeth gleaming.

'You never cease to surprise me, Flora McNeill. Or humble me. You have courage enough for the pair of us.'

He shrugged out of his robe and he stood there, allowing her to look her fill. And she took full advantage, feasting her eyes on his torso——the wide span of his shoulders, the dark hair that spread over his muscled chest, then narrowed down over the ridges of his flat abdomen until… Her breath seized and she felt a quiver run through her core. He was truly magnificent, his erection jutting out from a thatch of dark hair. He had been inside her. Once. And now she longed for him to be inside her again. This time, she would allow herself to enjoy her husband and his loving. She would not be scared to respond to him. Her gaze continued down, taking in his narrow hips, straight, hair-dusted legs and——she pressed her lips together, raising her eyes to his face. Lachlan glanced down and then up. Their gazes fused.

'All of you.'

Lachlan grinned and he kicked off his slippers.

He came towards the bed and took her hands, and pulled her up to stand face to face with him. Except her eyes were level with that mouth-watering chest, he was so much taller than her. His spicy male scent surrounded her and she felt the sudden urge to strip off her nightgown and press her naked flesh to his.

He laced his fingers through hers.

'Look at me,' he whispered.

She looked up, into his eyes. Then, his gaze never leaving hers, he released her hands and untied the ribbons at her neck. He pushed her nightgown down, exposing her shoulders, leaving her arms trapped to her sides. His eyes went impossibly dark—black—as he trailed his fingers with a featherlight touch down the sides of her face, across her jaw, neck and shoulders. Her skin sizzled beneath his touch.

'You are so beautiful.'

His head lowered and he nibbled and licked the same path as his fingers. Gently, he untied the ribbon securing her hair and shook it free, spreading it out across her shoulders, combing his fingers through the heavy tresses.

'I adore your hair. The feel of it. The colour. Silken fire.'

He pushed her nightgown lower and her breasts popped free as it slithered to the floor. His sharp intake of breath spoke for him and her eyes closed and her head tipped back as he closed his hands around them. And that memory from their wedding night...that tug of anticipation in her womb as he pinched her nipple...it had been no fantasy. Then his mouth was on her and her legs turned weak. His arm at the back of her waist kept her upright as he licked and nipped and suckled and everything... *everything*...disappeared in a haze of pure feeling.

He swung her into his arms and then lowered her to the bed, following her down, his hands and mouth cruising her body—tasting, kissing, nibbling—as she grabbed at whatever part of him she could reach, frantic fingers clutching his heated skin. She wanted him inside her. Now.

'Please.'

It was a whimper. She was begging. She didn't care.

And when he parted her legs and stroked her, the fire inside blazed higher. She moaned, her thighs spreading wider, offering, but he slid down, leaving her hands empty, clutching at empty air before fisting in the bedsheet at the first sweep of his tongue. Her heart pounded. Desperate moans came from far away. Large hands at her hips held her still as she strained to move. Her back arched as heat and urgency filled her, pushing her closer and closer to some unknown edge.

'Can't take it…stop…stop…' She grabbed his hair with both hands, not to push him away, but to keep his head in place. 'Don't stop…*please* don't stop…'

He didn't stop.

She reached the edge. Clung on for dear life.

He stopped. Raised his head.

Don't stop! A frantic plea…in her head.

'Let go, sweetheart.'

His mouth closed around her again and she let go with a scream as she flew over that edge and all that heat and urgency inside her exploded, surges of pleasure pulsing through her. Lachlan's lips found hers as the waves that rippled through her slowed and faded. He settled on her, his hips between her widespread thighs.

She was shattered. Exhausted. She wanted more. She wanted him.

Greedily, she reached for his buttocks, hot and firm in her hands as she urged him to fill her. As he slid inside, she drew in a deep breath and her head tipped back, her neck bowed. *This* felt right. *This* she remembered from before, but *this* was a thousand…a million…times better.

Later, as they lay together, sweat damp and sated, Flora found more courage than she'd ever dreamed of as they talked and they played and they explored. And they laughed.

* * *

Flora awoke the next morning to a large, warm male body in her bed. Although the steady sound of breathing and the weight of the arm slung over her suggested he still slept, the solid length of flesh nudging her bottom suggested he still had not had his fill of her. Glorying in the pleasure of feeling well loved, she turned sleepily in his arms and studied his face.

Relaxed, his hair tousled, he looked…content. His eyelashes, she saw with a stab of envy, were thick and dark and long as they fanned against his cheeks. His jaw was dark with stubble and his lips…she tore her gaze from them, a blush sweeping her body as she remembered the cries they had wrung from her. Who would have thought such a thing would be so enjoyable? Or so much fun? They had laughed together more last night than they had in the whole of their marriage so far.

He stirred and mumbled something unintelligible and a huge wave of affection and protectiveness swept over her. That last made her frown. It seemed bizarre, for a tiny woman such as her to feel protective towards a man as powerful as Lachlan. But she did and she recognised that, although physically he was bigger and stronger than she would ever be, emotionally he was still fragile. And—she realised with a jolt—she loved him. The feeling had crept up on her so slowly she could not say when it had happened. Joy and contentment filled her. She had rediscovered all the confidence she had lost. She felt more courageous than she'd ever thought possible and she was certain there was nothing she could not say to her husband.

Unlike poor Mother, who barely dared to voice any opinion at all to Father.

She was fortunate indeed. The only words she was not quite brave enough to say were the words, 'I love you.'

Not yet.

With a secret, wicked smile she reached between them and closed her fingers around his hot, hard length—silky smooth skin sliding over solid flesh.

His eyes opened.

'Good morning, Lachlan.'

His mouth curved. His arms tightened. His lips touched hers.

And then she was swept away on an irresistible wave of pure passion.

When she awoke again, she was alone and Bandit was curled up on the end of the bed. She sat up and peered groggily towards the window where the light filtering through a narrow gap in the curtains suggested the morning was not too far advanced. The door to her boudoir stood open and she smiled to realise that Lachlan must have let the little dog out. He tried to hide it, but he had a soft heart.

'Has Mr McNeill gone to the distillery yet?' she asked later as Muriel laced her corsets and helped her on with her morning gown.

'Nay, milady. He sent word for Mr Fraser to attend him here this morning and he told him only to bother him in the next few days if there was something he couldna deal with on his own. He said he wants to be here to help Mrs McKenzie and young Davy to settle into their new home.'

Flora batted away her immediate reaction—a stab of hurt that he had not done the same for her on her first day at Lochmore. She was his wife now, in every sense of the word. She hugged that knowledge to herself. Anna might be his sister and share a bond from the past, but the future belonged to Lachlan and Flora.

'Where is Mrs McKenzie now? Has she broken her fast yet?'

'No, milady. The master said to let her sleep. Young Davy is up and about, though. He ate breakfast with the master and Tilly is caring for him now. The master,' she added, 'is in his study.'

'Thank you, Muriel.'

She could not wait to see her husband again. And she had an idea she wanted to discuss with him—the idea that had disturbed her sleep in the hotel in Glasgow. *That* could not wait either.

'Good morning, Lachlan.' Flora smiled brightly as she approached his desk.

He looked up. His bemused expression quickly cleared and he returned her smile, got to his feet and rounded the desk to her. Before she realised what was happening, his arms were around her and his mouth on hers. She slid her hands up his chest to his shoulders and then threaded her fingers through his hair as she melted in his embrace, thrilled by his spontaneity.

'Mmm...' He lifted his head and gazed down at her, his dark eyes warm. 'Good morning, Flora. To what do I owe the pleasure of this early visit? I left you sound asleep.'

Pure male satisfaction rang in his voice. Flora bit back her smile as she toyed with the top button of his waistcoat, her other hand still on his shoulder, viscerally aware of his solid masculinity. Heat flared between them, leaving her craving more of his kisses. More of his touch. More of him.

She focused her thoughts. 'There is a matter I have

been thinking about. I should like to discuss it with you, if you have the time?'

His eyes crinkled. 'Of course I have the time.' He ducked his head, searching her eyes. 'Have you eaten yet?'

She shook her head. Without another word, Lachlan turned her around and propelled her out of the door and along the passage towards the morning parlour. After a frosty night, the sky was clear of cloud and the room was bathed in the pale light of the November sun.

'We can talk while you eat.'

Once Flora had settled at the table with a cup of freshly brewed tea and a bowl of porridge, Lachlan sat next to her and raised his brows. 'So,' he said. 'You have my undivided attention.'

'I have been thinking about your family. The dreadful circumstances...the deaths—' Her throat closed up, trapping her words. She coughed. Sipped her tea. 'I am horrified by what your family endured, but...' She frowned, staring at her bowl as she gathered her thoughts. 'But more than that...it breaks my heart that there are more— *so* many more—families facing the same struggle every day.' She searched his face. 'I saw that with my own eyes in Edinburgh. Forgotten people. Not living, merely existing, without hope. And women who have no choice but to follow that path Anna was forced down.'

She ate a spoonful of porridge. This was it. What if he dismissed her suggestion? Somehow, this plan—the details of which she had been mulling over ever since they had found Anna—had taken on huge importance to her. She wanted to be heard and she longed for him to take her seriously.

He waited silently for her to continue.

'Some of the ladies I spoke to at Sir Keith's house

party—the wives of the businessmen there, not the others—' She risked a quick grin and was gratified by the twitch of his lips in response. 'And also many of the guests at Aunt Tessa's soirée…they spoke of educational foundations and of philanthropic organisations and it was suggested I might like to join their committees.'

'If that is what you would like to do, Flora, I shall not stand in your way.'

'But it is not. I thought—I should need your agreement, of course—but I thought…that is, I should like to…'

Lachlan's hand covered hers on the table and squeezed. 'Just tell me, Flora. Whatever it is you would like to do, we will try to find a way to make it possible. But I cannot give you my opinion unless you actually speak the words.'

'I should like us to set up our *own* charity to help poor families in Glasgow, particularly women who find themselves on their own with children to support. I thought… maybe we might set up a fashion business that will provide such women with decently paid piecework they can do at home? And we could use any profits to help those who cannot work. I'd like to do more than just sit on a committee and talk about doing good. I should like to make a difference.'

Lachlan shoved his chair back abruptly and crossed to the window. Flora watched him carefully, trying not to jump to the conclusion that she'd angered him. Now she'd come this far she knew if she was ever to find her voice in this marriage, this was the time to stand firm. Lachlan's back expanded as he drew in a deep breath, then he returned, sat down again and took her hand.

'When we married I knew you had led a sheltered life and I feared you could never hope to understand the struggle and hardships of my childhood. You have proved me wrong. I now know the kindness and generosity in your heart—I saw and felt your distress in Edinburgh. Not only do I think it's a wonderful idea, I can tell you that it is also my dream to do exactly as you have suggested. It was always my plan to set up a charity using the profits generated from Carnmore Whisky and that is one reason it is so important to me that the business expands and is successful.'

He gazed down at their joined hands, playing with her fingers.

'One of my deepest regrets is that I never knew that my mother was ill, or that she had passed away and left Anna alone. Ma couldn't read or write and so we couldn't keep in touch. I believe one of the best ways of improving the lives of the poor is to ensure the workers are paid sufficient wages to afford a roof over their heads and enough food to eat. Everyone benefits—they spend that money in the place they live and shops and traders prosper, too. And it would remove the need for children to earn so they will have the time to be better educated. Then, when they grow up they will be in a position to improve their lives, as I have. Although—'

He stopped speaking as the door opened. Anna, holding Davy's hand, hesitated on the threshold, looking from Lachlan to Flora and back again, her expression uneasy.

'Is it all right to come in?'

Lachlan leapt to his feet and Flora—although she was sorry Anna felt uncomfortable at interrupting them— tried hard to quell her dismay at the interruption. It had finally felt as though she and Lachlan were truly communicating. There had been a meeting of minds—she had been heard, her ideas given credence and, at last, she felt as though she could make a difference.

She smiled at Anna nevertheless. 'Good morning, Anna.'

'Did you sleep well, Anna?' Lachlan watched his sister with a kind of hungry intensity.

'Davy was restless.'

'He will settle,' said Lachlan. 'It was a long, tiring day for us all yesterday. Sit down, have some breakfast. I can't wait to show you around the castle and the grounds.'

It seemed to Flora that Anna suppressed a shudder, but she sat at the table as bid and Lachlan ladled porridge into a bowl for her.

Flora held out her hand to Davy. 'Come and sit with your Auntie Flora, Davy, while your mama eats her breakfast.'

As she lifted Davy to her lap, Lachlan said, 'I have been thinking, Anna—Tilly is good with Davy, so if you are happy with her, I can make her change in duties permanent.'

Anna frowned. 'There is no need to go to such trouble for us, Lachy.'

'It is no trouble. This is your home now. The nursery suite will be perfect for Davy and I hope it won't be too long before he's not the only child at Lochmore.'

'I told ye yesterday, Lachy. I dinna want to stay here for ever.'

'Nonsense. You'll love it here. It's only because it's all so strange.'

Anna appeared to withdraw into herself at his eager words and Flora bit her tongue against warning Lachlan not to push his sister too hard.

'You'll soon feel at home, you'll see. We'll go down to the beach later—Davy will love running round with Bandit, even though it's chilly out there.'

'Ye dinna mean to keep us prisoner here, do ye, Lachy?'

Anna spoke as though in jest, but Flora feared there was a serious point underlying her question.

The days blended one into the other as November advanced and it was increasingly obvious that Lochmore—the size of it, the wildness, the loneliness—all terrified Anna. She missed the hustle and bustle of the city and wanted nothing more than to return to Glasgow and she argued frequently with Lachlan over her future. Flora tried hard to make friends with her sister-in-law, but Anna never seemed comfortable in Flora's company.

Despite the increasingly fraught atmosphere, Flora was happier in her marriage than she had ever been and had even accompanied Lachlan on a couple of business trips to secure lucrative new markets for Carnmore Whisky and to investigate ways to set up their charity. But their absence from the castle led to more friction with Anna who felt so unsafe left at Lochmore on her own with just Davy and the servants that she eventually begged Flora to help her persuade Lachlan to see sense and allow her to return to Glasgow. Lachlan, however, would not hear of it.

'She will soon change her mind,' he said when Flora tried to reason with him. 'They belong here with us, where I can take care of them.'

Flora, however, understood only too well how impotent Anna must feel when Lachlan ignored her feelings and desires, dismissing her needs over his.

'Anna is entitled to her views, Lachlan. You cannot make her stay against her wishes.'

'How can you deny they are better off here? Look at what we can offer them. She'll get used to Lochmore. She just needs time.'

And despite Flora's growing love for her husband,

his intransigence where his sister was concerned raised niggles of doubt in her mind. Although he appeared to value Flora's opinion, did he truly do so? He dismissed her warnings about Anna out of hand. He gave no credence to his sister's repeated requests to move back to Glasgow. He behaved, in those instances, as Flora's father had done all his life.

'You are being stubborn, Lachlan. If you do not take care, you will drive Anna away and then you will lose her and Davy again. Look at it from Anna's point of view— she is a grown woman. Surely she is entitled to have her views taken into account? You are in danger of smothering her with your need to protect her.'

'I've said all I intend to say on the matter.'

Chapter Nineteen

One afternoon, some three weeks after Anna had come to live at the Castle, Flora came across a frantic Tilly, scurrying along the upper corridor.

'Tilly? What is wrong?'

'Oh, milady! Master Davy—he slipped away when I wasn't looking. I don't know where he is. I thought he might have come up here.'

A huge, terrified sob erupted from her and Flora gripped her shoulders, giving her a little shake. 'Where did you last see him?'

'We were in the ballroom, milady.' Her face flushed. 'I know we shouldn't be in there, but there's room for him to run around when it is cold outside. I didn't think there'd be any harm in it. Bandit was there, too, and Master Davy had his ball and his skittles and his little wooden engine. I only—' She clapped her hands to her face and wailed loudly.

'Hush, Tilly. Where is Mrs McKenzie?'

'Resting, milady. She had the headache. Oh, milady! Where can the poor little mite be?'

'Try to stay calm, Tilly. He's probably just followed Bandit somewhere. He must be somewhere in the house—he is too small to open any of the outer doors.

You search up here and I shall go downstairs and have another look.'

Flora ran down the staircase and to the ballroom. The huge double doors were standing open and there, in the middle of the room, lay Davy's abandoned toys. Through the French windows that had been cut into the thick outer wall Flora caught sight of two gardeners, sweeping the paths in the knot garden. One of them straightened and looked towards her. His grin froze on his face and Flora's brows arched. No doubt he was the reason Tilly became distracted.

She turned away, then gasped, fear clutching her heart. The door below the minstrels' gallery looked shut, but it was unlatched. Heart in mouth, she rushed to the door, beyond which were the spiral stairs that led down to the cellars. She'd not been in the tunnels since Lachlan had taken her down there, but she remembered the vaulted stone ceilings and the tunnels that led, maze-like, under the castle. If Davy got lost down there, he would be petrified.

Every instinct she possessed was urging her on... screaming at her to *hurry*. She felt around for the candle, struck a match on the sandpaper block to light it and sped down the spiral steps.

Which way?

'Davy? Are you down here? Bandit?'

Her voice echoed back at her, sending a shiver down her spine. There'd been no time for Lachlan to replace the rotten doors as he'd intended. Bandit loved the beach and, having been down here before, would surely head straight for the Sea Gate. If Davy was following him... She shielded the candle flame against draughts and raced along the tunnel, grateful for the faint wash of daylight ahead that guided her. She ran on, panting now, to where her tunnel met another. Stronger light to her right sent her in that direction and she at last reached the end. She ran out on to the rocks and around the jutting pinnacle that disguised the Sea Gate from the beach. Frantic now, she scanned the rocks, the steps and the beach.

There he was!

Davy was on the beach, Bandit prancing around his heels, as they both headed for the sea.

Her swell of relief gave way to concern as she took in the wind-whipped, white-topped waves.

'Davy!' she screamed. 'Stay there!'

Heedless now of her own safety and cursing her full, unwieldy skirts, Flora raced as fast as she could down the steps to the sand. Davy had halted, looking back at her, his mouth turned down and, as she neared him, she saw the tears begin to fall. She snatched him into her arms, hugging him close, relishing the warm weight of him.

'Oh, Davy! Don't you *ever* wander off like that again, do you hear?' She hugged him even closer, pressing her lips to his wispy curls. A howl erupted from him and she jiggled him a bit, hushing him as Bandit danced around her feet yapping. 'It's all right. Auntie Flora isn't cross. I was just scared.' She turned back to the castle, suddenly aware of the freezing cold wind that blew in off the sea and the gathering clouds. 'Let's get back indoors quickly,' she said, kissing his cheek. 'We shall ask Cook for some hot chocolate to warm us up, shall we?'

She began to plod back across the sand, Davy balanced on her hip, Bandit bounding around her, tongue hanging out, stubby tail constantly on the move.

'Davy!'

Even at that distance Flora could hear the utter terror in Anna's scream. She flew down the path to the beach and snatched Davy from Flora so violently Flora almost unbalanced.

'I hate this place!' Anna shrieked. 'We're leaving. Today!'

And with that she stumbled away from Flora, heading back to the castle. Flora followed her through the chapel gate, unable to face the narrow spiral stairs that always brought back scary memories of when she found her brooch.

By the time she got home, the castle was in an uproar. Servants were scurrying about in nervous silence and Lachlan, a thunderous look on his face, grabbed Flora's arm as soon as she appeared, guiding her into his study and shutting the door behind him with a decisive bang.

'What happened? Anna is raging about it not being safe here.'

Flora recited the events of that afternoon. 'Anna was frantic. Lachlan, I did try to warn you about—'

The door flew open, cutting off Flora's words. Anna marched in and plonked her hands on her hips, glaring at Lachlan.

'My poor wee laddie is beside himself, crying his eyes out. Ye can loan us the carriage or we'll walk, Lachlan, but either way we're going and ye canna stop us.'

Lachlan crossed the room in two strides, grabbing Anna's shoulders, feeling like he'd been punched in the gut. 'You can't go, Anna. We have only just found each other. You belong here with us…we're your family.'

'*Davy* is my family and it's not safe here for him.'

'Of course it's safe. This is the perfect place for Davy to grow up. You've had a shock. You'll see things differently when you've calmed down.'

She averted her face. 'This isna my home. It'll never be my home.'

He must keep trying to get her to see sense. 'How can you know that? You've only been here a few weeks.'

He ignored Flora's soft, 'Lachlan...', and her hand on his arm.

'You're upset now. At least wait until the spring.' His full focus was on his sister. 'You'll see it differently then.'

Anna stared at him. 'It'll make no difference to me. I dinna want my laddie to settle, only to uproot him again.'

Frustration boiled through him. 'But where would you go? Not...not back to Hopkins?'

'Of course not, Lachy. I'm nae fool.' Anna jerked away and Flora grabbed Lachlan's arm to prevent him taking hold of his sister again. 'I hate it here.'

'Tell me what to do to make it better then. I'll do anything.'

Anna rolled her eyes. 'Will ye *never* listen to me, you stupid stubborn oaf? I dinna want to stay here with you. I want to begin a life of my own, with Davy.'

Lachlan turned to Flora. 'Say something, Flora. Persuade her to stay. Please.'

Anna laughed bitterly. 'Your fine lady wife willna be sorry to see the back of us, Lachy. Ye can dress a whore in fancy clothes, but she'll always be a whore.'

Flora looked as stunned as if Anna had slapped her. 'Anna, that's unfair. I have never—'

'But you think it! I know you do! Every time you look at me.'

'You're wrong, Anna. When has Flora ever given you a reason to think she doesn't accept you?'

Anna snorted. 'It's only a matter of time. Her sort will never accept my sort. Anyway, it makes no difference now. I hate all this space and the quiet and the weather. I've made up my mind.'

'You can't just leave.' He grasped any straw he could think of. 'Give me time to find you somewhere to live. I'll find you a place in the new year—'

'If ye think I'll stay here until after Hogmanay, Lachlan, you've got rocks in your head.'

'But you can't wander the streets with a child in tow.'

'It's no use trying to talk me out of it, Lachy. My mind is made up.'

He gazed at Flora, willing her to say something... *anything*...to sway his stubborn sister, but all she did was offer a rueful smile with a sympathetic lift of her brows.

'Well, you'll not go alone. I'll come with you and find you somewhere respectable to live. I can give you an allowance—'

'*No*, Lachy. I have my pride. Come with us to Glasgow tomorrow and find us somewhere to live if you must. I'll accept an amount to tide me over, but I willna accept more of your charity.'

She marched to the door, then paused before leaving the room. 'Thank you for rescuing us, though. Never think I'm not grateful to ye, for I am.'

Lachlan could scarcely believe what had just happened. He'd truly believed they were set for life...that Anna and Davy would settle here at Lochmore with him and Flora. Now, he felt as though his heart was being ripped from his body. He turned to Flora, quietly watching him.

'Why didn't you help me persuade her to stay? Or is she right? Do you *want* her gone?'

Flora frowned. 'That is unfair, Lachlan. I have been nothing but friendly and welcoming to your sister. It is Anna who won't accept *me*.'

Rather than soothing him, her voice of reason stirred

anger, deep in his gut. And mixed with that anger was fear and all his old insecurities—the ones he thought he'd banished for good—reared up. He wasn't even good enough for his own sister—how could he ever be good enough for an earl's daughter? His spirits plunged, deep and dark...the whole thing seemed so futile. He would never be good enough...

Flora came to him with quick steps and an anxious look, reaching for his hand. 'I tried to warn you what would happen if you pushed her too far, but you refused to even listen to what she had to say or to try to understand. I—'

He ignored her gasp as he snatched his hand away.

'Lachlan... I am sorry, but you need to accept that Anna is no longer your little sister—she is a grown woman and a mother and she is capable of making her own decisions. If she chooses to leave, you cannot stop her.'

Lachlan forced his chin up, blanking his expression.

'You're right. It is her decision. Now, if you will excuse me, I have work to do.'

He knew his cold response would hurt her and at some level he was aware he was being unreasonable, but he felt incapable of considering her feelings when his own were in such turmoil.

'I know it will hurt, but if you help her now and you part as friends, you will not lose Anna or Davy.'

'Thank you for your advice.'

He turned his back, selecting some random papers from his desk and pretending to be absorbed in them. It was not until he heard the soft click of the door as it closed behind Flora that he moved, dashing the papers to the desk before crossing with leaden steps to the window where he gazed blindly out, his thoughts blank.

He had no idea how long he stood there, but the clock striking six finally penetrated his misery and he went upstairs to change for dinner.

The meal was eaten in silence and the two women he loved withdrew to the drawing room, leaving Lachlan with his bleak thoughts and his whisky. When he finally followed them to the drawing room it was empty and he climbed the stairs to his bedchamber. He felt so helpless. Why would Anna not listen to him?

He undressed swiftly and went to Flora, longing to lose himself in her soft, slippery heat.

'Lachlan.'

The pleasure in her voice and the welcoming smile on her face were balm to his soul.

He did not want to talk. Even though he suspected he was being unfair, he couldn't help but blame Flora for clearly supporting Anna's decision. All he wanted now was to forget everything. He set about ensuring his wife was fully satisfied before thrusting inside her and reaching his own climax. He groaned at his release and then kissed her soundly, but as soon as she turned in his arms to snuggle into him, reality impinged again. He sat up and swung his legs out of the bed.

'Lachlan?'

The puzzled hesitation in that single word wrenched at his heart, but he could not bring himself to offer her comfort, not when he was so cut up inside.

'Yes?' He sat on the edge of the bed, his back to her.

'Have I...? You do not...? Please tell me you do not blame me for Anna wanting to leave. I promise I have done nothing to encourage her to go.'

'Of course I don't blame you.' But he could not fully forgive her for taking Anna's side. 'But I am not tired so I shall go downstairs and read for a while until I'm sleepy. I'll sleep in my own room tonight so I don't disturb you.'

He looked back at her then, forced a smile and swiftly kissed her lips. Part of him wanted nothing more than to settle down with her in his arms but the other part was busily retreating and rebuilding those barriers between them. And he had no idea how to stop it.

Chapter Twenty

Flora played a few scales on the pianoforte to loosen her fingers ready to play. Lachlan was at the distillery. He went most days since their return from Glasgow, where they had settled Anna and Davy in a neat four-storey Georgian town house in a respectable street. Flora had come up with the idea of Anna taking in lodgers to give her an income. Anna had been grateful for a sensible solution to her need to earn a living, but Lachlan was unhappy that Flora had made it easier for Anna to be independent.

Flora sorted through her music. She wasn't in the mood for a delicate, happy tune—she needed a robust piece to work out her frustrations and worries about her husband. She couldn't get through to him. He seemed to be slowly but inexorably slipping away from her. Ever since Anna left Lochmore he had seemed to retreat further into himself every day, yet whenever Flora tried to talk to him about it, he insisted there was nothing wrong. The intimacy that had been so hard won seemed to be fading away and Flora had no idea what to do about it.

Or maybe, she thought—gritting her teeth as she bashed out a few thunderous passages from Chopin's

Revolutionary Etude—she had fooled herself into believing she and Lachlan were falling in love after he had finally confided in her and told her the full story of his past. Maybe, like her father, he didn't value her opinions at all and it had all been an act to dupe her into accepting Anna and Davy into their home. Now he no longer needed to keep up the pretence because his sister had gone.

Tears burned behind her eyes. She forced herself to play on even though the score had blurred and false notes reverberated around the room. She didn't want to believe it, but why did he, once again, hold her at arm's length? Emotionally, if not physically, for he still visited her bed most nights. But even that was not the same, for she could sense he was holding back, even when they were in the throes of passion. And it broke her heart when she compared their recent lovemaking to that of the first few weeks after Anna and Davy had come to Lochmore. It was the difference—and she blushed at the crude comparison—between riding a horse of warm flesh and blood, and sitting astride a stone wall. Every human emotion was battened down as he went through the motions and, try as she might, she could not coax him into releasing them.

Lachlan had thrown himself back into his work and he had shut her out while pretending he had not. She again felt isolated in her own home—afraid of speaking out in case she said the wrong thing. She was back in the situation she had most feared and seemed helpless to do anything to remedy it.

She played on to the end of the piece, uncaring of the number of times her fingers stumbled over the passages. As the final notes faded and the silence descended, Flora reached a decision. She flatly refused to revert to that timid bride, scared to speak up for herself.

She shoved back the piano stool and strode from the room.

'Drummond. Please send word to the stables to bring the carriage round immediately. And ask Muriel to come to my room and help me to change.'

She didn't wait for his reply, but hurried upstairs, where she selected a dark green velvet afternoon dress suitable for visiting. Her original intention had been to go straight to the distillery and confront Lachlan. But that, she had realised, would be a mistake. Confrontation wouldn't help. It risked driving a bigger wedge between them and the distillery was the last place for a heart-to-heart talk. But she needed distraction from her endlessly circling thoughts and maybe Joane could help Flora understand why Lachlan was shutting her out again. They had met a few times since their first meeting—both at Joane's house and here at the Castle—and Flora knew she would feel better after a good dose of Joane's straight-forward common sense.

Muriel helped Flora into her afternoon dress and tidied her hair. Then she went to the wardrobe to fetch Flora's ermine palatine and matching muff.

'Thank you, Muriel.'

Flora went to her dressing table and pinned her brooch to her gown, struggling as usual to fasten the stiff catch. She had taken to wearing it again, the comfort it gave her increasing in proportion with the growing emotional distance between her and Lachlan. She then swung the palatine around her shoulders, put on her bonnet, picked up her muff and hurried downstairs.

It was a short journey to The House, as everyone seemed to call the Duke and Duchess's home, built just outside Lochmore Village. The carriageway swept up to the elegant Georgian manor which Flora always thought would look more at home nestled among the mature woodlands and verdant pastures of England than here, on the edge of the Scottish Highlands. As soon as Flora entered the salon, however, her courage failed her and doubts mushroomed. How could she possibly speak about such private matters as her marriage to Joane, no matter how friendly she seemed?

'Flora! Good afternoon, my dear. What a pleasant surprise.'

'Good afternoon, Joane. I hope I have not called at an inconvenient time?'

'Not at all.' Joane's great grey eyes swept Flora's face. She felt a blush rise—those sharp eyes were not easily fooled. 'I am delighted to see you. Please be seated.'

'Thank you. I shall not stay long.' Flora sat on a sofa. 'I—I just fancied a drive and I was passing, and…'

Her voice faltered. Joane had remained standing and now she tipped her head to one side. 'What is it, my dear?'

Flora's throat ached with misery. 'Nothing,' she said, even though she longed to confide in Joane. 'I am…'

Flora fell silent as Joane sat next to her and took her hand.

'Come now. I have three daughters. I can always tell when something is troubling them.'

She could not resist the sympathetic tone. Flora spilled out everything.

'I tried to be friendly and welcoming, but Anna never seemed at ease with me even when I supported her against Lachlan. And he, stubborn man, wouldn't listen to what she wanted. Why couldn't he simply accept that she would rather live in Glasgow than at Lochmore? She *hated* the countryside.'

A maid brought in the tea tray at that moment and Joane waited until she had poured their tea and left the room before she spoke.

'I suspect your Lachlan doesn't see it in simple terms of where Anna chooses to live. He takes it personally— as a rejection of him, not of Lochmore.'

'But...he knows where she is. He can visit her. Shouldn't that be enough for him?'

'Foolish girl, of course it isn't enough.' Joane's eyes twinkled. 'How can he possibly make proper amends for not being there when she needed him if she won't allow him to *take care* of her? All he is guilty of, Flora, is wanting to smother his sister and nephew with love.'

She supposed Joane had a point.

'But I still don't know why Anna took me in such dislike. It would be nice to be on more friendly terms—I know how important family is to Lachlan.'

'I doubt she disliked you, Flora. It was probably that she couldn't bring herself to believe that an earl's daughter could ever accept her as a friend.' Joane sipped her tea, her brow wrinkled thoughtfully. 'You told me Lachlan's family were poor...maybe uneducated?'

Flora nodded. She had not told Joane about Lachlan's transportation or Anna's past as a prostitute, but she *had* told her of their family's eviction from their tenanted farm that ultimately led to their struggle to survive in the Glasgow slums.

'Lachlan, too, must have felt unworthy of an earl's daughter, but he at least has the satisfaction of being a wealthy, successful businessman. But all Anna would see is the huge disparity between you and her. *She* needed rescuing from her poverty. *She* was living as a supplicant in your home—poor does not equate to lacking in pride.

I wonder if Anna was afraid to accept your friendship in the belief you would, sooner or later, reject her?'

That made sense, particularly when Anna had been forced into prostitution. It was such a relief to be able to discuss this with Joane.

'Don't forget,' Joane continued, 'everyone she has ever loved has either died or left her and, even though Lachlan was desperate for her to stay, she would know, if pushed, he would choose his wife over his sister.'

'I'm not so confident he would make that choice.'

Joane settled those grey eyes of hers on Flora. 'Of course he would, foolish girl. Anyone can see he is besotted with you.'

Her words sent a tingling glow right through Flora.

'But he will not *talk* to me.'

Joane laughed. 'Of course he won't. He's a man. They hate to talk about their feelings. It makes them feel vulnerable. They prefer to be all manly and take action, but your Lachlan can't take action because Anna—most unreasonably!—hasn't fallen in with his plans and so he's ignoring his feelings by throwing himself into his work.' She patted Flora's hand. 'I have every confidence you will get through this little hiccup.'

Little hiccup?

But talking to Joane had given Flora the incentive to take action rather than letting her problems overwhelm her. She refused to return to being the timid girl afraid to speak her own mind and she would not allow Lachlan to exclude her any more.

'I wonder if it will help if Anna and I *can* become friends after all? Now she isn't living at Lochmore maybe it will be easier? And then Lachlan will realise I never *wanted* Anna and Davy to leave; I only trusted that she knew what was best for her.'

'Anna leaving might have been the only way you two ever could become friends.' While Flora puzzled over Joane's meaning, she continued, 'I see you are wearing that brooch again. May I see it?'

Flora looked down and realised she had been, quite without volition, running her fingertips over her brooch, every curve and indent as familiar to her as her own face. She unpinned it.

Joane examined the brooch. 'I still cannot think where I have seen another like it…it is teasing me, right on the edge of my mind, but… I cannot… No…' she handed it back '…it will not come to me.'

'Have you heard from Benneit?' Flora asked as she fumbled to work the brooch's catch.

Joane's eyes sparkled. 'Yes, only yesterday. They still intend to return in January and I cannot wait. Which reminds me… I've had some of the family portraits cleaned, including one of Benneit as a young man. Would you care to see it?'

'Yes, indeed.'

In the gallery Joane stopped in front of a large, full-length portrait of a young man dressed in the long tailcoat and knee breeches fashionable from thirty years ago. He was tall and handsome with broad shoulders and an expression on his face that said *Cross me at your peril*. He was clean shaven and his black hair looked windswept.

'I cannot wait for his return.'

'He was very handsome,' said Flora. 'Oh! I did not mean…not that… I am sure he is still a fine-looking man.'

Joane laughed. '*I* still think him handsome, although his hair is silver now and receding a little at the temples. I like to tease him about it.'

Flora felt a touch of envy at Joane's clear devotion

to her husband. She could only pray she would feel the same about Lachlan when they had been together as long.

'I ought to go,' she said.

'I will see you out.' Joane led the way along the gallery, but then paused before another portrait, this time of a striking lady with jet-black hair and flashing eyes. 'This is Benneit's French ancestor, Marguerite. Do you remember me telling you we named Marguerite after her?'

'Yes. I remember. I have seen her tomb, and that of her husband, Ewan, in the new chapel at Lochmore.' Flora studied the portrait. The woman's clothing was unfamiliar—a dark red gown with gold-coloured undersleeves and a square neckline decorated with pearls, and a strange cap the top of which was shaped like the gable of a roof and with sides that hung down past Marguerite's ears. 'She is very beautiful. How long ago was she mistress of Lochmore?'

'Oh, over three hundred years ago, I should think. I often wonder how a French lady came to be wed to a Scottish earl. It would be fascinating to be able to go back and meet our ancestors, would it not?'

'Indeed.'

They returned downstairs and, by the front door, Joane hugged Flora and then kissed her cheek.

'I do hope our little chat has helped you, Flora dear.'

Flora's heart cracked. Why, oh, why could her own mother not be more like Joane? Even though Mother had not been affectionate, Flora felt her loss as a great gaping wound in her life. She still missed all of her family.

'It has. Thank you for listening to my woes.' She forced a smile. 'I shall try hard to find a solution.'

During the journey home, Flora closed her eyes to think over what Joane had said. She had helped Flora understand that because Anna feared rejection she protected herself by keeping Flora at arm's length. Lachlan's reaction was harder to fathom—it was as though he believed that now Anna and Davy had gone he had no family left.

But what about me? Aren't I his family now?

Her whirling thoughts slowed and steadied. *Family.* Was that the key? Ever since their marriage, Lachlan had been possessed by the need to find his sister. Flora pondered all she had learned about his past...the loss of his father, his other sisters, his mother. He had lived among strangers from the age of fifteen—in prison, on board the prison ship and in Australia, both during and after his sentence.

He'd struggled to share his innermost feelings with her, but he had begun to change because—and the truth hit her like a lightning bolt—he was exactly like Anna. He had protected his heart by keeping everyone, even his new wife, at a distance. But he had let down his defences after he found Anna. He had begun to feel safe, with his family around him. But now...*now* he felt he had lost Anna and Davy all over again. In his eyes, as Joane said, *they* were rejecting *him*. Exactly what Anna feared might happen if she allowed Flora to become a friend.

A sense of urgency fired her blood. If she could not find a solution—if she could not, somehow, break through the barrier Lachlan had erected between them—she was in danger of once again being relegated to the background of his life. And that she could not bear.

He annoyed her.

He frustrated her.

There were times when she wanted to *hit* him.

But, beneath all of that, humming in her blood and in her heart, was a deep affection for this complex, taciturn husband of hers.

She respected him.

She *loved* him.

He was worth fighting for.

And if he wouldn't *listen* to Flora, then she would *show* him how much she cared. She would prove to him that he was worthy of her love and she would find a way to give them the family they both craved. She would make him feel safe.

Anna might no longer live at Lochmore, but Glasgow was not so very far away. *Anna leaving might have been the only way you two ever could become friends.* Flora hadn't understood Joane's meaning at the time, but now she understood that their relationship could never be equal while Anna was living in Flora's domain. Now Anna had her own home and an independent income, might she have the confidence to meet Flora on more equal terms? But, knowing Anna's pride, would her new situation be enough or was more needed? One thing was for sure—it would be up to Flora to make the first move. She determined to find a way to prove to Anna she was a valued member of Flora's family, as well as Lachlan's.

Then there was Flora's family. And just as Lachlan craved closeness with his own family, so did Flora. Mother had written twice since her wedding—neither letter contained any hint that she missed Flora nor was there any message from her father. In fact, there was nothing of a personal nature, just inconsequential news about the castle and its inhabitants. Flora felt sick at the thought of confronting her family but, if she wanted to change their relationship, she must at least try. And soon, before she lost her nerve.

Back home at Lochmore, Flora couldn't settle. Lachlan wouldn't be home for a few hours and she was too restless to simply sit and wait for him. She donned her old cloak and wandered outside. The clouds threatened rain and she didn't want to risk getting wet so where…? She paused. She'd never properly explored inside the old chapel—picking through old furniture was just the sort of activity to while away time on a dreary afternoon.

The heavy oak door protested as she opened it. She shut the door behind her and peered around the interior which was only dimly lit by the daylight filtering through the dusty windows. A lamp and tinderbox sat on a dresser and it cast enough light for her to see as she picked through the stacks of old-fashioned furniture. There was little of interest, if she was truthful, although she did linger over a beautifully carved cradle, wondering how many babies had slept in it over the years. Maybe she could clean it up and reuse it?

She fetched the lamp, intending to carry it closer to the cradle to check for the tell-tale signs of woodworm but, as she did so, the light dimmed.

Always.

Flora stifled a scream, but the lamp flared again almost immediately and her thudding heart steadied. All was quiet. She gazed around the chapel, feeling a little foolish. *Had* she heard that whispered word, or was it inside her head?

She put her free hand to her chest and there, beneath her cloak, she felt the outline of her brooch and she felt… joy. The lamp beam touched on a doorway in the corner of the chapel and her feet carried her over to it. Inside, she saw spiral steps leading down. She swallowed. The urge to go down…to explore…was strong even though the dark, narrow stairwell evoked memories she would rather keep at bay.

Lachlan had told her there was a crypt beneath the old

chapel and that it was walled off from the tunnels beneath the castle. There was nothing to fear. She had been in the McCrieff crypt many times. This crypt would differ only in that the tombs would be of long-dead Lochmores, with no one to remember them or even to care.

She stepped on to the first of the tightly spiralling stairs and, although her breathing grew erratic, the feeling of rightness became stronger with every step. The lamplight played across the tombs set in alcoves along the long walls and Flora shivered at the carved stone effigies, their eyes staring blindly into endless night.

Step by step, she was drawn deeper into the crypt, towards a bigger alcove at the back—an alcove that housed a double tomb. Rubble littered the floor, as though a wall had once walled up this alcove.

Flora cried out, bending double as a dizzying, aching sadness whirled within her.

Always.

The hushed whisper seemed to linger in the freezing air. Flora clutched tight at the lamp and yet, in among the anguish, she felt—again—joy and a deep sense of belonging.

She raised the lamp and its light glinted off something metallic that nestled between the crossed hands on the stone breast of an effigy.

My brooch!

She clutched her chest. No. She could feel it, still pinned to her gown. Impelled to look further, she tore her eyes from that other brooch and a whimper escaped her. The other half of the tomb was open, its cracked lid abandoned on the floor. As if in a dream, Flora took one step. Then another. As she neared the open tomb the wavering lamp light gradually revealed…nothing! That empty space wrung a shuddering moan from her lips, a moan that seemed to originate from deep, deep inside her. Then her toe stubbed against something hard and she looked down at the discarded lid and its carved stone figure. Like the other effigy, its hands were crossed on its breast but, in the indentation between them, was... nothing. As the chill clawed at her nostrils, her throat, her lungs, Flora fumbled beneath her cloak. Her breaths ripped across the silence as she finally unfastened her brooch.

Always!

No whisper. No plea. A demand.

She crouched down, her hand trembling, and yet it felt right as she placed the brooch in that empty space.

The lamp flickered and all went black.

Flora stumbled away, back to the dimly visible stairs, up to the gloomy chapel and out into the fresh air. She slammed the door behind her and, trembling, she sank to the ground.

The sound of whistling roused her after she knew not how long, and sent her scrambling to her feet, shivering. She stared at the chapel door, her heart still racing.

What happened?

She wasn't about to go back and find out. She hurried around the corner of the building and there was Rab, whistling as he raked leaves—as every day and normal as she could wish for. He touched his cap and she smiled a greeting. But, as she passed him, she couldn't help a little curiosity.

'Rab... I've just been exploring the old chapel. Do you know anything about the empty tomb?'

The old gardener leaned on his rake and scratched his beard. 'There's them that say it's never been occupied, milady, but I dinna know anyone who knows for certain. Mind,' he added with a shrug, 'even if it *did* hold a body